FATHER'S DAY MURDER

Lucy was just finishing her dessert—a thin wedge of very rich chocolate cake sitting in a pool of raspberry sauce—when a man stepped to the microphone in the front of the room and asked for silence. The program, he said, was going to begin in a few minutes, as soon as the waiters finished clearing.

Hearing this news, Junior got to this feet and left the hall, presumably in search of his father. It was only a moment or two later that he returned in some agitation.

"We need an ambulance," Lucy heard him say to the man in charge of the program. "My father's collapsed."

Several people hurried out of the room, along with several members of the Read party. People from the other tables, however, began drifting to the door, curious to see what was going on. That brought the emcee back to the microphone.

"Please stay in your seats," he said. "We're going to start the program with a short film, a biography of Luther Read."

It was eerie, thought Lucy, watching the images of Luther Read flicking across the screen. Maybe he was dead or maybe he was fighting for his life, but in the darkened room he was an enormous, living presence. Then the film ended. The final image of Luther Read's smiling face had hardly faded when the announcement came.

"Luther Read, our Newspaperman of the Year, is dead."

That was incredible enough, but an even more shocking announcement followed.

"Remain in your seats, please, as the police will be collecting information from everyone . . ."

Books by Leslie Meier

MISTLETOE MURDER

TIPPY TOE MURDER

TRICK OR TREAT MURDER

BACK TO SCHOOL MURDER

VALENTINE MURDER

CHRISTMAS COOKIE MURDER

TURKEY DAY MURDER

WEDDING DAY MURDER

BIRTHDAY PARTY MURDER

FATHER'S DAY MURDER

STAR SPANGLED MURDER

NEW YEAR'S EVE MURDER

BAKE SALE MURDER

CANDY CANE MURDER

ST. PATRICK'S DAY MURDER

MOTHER'S DAY MURDER

Published by Kensington Publishing Corporation

A Lucy Stone Mystery

FATHER'S DAY MURDER

Leslie Meier

KENSINGTON BOOKS
http://www.kensingtonbooks.com

KENSINGTON BOOKS are published by

Kensington Publishing Corp.
119 West 40th Street
New York, NY 10018

All Kensington titles, imprints, and distributed lines are available at special quantity discounts for bulk purchases for sales promotion, premiums, fund-raising, educational, or institutional use.

Special book excerpts or customized printings can also be created to fit specific needs. For details, write or phone the office of the Kensington Special Sales Manager: Attn.: Special Sales Department. Kensington Publishing Corp., 119 West 40th Street, New York, NY 10018. Phone: 1-800-221-2647.

Kensington and the K logo Reg. U.S. Pat. & TM Off.

ISBN-13: 978-0-7582-7297-3
ISBN-10: 0-7582-7297-9

First Kensington Books Hardcover Printing: June 2003
First Kensington Books Mass-Market Paperback Printing: May 2004

10 9 8 7

Printed in the United States of America

Chapter One

"Wouldn't you like to kill him when he does that?" Phyllis was referring to her boss, Ted Stillings, editor-in-chief and publisher of the weekly Tinker's Cove *Pennysaver*, who had just announced his arrival in the office by throwing his head back, pounding his chest, and yelling like Tarzan. Behind him the little bell on the door jangled merrily, and dust motes danced in the stripes of afternoon sunlight that streamed through the old-fashioned brown-wood Venetian blinds covering the plate-glass windows.

"Only if I can torture him first," replied Lucy Stone, the paper's investigative reporter, feature writer, listings editor, and photographer. "Quick, pass me the hand-cuffs and the duct tape."

Phyllis, whose various job descriptions included reception-ist, telephone operator, and advertising manager, smoothed her pink beaded cardigan over her ample bust and began searching in her desk drawer.

"Darn. I must have loaned them to somebody," she said, shaking her head. Not a single tangerine lock escaped from the hair spray she'd liberally applied that morning.

"Enough with the sarcasm," admonished Ted. "I've got big news."

"Uh-oh," said Phyllis in a resigned tone. "That probably means more work for us."

"Not today it doesn't," insisted Lucy, who as the mother of four had learned early on the importance of setting limits. "I have to get Zoe to ballet, and Sara has horseback riding. I absolutely, positively have to leave at three. Not a minute later."

"Will you two shut up?" demanded Ted. "I have an announcement to make."

Phyllis rolled her eyes. "So what's the problem? Cat got your tongue? Spit it out."

"We're waiting," said Lucy, drumming her fingers impatiently on her computer keyboard.

"I get no respect here," fumed Ted. "I might as well be home."

He sat down at the antique rolltop desk he'd inherited from his grandfather, a legendary New England newspaper editor, and put his head in his hands.

"This is the biggest thing to happen to the *Pennysaver* since . . . well, I don't know when, and nobody's interested. Nobody cares."

"We care," chorused Lucy and Phyllis.

"Please, pretty please," cajoled Lucy. "Please tell us." Ted lifted his head.

"Only if you're really interested."

"We're really interested," said Phyllis with a big sigh.

"You don't sound interested." Ted was pouting.

Lucy checked her watch. "I don't have all day, Ted," she reminded him.

"Okay." Ted straightened up. "Drumroll, please."

Lucy tapped two pencils against the edge of her scarred wooden desk.

"Today," began Ted, making a little bow and displaying a sheet of paper with an impressive engraved letterhead, "I have the honor of informing you that the Tinker's

Cove *Pennysaver* has been named 'Community Newspaper of the Year in Category Five, Circulation Less than Five Thousand' by the Trask Trust for Journalism in the Public Interest."

"You've got to be kidding," said Phyllis, raising the rhinestone-trimmed reading glasses that dangled from a chain around her neck and holding her hand out for the official letter.

"Wow," said Lucy, honestly impressed. "Congratulations." She knew how Ted had struggled through the years to keep the *Pennysaver,* which had a lineage reaching back over a hundred years to the yellowed and crumbling *Couriers* and *Advertisers* in the morgue, a going concern. Only someone with a genuine dedication and commitment to local news would have continued to soldier on in such a difficult economy against TV, the Internet, and numerous slick and sophisticated competitors.

"It gets better," said Ted, passing the letter to Phyllis. "The award includes a grant to attend the Northeast Newspaper Association conference in Boston."

"It's true," said Phyllis, lowering her glasses. "Just my luck, the conference is for editorial staff only." She sucked in her heavily powdered cheeks and pursed her Frosted Apricot lips. "I suppose that leaves me out."

"Sorry," said Ted, not bothering to sound too sympathetic. "Someone has to watch the store. But Lucy, I think you should definitely go. It's a great opportunity to polish up your writing and reporting skills and to meet other journalists. Opportunities like this don't come along every day, you know."

Lucy knew. She couldn't remember the last time she'd left the little Maine town. And she'd hardly ever left her family for more than a day, and then only to give birth or tend to her ailing parents.

"Where is it? And when is it?" she asked.

"Boston. The second week in June."

"Oh, I'd love to go to Boston," she admitted. "But June?

I can't get away in June. Elizabeth and Toby will be home from college. Sara and Zoe will be finishing up the school year. It would mean missing the middle school awards ceremony and the ballet recital—"

"That's not what I call a problem," said Phyllis, cutting her short. "I'd call it a gift from God."

In spite of herself, Lucy laughed, recalling long hours spent perched on uncomfortable bleacher seats in the stifling gymnasium watching an endless procession of students receive awards for everything from perfect attendance and positive attitudes to the Zeiger Prize for Improved Penmanship.

"It means a lot to the kids," she said lamely.

"They have a father, don't they?" continued Phyllis. "He can go."

"You're right," said Lucy. "Bill will go." She sighed.

"There's some problem with Bill?"

Phyllis was sharp; there was no denying it, thought Lucy.

"It's just that . . . well, you know Toby is going to be working for his father when he gets home from college."

Bill Stone, Lucy's restoration carpenter husband, was still recovering from a nasty fall. It had been decided that Toby, who was struggling in college, would take a year off from his studies and assist him on the job.

"Well, I don't have a good feeling about it," said Lucy, voicing a thought that had been nagging her for some time. "They're both pretty strong personalities."

"Both stubborn as hell, you mean," said Phyllis.

"I'm worried they might have a little trouble adjusting."

"Probably fight like cats and dogs."

"Exactly. But if I'm there I can be a buffer, smooth things out."

"Honey, you can just forget that idea," said Phyllis, fixing her with a level gaze. "They'll work things out a lot faster if you're not there."

"I was hoping to keep it in the family and out of the courtroom," said Lucy darkly. "And then there's Elizabeth."

Phyllis cocked her head expectantly.

"Well, you know she didn't much like working as a chambermaid at the Queen Vic Inn last summer? I've got to help her find a new summer job."

"You mean make sure she gets a summer job."

"Right."

Phyllis shrugged. "No work, no spending money, it's that simple."

"I wish I had your confidence," said Lucy, staring at the calendar photo of scullers on the Charles River, with the Boston skyline in the background. Flipping through the pages she saw a shot of the swan boats in the Public Garden, street musicians performing in Copley Square, and a nighttime photo that transformed Storrow Drive into swirling ribbons of red and white light.

"How would I get there? I've never driven in the city. Besides, Elizabeth will need my car to get to the summer job she doesn't have yet."

"Go with Ted," suggested Phyllis.

"No can do," said Ted, looking up from his computer. "Pam and I are going a few days early, kind of a mini-vacation."

"Take the commuter jet."

Lucy considered this. "That's a good idea, but I bet it's awfully expensive."

"All your expenses will be paid," snapped Phyllis. "Right, Ted?"

"Well, within reason. Workshops, registration, lodging, meals, transportation." He paused. "No jets. Bus."

"Bus?" Lucy hadn't traveled by bus since she was in college.

"Sure. There's two or three every day. And the bus, unlike the plane, takes you right into town. To South Station."

Lucy studied the June calendar photo of a narrow street on Beacon Hill lined with rosy pink town houses. She wanted to walk down that street, perhaps the very same street where Paul Revere or Louisa May Alcott or Robert Lowell had walked. She flipped a page, revealing a photo of the fashionable boutiques and outdoor cafés on Newbury Street. In the foreground, a fashionably dressed couple were strolling arm in arm. She was suddenly uncomfortably aware of the blue jeans and polo shirt she was wearing, her usual outfit for work.

"I have nothing to wear," she wailed.

Phyllis raised an eyebrow. "Girlfriend, then you better get off your fanny and go shopping."

"You win," said Lucy, laughing. "I'll go!"

That night at dinner Lucy could hardly wait to share the good news.

"Guess what?" she began as she unfolded her napkin. "Ted wants me to go to a newspaper convention in Boston. All expenses paid."

"Boston?" Zoe, seven years old and in second grade, was suspicious. "How long will you be gone?"

"How come we don't get to go?" demanded Sara, who had just turned fourteen and had a permanent chip on her shoulder.

"Exactly when is this shindig?" inquired Bill, scooping mashed potatoes out of the bowl and piling them on his plate.

"It's a week long, the second week in June, and Elizabeth will be home then so she can help out."

"Elizabeth never does anything," complained Sara, pretty much hitting the nail on the head. A year at Chamberlain College in Boston had done little except convince Elizabeth that she was disadvantaged because her parents had refused to fund a trip to Cancún for spring break and had insisted she come home to look for a

summer job. A search that had been far too halfhearted
to be successful.

"A whole week?" Zoe scowled, pushing her peas around
on her plate.

Lucy was beginning to think the convention wasn't a
very good idea as she watched Bill consult his pocket
calendar.

"Do you know what this means?" he asked, tapping
the calendar.

Suddenly Lucy knew exactly what it meant. An entire
week without household responsibilities. No loads of
laundry, no suppers to cook, no family crises. No complaints and no reproaches. No explanations. A week with
no one to answer to but herself. Freedom.

"What's the problem?" she demanded. "I'll only be
away for five nights, five weekday nights. The kids aren't
babies anymore; they'll all help out. You go away, to
restoration carpenter's workshops and antique house
conferences and buying trips and I don't know what
all. . . ."

"It's the week before Father's Day."

This was news to Lucy.

"I bet you never even thought to check."

Lucy looked at the wilted lettuce leaf remaining on
her plate.

"They call it Father's Day, but this year I guess it will
be Passover."

This was a favorite complaint of Bill's, who always
feared he would be "passed over" and ignored on birth-
days and holidays.

"I hadn't realized," admitted Lucy. "But Father's Day
is always on Sunday, and I'll be home Friday or Saturday
at the latest. It will be the same as always. Even better.
The best Father's Day ever."

"Promise?"

"I promise," said Lucy.

Chapter Two

Maybe going to the newspaper convention wasn't such a good idea after all, thought Lucy, carefully folding her best dress and tucking it in her suitcase. It was a flowery-print silk sheath that she'd bought at Carriage Trade's end-of-season sale last August. It was perfect for an occasional summer theater show or cocktail party, the sort of event she was likely to attend in Tinker's Cove, but she wasn't convinced it would do in Boston. It screamed summer resort wear rather than urban sophistication.

Too bad, she told herself firmly; it would have to do. According to the schedule Ted had given her, there would be only one dress-up occasion at the conference: the awards banquet. She was certainly not going to buy a new outfit for one event, especially when she had a perfectly good dress in her closet. A lovely dress. A designer dress. A dress splashed with gaudy pink and fuchsia and orange blossoms.

Lucy gave her hair a good brushing, studying herself in the mirror. She saw an average sort of person—average height, average weight, not as young as she used to be and not as old as she hoped to be—someday. Her shining cap of dark hair was her best feature, she thought, mostly because she didn't have to do much with it. She got it cut once a month, rinsed in some hair color now and then to cover the gray that had begun to appear, and that was it.

Lucy gave her reflection one last look and decided she looked presentable, dressed for comfort on the bus in jeans and an oversize white shirt. She slipped the brush into the suitcase and was zipping it up when she heard a thunderous crash outside.

Involuntarily, her stomach clenched. What now? she wondered, as she ran to the window to see what had happened. At first nothing seemed different, only that the backyard looked rather empty. Then she realized that the toolshed, which had been covered with climbing rambler roses, had somehow collapsed. The roses were still there, still in bloom, but not as high as they used to be.

Bill and Toby were standing in almost identical positions, arms akimbo, examining the damage. Kudo, the dog, was running in circles and barking furiously.

"Shut up!" yelled Bill, advancing at the dog.

Kudo gave a protesting yelp or two, then scooted off in search of safer ground. Toby was thinking of following him—Lucy could tell by a slight shift in his weight and a definite angle toward the house—but Bill had him in his sights. She'd better get down there fast, she decided, before things got nasty.

Bill had already worked up a good head of steam when she stepped out onto the back porch.

"Why'd you say it was all set when it wasn't?" he yelled at Toby.

Toby shook his head, shrugged his shoulders, and held out his hands. "I thought it was set."

"How could you think that? There was nothing to hold it up once I took out the corner post. How stupid can you be? Did you think the air would hold it up? Did you think Newton's laws have been repealed? Dr. Gravity took the day off?"

Toby's face was red, and Lucy knew he was struggling to keep his temper.

"I didn't understand," he said, shaking his head. "I thought you'd done something. I thought you had it under control."

It sounded reasonable enough to Lucy. Kids expected their parents to take care of things for them. There was a roof over their heads, dinner on the table, clean clothes in the drawers. Dentists' appointments got made; all they had to do was show up and open wide. That dynamic had changed, of course, when Toby started working for his father. Now he was supposed to earn his keep.

"No!" barked Bill, pointing a finger at him. "That was your job." He jabbed a finger at him. "You! You were supposed to put in a brace."

Toby's face was beet red and his chin was quivering.

"Why didn't you explain that to me, Dad? Why?"

Bill threw up his hands. "God almighty, do I have to explain everything? This is a job your average idiot could do with his eyes closed and one hand tied behind his back."

Toby didn't answer; he fled to the rattletrap Jeep he'd bought with money borrowed from Sara, the family miser, and sped off, spraying gravel.

Bill turned to Lucy. "Can you believe that kid?"

Lucy didn't want to answer. She figured anything she could say would only make Bill madder, so she just shook her head.

"Can't you say something?" demanded Bill.

She was spared having to answer by Kudo, who suddenly ran by with a limp chicken in his mouth. Proof positive that once again he'd gotten into Mrs. Pratt's chicken house.

"I'll call and find out how much damage he did," said Lucy, heading for the house.

"You'd better catch him and tie him up first," said Bill, picking up the crowbar. "You know, Lucy, I can't guarantee that beast will be here when you get back from Boston."

Lucy had heard these threats before and didn't take them seriously. She knew Bill was really fond of Kudo. She suspected that he pretended to be antagonistic so he wouldn't be asked to help take care of the dog. She shrugged and went inside to get the box of dog treats she kept handy for calling the dog. He could hear her shaking it from miles away, and the sound never failed to bring him home, drooling with anticipation. When she came back out of the house, however, she realized Bill's truck was gone.

"Great," she muttered, shaking the jar furiously. Now she didn't have a ride to the bus.

A half hour later she had locked the dog in the house and had tracked Elizabeth down at her friend Jenna's house. Impressing upon her the gravity of the situation—that she was going to miss the bus unless Elizabeth returned home immediately with the Subaru—took a bit of doing.

"But, Mom, you said I could have the car while you're gone."

"I'm not gone yet, Elizabeth. And unless you take me to the bus stop I won't be gone at all."

"Okay, Mom. I'll be right there."

She had plenty of time, she told herself, trying to stay calm. At least forty-five minutes. Plenty of time. No reason to panic. She'd go upstairs and get her suitcase and Elizabeth would no doubt be pulling into the driveway when she came down. After all, it was only five minutes to Jenna's house.

But when Lucy came out on the porch with her jacket and purse slung over her arm and towing her wheeled suitcase, there was no sign of Elizabeth or the car. She went back in the house and reached for the phone.

"Jenna," she said, struggling to keep a level voice. "Is Elizabeth still there?"

"Oh, hi, Mrs. Stone. Yup, Elizabeth is right here."

"Could I please speak to her?"

"Sure thing."

When she heard Elizabeth on the other end of the line, she could barely contain her fury.

"Right now. This minute. Get in the car. Understand?"

Elizabeth understood. Minutes later she rolled into the driveway, loud music pouring from the station wagon's open windows. Lucy threw her suitcase into the back and climbed into the passenger side.

"There are hamburgers for supper. Dad can grill them. There's macaroni salad all made, and you can slice up some tomatoes."

"Sure thing, Mom."

From her spritely tone and the way her head was bobbing along to a Janet Jackson tune, Lucy doubted she'd heard a word.

"I'm serious, Elizabeth. Don't forget to pick up Sara and Zoe. Sara gets done with her volunteer job at the animal shelter at four, and you can swing by the Orensteins' for Zoe then, too."

"Right, Mom."

"What did I just say?"

"Grill the tomatoes, slice up the gruesome twosome."

Lucy let it go.

"You know, the only reason I'm letting you use my car while I'm away is so you can get yourself to work."

"I know, Mom. I know."

Elizabeth had taken a job as an au pair for a wealthy couple, Junior and Angela Read, who were summering at his family's enormous shingled "cottage" overlooking the ocean on Smith Heights Road. Elizabeth would be responsible for taking care of their three-and-a-half-year-old son, Trevor.

"It wouldn't hurt you to take a look at that old Gesell

book I gave you. Trevor's at a tricky age." She remembered that when Toby was three and a half she'd been convinced he had gone deaf because he never seemed to hear what she was saying and insisted on ignoring her and stubbornly going his own way. It was only after consulting the child-care books that she'd discovered such behavior was normal. What the book's authors had neglected to mention was that he might never grow out of it.

"Don't worry, Mom. We'll be at the yacht club most of the time."

"You do understand that the Reads aren't sending you to the yacht club to get a tan and flirt with the boys, don't you? They'll expect you to take care of Trevor."

"I know. I know. How hard can it be to take care of one little boy? Besides, he'll probably take a lot of naps and stuff."

"Sure," said Lucy, stifling the impulse to burst into hysterical laughter.

The bus was just coming into view when they pulled into the Quik-Stop parking lot.

"Oh, God, I almost forgot Father's Day."

Lucy already felt a little pang of guilt. She wasn't going to be home on Friday after all; Ted wanted her to stay for the morning workshops which meant the next bus didn't depart until Saturday morning.

"It's okay, Mom. I know what to do. Honest, I've been around for nineteen Father's Days. In fact, I've already got a great idea for a present."

"Good. Don't forget the cards. He loves them, and they have to be homemade. The funnier the better."

"Of course, Mom."

"Bacon and sausage—he'll want both."

"Right."

"Plenty of eggs."

"Right."

"Doughnuts from Jake's . . ."

"Absolutely. There's not enough cholesterol in bacon, sausage, and eggs. Got to have doughnuts, too."

Lucy smiled at Elizabeth's joke and got out of the car just as the bus pulled into the parking lot. She was lifting her suitcase out of the back when she remembered the most important thing.

"Don't forget the Bloody Marys!" she said, leaning on the driver-side door. It certainly wouldn't be the perfect Father's Day without Bill's traditional eye-opener.

"Mom, aren't you forgetting something?"

Lucy's mind went blank with terror.

"My toothbrush? Did I remember to pack it?"

"No, the liquor. I can't buy vodka and neither can Toby. We're underage."

"Right, right." The bus motor was rumbling. "I'll get vodka. I won't forget. You get the rest of the stuff."

"The bus is gonna leave, Mom. You better hurry."

Before she could say good-bye, Elizabeth had driven out of the parking lot.

Lucy felt alone and deserted. It wouldn't have killed Elizabeth to wait a few minutes so she could wave to the departing bus. Maybe even say an encouraging word, like "Have a good time" or "Don't worry about a thing."

Lucy trundled her suitcase around the bus and gave it to the driver, who stowed it in the baggage compartment, and bought her ticket. He punched it when he gave it to her, telling her she would need it when she debarked in Boston. Then she climbed on board and took a seat next to a window. The driver clambered aboard, released the brakes, which gave a huge hiss, and they began to roll.

Alone in her seat, Lucy reached for her cell phone. Things had been so confused when she left that she wanted to make sure everything was all right. Maybe she could catch Bill, just to touch base and let him know she'd left the hotel phone number on the refrigerator. Or Toby, to tell him that his father wasn't really angry at him; he had just been upset about the shed collapsing. Or she could call Zoe, at her friend Sadie's house, just to say good-bye and remind her to be a good girl.

Lucy was fingering the phone, trying to decide which number to call, when the bus began the long climb past Red Top Hill and on toward the interstate. From where she sat she had a clear view of the little New England town with its white church steeples rising above the leafy green trees and the Main Street shops with the sparkling blue harbor beyond.

It looked, she thought, like a picture postcard. Or the opening scene from a movie. The credits had finished rolling, the heroine had boarded the bus leaving her small-town past behind her, and the adventure was about to begin.

Chapter Three

Lucy's first stop when the bus finally pulled into South Station six hours later was to find the ladies' room. Then, with face and hands freshly washed, hair combed, and a fresh application of lipstick, she went out to find a taxi. The city air, heavy with the pungent exhaust of diesel engines, made her eyes sting, and she felt a little pang of homesickness for Tinker's Cove, where the ocean breezes kept the air sweet and fresh.

"Park Plaza Hotel," she told the cabbie, who immediately started the meter. Shocked at the amount it already showed and remembering Ted's admonition that she had to watch her spending, she asked if it was a long trip.

"Nah," he said, pulling away from the curb. "Sunday evenings there's not much traffic. It should be quick."

Relieved on that score, Lucy leaned back in her seat and prepared to enjoy getting reacquainted with the city. Boston, she knew, was one of the nation's oldest towns and was filled with treasures like Faneuil Hall, Old Ironsides, and Paul Revere's house, though Bill maintained there wasn't really much of the original structure left in the Revere house, and she supposed that since he was a restoration carpenter he would know.

She and Bill had brought the kids into the city a few times over the years, to see Red Sox games at Fenway Park and to visit the Museum of Science, the New England Aquarium, and other attractions, but each trip had been a tense exercise in map reading as they tried to find their way through a maze of unfamiliar roads filled with notoriously unpredictable Boston drivers who considered using a turn signal tantamount to giving away a state secret. Most traumatic of all had been their trip last fall to bring Elizabeth to Chamberlain College, when the stress of the city driving had been compounded by the emotional trauma of separation. Lucy had fought tears for the entire trip, and had hardly noticed her surroundings.

Today, however, she was buoyed by a sense of adventure and looked around eagerly, hoping to spot a familiar landmark. Instead she was dismayed to see that more of the roadways had a makeshift appearance and were lined with long chains of scarred concrete Jersey barriers.

"What's going on?" she asked, remembering the cranes and numerous road construction projects she'd observed from the bus. "These roads are a mess."

"You said it, lady. They call it the Big Dig, but the Big Boondoggle is more like it."

"Big Dig?"

"You never heard of the Big Dig? Where are you from?"

"Maine," said Lucy, grabbing the door handle and holding on for dear life as the driver whipped around a sharp corner and slammed on the brakes in front of the hotel.

"That explains it," said the cabbie, turning around to face her. "They're gonna put all the highways underground. They've dug up most of the city. It's costing a lot of money and making for a lot of aggravation. That'll be four-twenty."

Lucy gave him five dollars. "Keep the change," she

said in a burst of extravagance. She'd feared the fare would be much larger.

He nodded his thanks. "You have a nice visit, and while you're here, take my advice and take the T."

"Thanks," said Lucy. "I will."

A handsomely uniformed doorman opened the door for her with a flourish and Lucy felt rather grand as she entered the lobby, even if she was toting her own suitcase. There was a short line at the desk and she looked around while she waited, taking in the enormous flower arrangement of real flowers on a center table, crystal chandeliers, and the elegant Swan Court restaurant, where white-jacketed waiters tended to the wants of well-dressed customers.

When it was her turn to step to the counter she tried to act as if checking into a hotel alone were something she did every day.

"I have a reservation," she said. "Lucy Stone."

The clerk, a skinny young man with a bad complexion in a hotel uniform that was too big for him, bent his head and clicked away at the computer. After endless, apparently fruitless searching, he raised his head.

"Do you have your confirmation number?"

Confirmation number? Eek! What was that?

"Uh, no," she said. "I don't think so."

The clerk looked over her shoulder. "Well, do you have it or not?"

Lucy followed his gaze and saw that the line of impatient customers was growing.

"No."

"Well, I can't help you then."

Lucy panicked. She was alone in the big city and she didn't have a place to stay. What was she going to do?

"Maybe it's under Stillings." She spelled it out. "Ted Stillings."

The clerk sighed and clicked the name in.

"It's not here."

"You don't have a room for Ted?" Lucy was horrified. "Try the *Pennysaver* newspaper. That's P-E-N—"

"Are you with the NNA convention?"

"Yes, I am. And so's Ted."

"Well, why didn't you say so." He glared at her before bending over the computer once again.

Behind her, Lucy imagined the people waiting in line were sharing her sense of relief.

"Here it is. Credit card please."

Lucy hesitated. "I thought the paper was paying for my room. . . ."

"For incidentals," he said, holding out his hand.

Lucy pulled her wallet out of her purse and found the card, hoping that there wouldn't be many incidentals, whatever they were. She was perilously close to her limit, and heaven only knew what Bill might charge while she was away. She was busily imagining him doing the unthinkable, charging groceries, when the clerk cleared his throat.

"This is your room number," he said, pointing to a number on the key card folder. "The elevators are behind you." He paused. "Have a pleasant stay," he said in a sticky, saccharine voice.

Lucy didn't think a reply was called for, so she went over to the elevator bank. She was waiting and wondering what her room would be like when she was approached by a tall, dark, handsome man whom she couldn't name even though he looked very familiar.

"You're Mrs. Stone, aren't you?" he asked.

"I am," admitted Lucy, silently reminding herself that this could be one of those situations her mother had always warned her about. "But how do you know me?"

He gave a disarming chuckle and smiled, revealing two deep dimples in each of his tanned cheeks. Lucy resisted the impulse to smile back and maintained an aloof expression.

"Excuse me," he said, extending a hand. "I'm Luther

Read, Junior, but everybody calls me Junior. Your daughter is our mother's helper. I've seen you waiting for her in your car."

"It's nice to meet you," said Lucy, taking his hand. "I am indeed the family chauffeur."

"Slow elevator," said Junior, bouncing on the balls of his feet. "So what brings you to Boston?"

"The NNA conference," said Lucy. "I work for the Tinker's Cove *Pennysaver.*"

Recognition dawned in Junior's eyes. "Lucy Stone. I read your stuff all the time, but I didn't make the connection." He chuckled. "I guess we'd better treat Elizabeth right or we'll be a page-one story."

Lucy smiled. "You can be sure that whatever Elizabeth tells me will be off the record." She paused and sighed. "Not that she's going to tell me much, and certainly not in sentences of more than one word. 'Where are you going?' 'Out.' 'Who are you going out with?' 'Friends.' 'When will you be back?' 'Later.' " She rolled her eyes. "You know how it is."

"Not yet. Trevor's only three."

"Well, enjoy him while you can," advised Lucy. "They grow up too fast."

The elevator doors were opening and Lucy was preparing to step inside when Junior took her by the elbow.

"Do you mind? There's somebody I'd like you to meet. I just spotted my father."

"Okay," said Lucy, allowing herself to be steered across the lobby to a couple who were seated on one of the oversize sofas that were scattered about. The man, a gray-haired version of Junior, rose as they approached.

"Dad, you'll never guess who I just met. This is the *Pennysaver*'s Lucy Stone! Right here in town for the convention. And how's this for six degrees of separation? Her daughter Elizabeth is our mother's helper this summer."

"I'm glad to meet you," he said, taking her hand.

"Junior here forgot to mention that I'm Luther Read, and this is my dear friend Monica Underwood."

Lucy's gaze turned to the crisply turned-out woman sitting on the sofa and she immediately recognized her. Monica Underwood was running for reelection as a senator representing Vermont in the United States Congress.

"You need no introduction, either of you," said Lucy. "It's an honor to meet you." Lucy took Monica's outstretched hand. "I've often wished we had someone like you to represent Maine."

"That's very kind of you," said Monica. "Won't you sit down?"

"Thank you," said Lucy, accepting her invitation.

She almost felt like pinching herself to see if she were dreaming. After all, she'd barely been in Boston for an hour and here she was chatting with the Reads, who as owners of the Pioneer Press Group were major movers and shakers in the newspaper industry, and sitting next to Monica Underwood, the controversial champion of doomed initiatives like the Equal Rights Amendment and universal health care and a tireless advocate for the underprivileged, unemployed, and uninsured. And they were all treating her as if she were their equal.

"It's a pleasure to meet you, Lucy," said Luther, taking an adjacent chair. "I've admired your work for some time."

"Thank you," replied Lucy, trying not to stammer. "I have to admit that I'm a little surprised to learn that you read the *Pennysaver.*"

"Of course we do. We're in the business, for one thing, and having the house in Tinker's Cove, we've always followed the local news in the *Pennysaver.* I must say you've really brought new energy and a fresh perspective to that venerable institution. You have a real knack for getting the story."

Lucy swallowed hard. "I think most of the credit should go to Ted—Ted Stillings—he's the editor and publisher."

"You're too modest," said Luther. "I've been in the business a long time and I know good work when I see it."

"It's true," said Monica, taking Luther's hand and giving it an affectionate squeeze. "Luther is going to be named Newspaperman of the Year at the banquet tomorrow night."

"Congratulations," said Lucy. "That's quite an honor."

"No one deserves it more," said Junior.

There was such honest respect and affection in his voice that Lucy was struck by it. It wasn't often, she thought, that a grown son expressed such open admiration for his father. She found herself wishing that Bill and Toby's relationship were more like Luther and Junior's.

"That's right," agreed Monica. "Luther hasn't just paid lip service to the democratic idea of free and open debate; he's made it a reality in the Pioneer Press papers."

"Not everyone would agree with you, my dear," said Luther. "Some of our readers and employees seem to feel we've carried openness a bit too far, especially when it comes to social issues like reproductive rights and homosexuality."

"What do you think, Lucy?" asked Monica, graciously drawing her into the conversation. "What's the line between reporting and advocating?"

Lucy, who had been content to bask in the presence of such exalted company, now found herself the focus of attention. She was groping for a reply when she was saved by Junior, who glanced at his watch and announced they had to leave.

"We've got to get up to the hospitality suite. It's due to open and Harold will be waiting for us."

"Right, right," said Luther, getting easily to his feet

despite his age. He turned to Lucy. "My brother Harold is a stickler for punctuality," he said.

"He's also the only Republican in the family," said Junior.

As the two men stood side by side, Lucy was struck by the resemblance between father and son. Both were tall and fit, exuding confidence and affability. And wealth, she decided. Not that they were ostentatious in any way, but it showed in their perfect white smiles and expensively flatering haircuts and the tailored fit of their clothes and the gleam of their buffed leather shoes.

"Lucy, I hope you'll join us for cocktails and hors d'oeuvres. We at Pioneer Press pride ourselves on our hospitality and always put out quite a spread, if I do say so myself."

It was tempting, and no doubt Ted would be thrilled if she cadged a free meal.

"Thank you," she said as the group headed back to the elevator, "but I haven't gotten settled yet."

"Of course," said Junior. "Come on down later, once you've got things sorted out. It's on the fourth floor. What's the number?"

"Four-oh-four," said Monica, leading the way into the elevator.

"The doors will be open into the wee hours, if previous years are any indication," said Luther, turning to Lucy. "I think that hospitality suite is the main reason I'm Newspaperman of the Year. Free food and drink will take you far in the news business."

"In politics, too," added Monica, as the elevator slowed. "It was nice to meet you, Lucy. I hope we'll see you later."

The doors opened and Lucy stepped out, turning to say good-bye. She hated to leave this happy bunch, all so friendly and smiling at her. She impulsively decided to accept the invitation.

"Sure thing," she said quickly, as the doors started to close.

Chapter Four

Then the doors closed and she was left alone in the elevator, ascending smoothly to the tenth floor. Lucy followed the sign when she got off the elevator, proceeding down a short hall and turning a corner, where she immediately found her room. At least she didn't have to walk all the way down the long hall, she thought, wondering if the elevators would be noisy at night. It took a few tries, but she finally got the key card to work and opened the door to her room. She closed it carefully behind her, fastening both the latch and the safety chain. She was a woman alone in the big city, and she wasn't going to take any chances.

Flicking on the light switch, she poked her head into the bathroom—white, tiny, and old-fashioned with a pedestal sink—and went straight to the window to open the drapes. Looking out, she was disappointed to see there was no view of the city, only four dreary brick walls punctuated with rows of windows. It was some sort of air shaft, she decided, that provided light and ventilation to the inside, less expensive rooms like hers.

Even so, she decided as she studied the furnishings,

it was much more luxurious than the master bedroom at home, even if it wasn't much larger. The furniture all matched, for one thing. And the bed was covered with a puffy maroon comforter and the pillows encased in white Euro-style shams. It was much more sophisticated than the candlewick spread on the bed she shared with Bill. Bed stands with bulky square lamps flanked both sides of the bed, and a matching floor lamp stood in one corner, next to a rather stiff-looking armchair. A fourth lamp, with an enormous square shade, stood on a long, low bureau next to the TV. The shade was askew— the lamp had been shoved too close to the wall—and Lucy automatically straightened it. She hated cockeyed lampshades, and, come to think of it, she didn't much like all the bits and pieces of cardboard that advised her she was indeed welcome at the Park Plaza Hotel and putting her on notice that this was a nonsmoking room and offering her several choices of room-service breakfasts. She gathered them all up and shoved them in a drawer. It was her room, after all, and she was going to be here for the better part of a week. She might as well have things the way she liked them.

Warned in advance about the high cost of hotel telephones by Ted, she perched on the edge of her bed and pulled her cell phone out of her purse and called home. The call went through and she waited while it rang at least ten times, but nobody answered. They must all be out, she decided, but where? What could they possibly be doing on a Sunday evening? Sara and Zoe ought to getting ready for bed—tomorrow was a school day—and Elizabeth ought to be helping them. Bill usually watched a newsmagazine show on Sundays; he hated to miss it. And Toby . . . well, the less she thought about what Toby did with his time these days the better.

Unless, she thought, he hadn't gone out. Maybe he'd stayed home, provoking a fight with his father. She could see the headlines now: *Deadly Domestic Dispute Rocks Village.*

Violence Erupts on Red Top Road. Neighbors Never Suspected Family Dysfunction.

That last one needed work, she thought, regaining her senses. Bill had probably taken the younger girls out for ice cream. Or down to the town pier to see the seals. Elizabeth and Toby were probably out with friends. There was no need to panic, not yet anyway. She'd call first thing tomorrow. If nobody answered, then she'd panic.

Next on her list was a call to Ted, informing him she had arrived. She made that call on the hotel phone, calling the desk and asking to be connected to his room.

"You got in all right?"

His voice was so loud, it startled her.

"Safe and sound."

"Great! Hey, congratulations! That series you did on the fishing industry got an award."

"Really?" Lucy was delighted. "First place, second, honorable mention? What?"

"Dunno. They'll announce it at the banquet. But you definitely won something."

"Wow."

"Don't let it go to your head," cautioned Ted. "There's no money in the budget for a raise or anything."

"I won't," promised Lucy. "Are you going to the hospitality suite?"

"Wouldn't miss it for the world."

"I guess I'll see you there, then. 'Bye."

Lucy carefully replaced the phone, then did a little victory dance around the bed. She'd won a prize. She was a winner! A prizewinning journalist. It was amazing. Fantastic. She was hot! No wonder the Reads had all been so nice to her. She was a star. A comer. A comet, blazing a trail of glory through the newspaper universe.

Well, at any rate, someone to watch. Someone to be taken seriously. A reporter readers could trust. One who generally got things right more often than she got them wrong. Someone, she decided as she opened her suitcase, who needed to calm down and get control of herself.

Now what exactly, she wondered, did you wear to a hospitality suite?

A short time later she was standing in the open doorway to the Pioneer Press hospitality suite, dressed in the polo-style shirtdress with the grosgrain ribbon belt she'd bought at the outlet mall. The saleslady had promised her it was a classic, but Lucy was beginning to think it was last year's classic look. Nobody else was wearing anything remotely like it.

"Lucy! So glad you could make it!" Junior clasped her hand and shook it energetically, radiating good fellowship and bonhomie. "The bar's in the corner and help yourself to the food."

Then he was gone. Lucy scanned the room, looking for Ted. Or someone she knew. Anybody. But except for Monica Underwood and Luther Read, she didn't recognize a single soul. She didn't feel as if she could presume on her slight acquaintance with them; besides, they were busy working the room, greeting important people. They seemed important, anyway, these tall men in their tailored suits and slicked-back hair with their reed-thin wives on their arms.

The type was familiar to her from home. The folks who had summer homes on Smith Heights Road and belonged to the yacht club. The men played golf and the women belonged to the garden club and organized house tours to raise money for favorite charities. They didn't mingle much with year-rounders like herself.

Lucy decided a glass of white wine might help boost her confidence, so she headed for the bar. Then, glass in hand, she began a slow circuit of the room, looking for someone to strike up a conversation with. Most everyone was in a group, engaged in lively conversation punctuated with bursts of laughter, but she finally spotted another loner, a heavyset woman with a glum expression.

"Hi! Nice party, isn't it?" said Lucy.

The woman stared at her through thick glasses, as if she'd made an indecent proposition, then abruptly turned and clomped off.

Oh, well, she'd done her best. She'd tried to be sociable, but now it was time for the prizewinning journalist to hit the buffet table. That was where Ted found her, stubbornly holding her own amidst the crowd of hungry journalists browsing among the platters of shrimp, cheese, and raw vegetables. There were also chafing dishes holding hot Swedish meatballs, bacon-wrapped scallops, and pigs-in-blankets.

"Some spread, huh?" said Ted. "We probably won't need supper after all this."

"I guess not," said Lucy, attacking the platters with new gusto. "But what about dessert?"

"There's a fruit platter on the other table."

The other table, Lucy saw, was surrounded by an even larger crowd of people. It was a positive feeding frenzy; she'd never seen anything like it.

"Maybe later," she said.

"I'm going to get in there before it's all gone," said Ted, diving into the fray.

Lucy retreated to a quiet corner, where she stood and nibbled on her supper of hors d'oeuvres. It was a funny sort of party, she decided. Except for the Reads and their crowd, probably publishers, not much socializing was going on at all. People were just eating and drinking as fast as they could. These were most certainly the reporters and editors at the bottom of the organizational pyramid. They put in long hours, they didn't make much money, and they weren't about to pass up a free meal. In fact, quite a few of them were snagging snacks for later, wrapping bits of food in paper napkins and tucking them away in purses and pockets.

Once Lucy had finished eating she didn't see much point in sticking around, so she put her plate on a table by the door and headed for her room. She still hadn't unpacked and she had a fresh bottle of bubble bath and an emergency chocolate bar in her suitcase. Just the thing to round out her dinner.

Chapter Five

When Lucy woke the next morning it took her a moment or two to remember where she was. She missed the warmth of Bill's body, his bulk, beside her. At home she liked to savor the first moments of her day, lying in bed and listening to the birds singing outside. Once she'd checked the clock, she always looked at the white-curtained window, gauging whether it would be sunny or cloudy. Then she'd consciously prepare herself for the day ahead by counting her blessings: being alive, being married to the man she loved, having four healthy children. Those things topped the list, but Lucy didn't stop there. She counted the house, the well-stocked pantry and refrigerator, the peas ripening in the garden, the buds on the rosebushes along the fence, the six new pairs of underpants neatly folded in her top drawer.

She tried the exercise in the hotel, stretching luxuriously under the crisp, white sheets, but it just made her feel homesick. It was already past seven, and at home she would have been up for an hour. She'd be hurrying Sara out the door to catch the school bus, reminding her of after-school activities and checking to make sure she had her lunch and homework. Then there would just be time for a swallow of coffee before she had to get Zoe, who took the eight-o'clock elementary school bus, started on her breakfast. It was a pretty complicated routine, and Lucy acted like a conductor, making sure everyone got fed and dressed and got a turn in the bathroom. She wondered how they were managing without her.

Probably not very well, but there was nothing she could do about it here in Boston. She rolled over and dug the card listing room-service breakfasts out of the drawer where she'd stowed it. The Businessman's Special with bacon and two eggs was an outrageous eighteen dollars, but she was seriously tempted by the Continental at a more reasonable twelve dollars. It would be an extravagance, but one that she herself could afford. The phone rang and she grabbed it eagerly, hoping it was Bill. Instead she heard Ted's voice, sounding a little thick, as if he'd been out partying the night before.

"G'morning," he said. "The registration desk opens at eight, so what say you get there first thing to beat the crowd and then we'll get some breakfast."

Lucy regretfully slipped the room service menu back into the drawer and checked the clock. It was almost seven-thirty, which meant that her leisurely morning was at an end.

"Okay. I'll meet you in the lobby in half an hour."

"Righto." Ted chuckled. "I'll be wearing a white carnation."

That must have been some night if Ted was still feeling no pain, thought Lucy as she hung up the phone. She hadn't expected her boss to behave like a stereotypical conventioneer; she thought he was serious about attending the workshops and honing his skills. Then again, maybe he was here to party while she did the serious work. She stretched and got out of bed, heading for the shower.

Her hair was still damp when she found the registration desk, located on the mezzanine. No one was manning it yet, however, so she wandered into the exhibit room. There, portable partitions had been set up, creating a gallerylike effect, but instead of paintings they displayed tear sheets from newspapers. They were arranged by category, and Lucy soon realized these were the stories and photographs that had been chosen for awards by the judges. The awards hadn't been announced yet, but all of the displays would receive prizes ranging from honorable mention to first place.

Lucy was especially fascinated by the photographs: a firefighter with an infant folded against his chest, the stoic and tearless face of a military widow receiving a folded flag as her two young children clung to her legs, and a charming shot of a grandmother and grandchild sharing the first ice-cream cone of the summer season. She got a pleasant surprise when she rounded the corner to view the exhibits on the other side of the partition and saw a familiar page from the *Pennysaver* with her byline. It was a story she had written over a year ago, about the impact of federal and state regulations on Maine fishermen. The judge's comment, scrawled in Magic Marker, read, *Carefully chosen quotes and real-life stories give these statistics a human dimension—top-notch reporting and writing.*

Lucy felt her cheeks warm with embarrassment and pleasure. It was true. They liked her work. She was good. She was a good reporter. Top-notch in fact. Wow. She stepped back to admire the page, taking in for the first time the three other stories in her category. They all had similarly flattering comments. Oh, well. Time would tell.

Hearing voices outside, she went back to the registration desk, where she discovered a short line had formed. Only one woman was staffing the desk, and she didn't seem terribly familiar with the process.

"I'm not even supposed to be doing this," she explained. "I can't imagine what's keeping Susan and Debbie."

"They're probably still in the Pioneer Press hospitality suite," suggested one man, and the others chuckled.

"Oh, I don't think so," said the clerk, who was flipping through a box of alphabetized registration packets.

Lucy was fourth in line, but at this rate she was going to be late. She sighed and looked down, only to be captivated by the shoes the woman in front of her was wearing. She'd never seen shoes like this before. They were witty and charming. Adorable, with tiny little curvy heels that reminded her of her very first pair of "high" heels. And the color, a wonderful coral, almost brick, that would go with absolutely anything. She shifted her position so she could see the toes and involuntarily gasped in pleasure. They were pointed, very pointed, and revealed a suggestive amount of toe cleavage.

Her gaze drifted upward, examining the rest of the woman's outfit. Not surprisingly, she was the very picture of urban sophistication in a short black skirt topped with a nubby beige twinset. Neat gold earrings were clipped on each ear, and her salt-and-pepper hair was expertly cut in a crisp boyish bob. A designer tote hung from her shoulder with one of those ubiquitous water bottles that everyone seemed to carry tucked in an outside pocket.

Lucy couldn't help thinking that she didn't fare very well in comparison. She was wearing her best khakis and had dressed up her polo shirt by tying a cotton sweater around her shoulders. Her feet were sporting sandals, which along with sneakers and patent-leather pumps comprised her entire summer shoe wardrobe.

"Name? *Name?*"

Lucy snapped to attention and gave her name, receiving in exchange a folder and an official NNA badge that dangled from a blue-and-white lanyard. Oh, good, she thought as she hung it around her neck, just the touch my outfit needs.

She found Ted in the lobby, taking a catnap on one of the sofas.

"That was quick," he said, blinking and yawning.

"Not really," said Lucy. "It's a quarter to nine. They didn't even open until eight-thirty, and quite a few people were ahead of me." She glanced at the Swan Court restaurant, where waiters were pouring deliciously fragrant coffee from silver pots. "Are we going to eat there?"

"At those prices? I don't think so. Follow me."

Lucy sighed regretfully as Ted led her out of the hotel and around the corner to a familiar franchise coffee shop. There was one just like it in Tinker's Cove, at the interstate exit. They got in line and Lucy ordered juice, coffee, and a bagel sandwich. Ted stuck to black coffee.

"You seem a little bit under the weather," she observed brightly, taking a big bite of the egg, cheese, and ham sandwich.

"Pam left last night, so I went out with some of the guys." He stared into the depths of his coffee. "Big mistake. I shoulda gone to bed after the hospitality suite."

"You were right—I didn't need dinner. I never saw so much food."

"Musta cost 'em a pretty penny," continued Ted, taking a sip of coffee. "I guess they want to go out with a bang."

Lucy put down her sandwich. "What do you mean?"

"Pioneer Press has been sold, you know. Everything but signing the papers and cashing the check."

"The whole chain?" Lucy could hardly believe it. And why, she wondered, had no mention been made of the sale when she'd talked to the Reads the night before? "Who's the buyer?"

"National Media. They're buying everything they

can. They want to be the premier national news outlet, maybe the only one, for that matter." Ted stared into his coffee. "So what's your first panel?"

Lucy opened the packet she'd been given at the registration table and studied it. " 'Interviewing Techniques, or Getting the Story They Don't Want You to Print.' Sounds interesting."

"Don't be late," said Ted.

Lucy checked her watch and discovered it was already a quarter past nine, and she had no idea where the panel was meeting.

"I guess I'd better get going," she said, crumpling up her paper wrapper and juice container and putting them in the trash. The coffee she took with her, just in case the panel wasn't as stimulating as promised.

A lot of other people had the same idea, she discovered when she found the meeting room, tucked down a flight of stairs underneath the lobby. Almost everyone seated at the rows of tables had either a covered take-out coffee cup or a bottle of water. One of the panelists seated at the front of the room, a young woman, was apparently expecting a drought—she had an enormous two-quart bottle of springwater.

The second panelist, an attractive woman in her thirties, arrived at nine-thirty, precisely on time.

"Our third panelist is running late," she said, "but we'll begin without him. I'm Catherine Read and, as most of you know, I'm the publisher of the Northampton *News*. That's Northampton, Massachusetts. We're a daily with a circulation that varies from twenty to thirty thousand, and we're owned by the Pioneer Press Group."

Lucy noticed that Catherine did indeed bear a resemblance to Luther and Junior Read, and guessed she must be Junior's younger sister. She wondered if she had gotten her job through hard work and ability or family connections. Maybe both.

"My esteemed colleague here is Morgan Dodd, who

is a reporter for the Framingham *Tribune*, a daily located right here in the Boston suburbs."

Lucy recognized the name; she'd seen it on the byline of one of the other stories selected for a prize. The same prize she'd been chosen for. They were competitors. She listened closely as Catherine continued.

" I might add that Morgan won first prize last year for her profile of Robert Andrade, the man who went to work the day after Christmas and shot seven fellow employees at Rayotex Industries."

Hearing this, Lucy's spirits sank a notch. Her chances of winning first place weren't as good as she thought.

The audience was impressed, however, and Morgan looked pleased at the buzz in the room. Her smile vanished, however, when the third panelist threw open the double doors at the rear of the room with a bang and staggered to the front. Lucy caught a definite whiff of alcohol as he passed, the same stale smell she associated with the district court on Monday morning, when the weekend catch of DUI's were arraigned.

"Here's our missing panelist," said Catherine in a spritely voice. "Sam Syrjala, editor of the Hartford *Gazette*. That's Hartford, Connecticut, and the *Gazette*, also owned by Pioneer Press Group, is a daily with a circulation of over a hundred thousand, making it one of the biggest papers in the group."

Syrjala didn't acknowledge this gracious introduction but collapsed into his chair. Unlike Morgan, who was neatly dressed in an edgy urban outfit complete with spiky hair and chunky shoes, and Catherine, neatly put together in a tan pantsuit and a silk camp shirt, he looked as if he'd slept in his rumpled seersucker suit. But even if he'd taken the trouble to dress in fresh clothes that morning, Lucy doubted it would have done much good. Seriously overweight and balding, with droopy jowls and bloodshot eyes, Syrjala was not a good-looking man.

"Well, let's get started," said Catherine. "Today's topic is interviewing techniques, and instead of sitting here and patting ourselves on the back for our past successes, I'd like to turn this panel over to you—the folks who are out there every day getting the stories. Then, as panelists, we can add our two cents' worth. How does that sound?"

It sounded pretty good to everyone except Morgan Dodd. Lucy noticed she was definitely miffed at losing a chance to talk about her prizewinning interview. Had it been an intentional slap in the face, or was Catherine simply trying to include as many people as possible in the discussion?

"Okay, let's get started," she said, adding an encouraging smile. "Would somebody, anybody, like to share an interviewing technique that really works—maybe something that puts the subject at ease?"

Nobody said a word. It was like being back in school, where everyone avoided making eye contact with the teacher. They examined their fingernails, they wrote in their notebooks, they tightened the lids on their coffee cups, they did anything except raise their hands.

Lucy couldn't stand it. Her hand shot up.

"Great, we have a volunteer," said Catherine, rewarding her with a big smile. "Would you mind introducing yourself?"

Lucy took a deep breath. "Well, I'm Lucy Stone, and I'm a reporter at the Tinker's Cove *Pennysaver;* that's in Maine." Lucy was rushing, sliding the words together. "One thing I've found really helpful is to let the subject know right up front that I'll be taking the photo at the end of the interview. A lot of people worry about having their picture taken, but if you tell them you're not going to spring it on them it gives them a chance to relax a bit."

"You take your own pictures?" asked a young fellow with a shaved head.

"Doesn't everybody?"

"No. I just give the name and phone number to the guys in photo."

Seeing nods all around, Lucy felt embarrassed.

"Well," she said, adding a nervous little chuckle, "the *Pennysaver* is pretty small. There's just me, a receptionist, and Ted, who's the editor and publisher."

"Who do you interview, anyway?" demanded Morgan. "Isn't the *Pennysaver* one of those throwaways?"

"Not in Tinker's Cove. It's been around forever, and used to be called the *Advertiser.* The owner changed it to the *Pennysaver* during the depression. There's also a Five Cents Savings Bank in town. I guess a penny used to be worth a lot more."

The others laughed at her little joke and Lucy began to feel better.

"I've heard of your paper," said Syrjala, rousing himself from the nap he'd settled into immediately after arriving. "Didn't you break that Ron Davitz story last summer?"

Lucy felt her cheeks redden. "That was me," she said.

"That was lucky, having a big story fall in your lap like that," said Morgan.

Lucy sat up a bit straighter. She'd risked life and limb to get that story and she wasn't about to pretend otherwise. "That's not the only story we broke that got picked up by the wires," she said. "There was the Metinnicut casino scandal and the cop who was dealing drugs and . . ." Lucy's voice trailed off; she didn't want to brag, after all. She shrugged. "Tinker's Cove isn't a typical small town. We have a lot of tourists and a lot of high-powered summer people."

Catherine Read looked as if she was about to speak, but was cut off by Morgan.

"Well, when I interviewed Robert Andrade, the workplace shooter, he was pretty much in a state of shock. Almost catatonic. The way I got him to talk was that I convinced him I was on his side. I pretended to sympathize with him and pretty soon it all came spilling out. How he hated his boss and how the others made fun of him and—"

"That poses an interesting question about the ethics of pretending to sympathize with an interview subject," said Catherine. "Let's hear from some of you other people."

The workshop picked up after that and the rest of the morning flew by. The panel went a little over its allotted time before Catherine finally closed it at a quarter past noon. Lucy was slipping her notebook into her tote bag when Catherine stopped by her chair.

"Thanks for helping to get the ball rolling," she said. "I always hate those awkward silences."

"Me too," said Lucy. "I sometimes wish I could just keep my mouth shut, but I always end up jumping in."

"Actually, that's not a bad interviewing technique. Do you use it often?"

"Always," said Lucy, laughing.

"Listen, would you like to have lunch with me? There's a Legal Seafoods around the corner that's pretty good, and I'd love to catch up on news from Tinker's Cove. My family has a summer home there, you know."

"I'd love to have lunch with you," said Lucy, who hated eating in restaurants by herself. "Actually, we have quite a bit in common—my daughter is working for your brother as a mother's helper."

Catherine considered this news for a moment, then brushed it aside with a little joke. "From what I hear about Trevor, she'll definitely have her hands full."

Legal Seafoods was crowded, and Lucy expected they would have to wait for a table, but the maître d' took one look at Catherine and led them to a quiet corner table for two. What was it with this family? wondered Lucy. Were they charmed or something?

"This isn't too bad," said Catherine, picking up the menu. "It's not near a window, but it's not by the kitchen door, either."

"It's fine," said Lucy, opening her menu and looking for something that wouldn't take too long to be prepared. "I've got another panel this afternoon and I don't want to be late."

"Not like Sam Syrjala," observed Catherine, showing annoyance for the first time. "Honestly, I don't know what people like my brother and my uncle see in him. Okay, so he was a legend in his day, but now he's really resting on past glories." Pursing her lips, as if she realized she'd spoken too freely, she opened her menu and deftly changed the subject. "What shall we have? I've heard the chowder is fabulous."

They both ordered salads and chowder with glasses of iced tea, then chatted while they waited for their food.

"Do you get to Tinker's Cove much?" asked Lucy conversationally.

"Not as much as I'd like," replied Catherine. "I think I may be working too hard. That's what people tell me, anyway."

"I guess it's always like that with a family business."

"You're right. You can't escape it. Every holiday somehow turns into a business conference." She laughed. "I can't complain, though. When it comes to fun—and by fun I mean good, old-fashioned hell-raising—there's nothing like the newspaper business, is there?"

Her eyes sparkled and she smiled when she said this, and Lucy responded warmly.

"You know, when I first started working for the *Pennysaver*, I simply couldn't believe I was getting paid to have such a good time. Running around, talking to people, writing it all down and then, every Thursday, seeing my stories with my byline, it all seemed too good to be true. I was in seventh heaven."

"I know exactly what you mean," said Catherine. "I actually hate to leave at night because I might miss something."

It was clear to Lucy that the Northampton *News* meant more to Catherine than a job or a title. Lucy wondered what her future plans were once the papers had been sold, and blurted out the question without thinking.

Catherine's smile vanished. "I know there are a lot of rumors about the company, but I really can't talk about it."

Ouch. Lucy felt as if she'd been stung. The little smile Catherine tacked on made it worse somehow. It was time to change the subject.

"Northampton's an interesting town," said Lucy. "I visited there when my daughter was looking at colleges. It has a reputation of attracting a lot of people seeking alternative lifestyles, especially lesbians and militant feminists, but there's this base of old-time conservative farmers. How do you handle that?"

Catherine took so long to answer that Lucy wondered if she'd stuck her foot in her mouth yet again.

"I don't know what you mean," she said. "The paper is committed to equal rights for everyone, regardless of race, religion, sexual persuasion, whatever. That's the American way."

Lucy knew that things were never that simple, but she didn't feel as if she could pursue the issue. No matter; Catherine wasn't going to give her a chance.

"So where did your daughter decide to go?" she asked.

"Chamberlain College. Here in Boston."

"Good choice. They have an excellent journalism department there. Is she interested in following in her mother's footsteps?"

Now it was Lucy's turn to laugh. "Not a chance. At this point she doesn't think much of her mother or her father, for that matter. As far as she's concerned we're Neanderthals. Lumbering brutes who stand between her and freedom."

"Parenting is a tough job," said Catherine. "But speaking of jobs, I was wondering if you're still happy in Tinker's Cove? I could really use someone like you in Northampton."

Stunned, Lucy dropped her soup spoon with a clatter.

"I'm flattered," she said. "But I'm in no position to relocate. My husband has a contracting business; I've got kids in school. . . ."

"I figured as much," said Catherine, "but I thought I'd give it a shot."

"Thanks for the offer," said Lucy, signaling the waiter for another spoon.

"So which workshop are you going to this afternoon?" asked Catherine, spooning up the last of her chowder.

"Libel," said Lucy. "A truly terrifying subject."

"Just remember," advised Catherine, "if it's true, it's not libel."

"If only I had your confidence," said Lucy, spearing a clump of lettuce.

Catherine signaled for the check and the waiter brought it promptly. Lucy reached for her wallet, but Catherine refused to let her pay.

"Thank you—everything was delicious and I had a lovely time," said Lucy.

"Thank you—for the pleasure of your company," replied Catherine, signing the check with a flourish.

Lucy was impressed once again by the unfailing politeness all the members of the Read family seemed to exhibit. Of course, she thought as she hurried back to the hotel for the workshop, good manners could work like a hedge, protecting one's privacy with an attractive, impermeable barrier. The conversation during lunch had hardly been freewheeling and spontaneous, thought Lucy, remembering how deftly Catherine had parried her questions. Instead of giving a workshop on getting the story, she thought wryly, Catherine could have given a workshop on how to deflect a reporter's questions.

Chapter Six

As she dressed that night, Lucy remembered Catherine's words: "If it's true, it isn't libel." It had taken five panelists more than three hours and countless convoluted sentences to essentially say what Catherine had succinctly said in six words. It had been all Lucy could do to stay awake while the lawyers and editors on the panel debated the fine points of the law. When it was over she had the same sense of freedom that Sara and Zoe felt when the school bell rang at three o'clock.

Not that she was quite as carefree as they were. She had a banquet to attend and, in addition to sharing in the Trask Award, which Ted would accept, she would also receive her award. Would it be like the Oscars? she wondered. Would there be a hushed silence while everyone waited for the winner to be announced? Would she have to give a speech? Or would it be like the awards assembly at the middle school, where the principal droned his way down an endless list of names? Judging from the number of winning stories and photographs on display, it would probably be the latter.

That was probably just as well. If winning first place

meant she had to make a speech, she'd prefer an honorable mention. She hadn't enjoyed being the focus of attention at the morning workshop, and was uncomfortably aware she might have tooted her own horn a little too loudly, giving herself the reputation of an investigative hotshot. The problem with reputations, she thought as she slipped her dress over her head, was that they were so darn hard to live up to.

Smoothing the silky sheath over her hips, she looked at her reflection in the mirror and smiled. She loved this dress—it fit perfectly, and the bright pink-and-orange poppy print was gorgeous. She'd been attracted to it the minute she saw it on the sale rack at the Carriage Trade, and had been delighted when she'd tried it on. It was perfect for outdoor theater and concerts, cocktail parties and cookouts, the sort of dress-up occasions that filled her summer calendar in Tinker's Cove. It was a casual, fun sort of dress that called for bare, tan legs, white sandals, and chunky jewelry, but it dressed up quite nicely for the city with her black patent pumps and a ladylike string of faux pearls.

Well, maybe it was a bit casual, but it would have to do, she decided as she dabbed on some pink lipstick and gave her hair one last lick with the brush. Her only other option was the black dress she wore to funerals, and tonight was a night of celebration, not mourning.

There was only one chore remaining before she could head to the party—she wanted to call home. This time the phone was answered on the first ring by Bill, who proudly announced he was in the kitchen fixing dinner.

"Where were you last night?" demanded Lucy, surprised at how upset she felt. "I called and nobody answered."

"We were over at the Orensteins'. Sadie's mom invited the whole family for a cookout."

"That was awfully nice of her," said Lucy, feeling rather left out. Juanita Orenstein was the mother of Zoe's best friend, Sadie. She was a warm, caring person, and the invitation was typical of her. Juanita wasn't much on cleaning house, but she wouldn't think anything of inviting five extra people for dinner. So why this little stab of jealousy, as if Juanita were trying to take over her family?

"Yeah. I took over the hamburgers you left for us and she had some stuff, too. She makes terrific potato salad. So how's the conference?"

Lucy didn't know how to answer. In only one day she'd had so many experiences and had met so many new people. It would take hours to tell him all about it.

"So far, so good," she said. "How are things at home?"

"Fine. No problems at all."

Lucy wanted to believe him, but she was doubtful.

"So things are okay with you and Toby? You were both pretty upset when I left."

"Oh, *that.*" Bill's tone was dismissive. "That was nothing. He's doing fine. He's a real asset on the job."

"Did you say 'asset'?"

"Yeah. What did you think I said?"

Lucy let it go.

"How's Elizabeth's job working out?"

"Great."

This didn't sound like Elizabeth. "No complaints?"

"Not that I've heard."

It might be true, conceded Lucy. It was only her first day on the job. And Bill was getting a bit hard of hearing.

"Sara and Zoe? How are they doing?"

"Fine, fine. Zoe's taking care of Kudo, feeding him and all that. And Sara's been a big help."

And hell's freezing over, thought Lucy, who remembered Sara's lack of enthusiasm when Lucy had first announced she was going to the convention. And Zoe had always been afraid of the huge dog.

"What are you doing for supper tonight? More potato salad?"

Now where did that come from? Besides, Lucy knew for a fact that Juanita put too much mayonnaise in her potato salad. No wonder Bill liked it. He liked anything so long as it was loaded with cholesterol.

"I'm going to make a stir-fry, soon as I find the wok."

"It's in the pantry. Top shelf." Lucy heard a sudden shriek in the background, as if the girls were fighting. "Are you sure everything's okay? I thought I heard Zoe scream."

"No, no, just the TV," insisted Bill. "Well, I guess I'd better get started cooking. Don't worry about a thing. Everything's under control."

The poor fool, thought Lucy, as she tucked her key card and banquet ticket into her tiny evening bag. He probably did think he had things under control. It was only an illusion, of course. He'd find out soon enough.

The mezzanine was crowded when the elevator door opened, and Lucy joined the crowd of conferees, most of whom were milling about with drinks in their hands and talking at the top of their lungs. She would have loved a glass of wine, but the crowd clustered around the bar was more than she could handle. When someone bumped into her from behind and she narrowly avoided a potentially disastrous collision with a woman holding a glass of red wine, Lucy decided she'd had enough of this crowd scene. It was great if you knew these people, she supposed, but she didn't. She was being pushed and shoved, the noise was deafening, and she was pretty sure all the oxygen was being used up. It was time to find her table and sit down.

The registration table, where late arrivals were still picking up name tags and packets, was set up in front of a pair of double doors, which Lucy assumed gave entry to the grand ballroom. The doors were shut, but Lucy didn't think anyone would mind if she slipped inside, out of the fray. She reached for the ornate gold handle and in a moment she was through, grateful for the rush of cool, fresh air. She leaned against the closed door for a moment while she recovered from the crush and got her bearings.

"Don't think you're going to get away with this!"

She snapped her head up, shocked at the speaker's angry tone. It was Junior Read, of all people, apparently very upset about something. He was facing his father, jabbing a finger at his chest.

Lucy gasped in shock at his behavior. It was the last thing she would have expected.

"Don't talk to me like that," roared Luther, equally angry. "Who do you think you are, anyway? What gives you the right? I've put my lifeblood into this company for over forty years."

The two men were surrounded by a small knot of people, all of whom were focused on their argument and unaware of her entrance.

Unaware, that is, until she dropped her beaded evening purse, which landed noisily on the polished parquet floor. Then all eyes were suddenly on her. Junior, Catherine, Luther, Monica, even Sam Syrjala, were all staring at her, as well as several others she didn't recognize. Her eyes darted around the room and she immediately realized her mistake. This was not the grand ballroom; it was a private function room set up for a small group of people.

"I'm so sorry," she stammered. "I'm in the wrong room."

Seconds later she was on the other side of the door, fanning her flushed face. What a faux pas, she realized, spotting the placard announcing *Pioneer Press Group: Private*. The Reads were obviously hosting a prebanquet cocktail party for invited guests, and she'd barged in like a gate crasher. How humiliating.

"Hi, Lucy! Where have you been hiding? I've been looking all over for you."

It was Ted, and Lucy had never been so happy to see him.

"I was looking for you, too, but I couldn't find you in this crowd."

"They're opening the doors, finally," he said, pointing to the opposite end of the mezzanine. "Let's get our table, shall we?"

"Good idea," agreed Lucy as the crowd surged forward.

The grand ballroom was indeed grand, thought Lucy as she surveyed the enormous cream-and-gilt-trimmed space. Scores of tables topped with spotless linen cloths and covered with glittering silver and stemmed goblets filled the lower level, which was ringed with a balcony, where even more tables were arranged behind an ornately curlicued black-and-gold railing. Enormous crystal chandeliers hung from the ceiling, and smoked mirrors lined the walls. She had never seen anything so gorgeous in her life; she felt as if she'd stepped into the Hall of Mirrors at Versailles. Not that she'd been there, of course, but this was how she imagined it must be.

"What number are we?"

Ted's voice brought her back to reality.

"Twenty-one, I think."

They cruised around the room, checking the numbered cards set in metal holders on each table, and exchanging pleasantries with people Ted knew. It didn't take long for Lucy to realize her dress was all wrong; most of the women were wearing beaded cocktail dresses or long evening gowns. In fact, she realized when they finally found their table and sat down, every single woman at the banquet was dressed in some variation of black. Black silk, black chiffon, black with beads, black with rhinestones, short black cocktail dresses, black evening dresses, and even black pantsuits. All black. There was no way she was going to get lost in this crowd, not in her pink-and-orange poppy print. In fact, she couldn't have chosen a dress that would make her stand out more.

"Do you want something to drink?" asked Ted.

"I'd love it," said Lucy, only to have her hopes dashed when Ted raised his arm and signaled a busboy holding a pitcher of water.

She sipped her water, trying not to feel self-conscious, and smiling at the others who joined them at their table. The room was noisy and she couldn't always catch the names, but Ted seemed to know everyone. There was a middle-aged couple from New Hampshire, a serious-looking man with glasses accompanied by two young fellows she guessed were rookie reporters, the glum-looking woman with a weight problem who had snubbed Lucy in the hospitality suite, and a pleasant older couple who sat next to Lucy.

"I'm Harriet Sims and this is my husband, Herb. We publish the Aroostook *Recorder,*" said the woman, who Lucy was relieved to see was wearing black with white polka dots. "Love your dress, dear. I don't know why everybody dresses as if they're going to a funeral."

"I've been to livelier funerals," grumbled Herb. "Five hours from now we'll be sitting here with nothing and Pioneer Press Group will grab all the awards."

"Now, you know that's not true. Ted's getting an award, aren't you, Ted?"

"And so is Lucy," added Ted.

"How wonderful!" enthused Harriet. "I bet it's for a human-interest story."

"Actually, it's about the new fishing regulations and their impact on Maine fishermen."

Harriet's eyes widened. "My goodness! Such a depressing topic."

"Fishing's over," said the serious man with glasses. "Times change. It's a different economy. Fishermen are going the way of the farmers and the lumberjacks and the railroad engineers."

"We're next," said Herb. "The independently owned small-town newspaper is fast going the way of the dodo."

"It's not just the small papers," said the overweight woman. "Look at Pioneer. Now they're gong to be part of National Media. It's the big fish swallowing the medium fish that swallowed the little fish."

"I heard that might not happen," said the man with glasses, capturing everyone's interest.

"Really? I thought it was a done deal," said Ted.

"Me, too," agreed Herb.

The man with glasses kept them waiting while he took a long drink of water. "Nope," he finally said. "What I hear is that the old man is having second thoughts, now that Monica Underwood is in the picture. Seems she'd like nothing better than a friendly chain of newspapers for spouting her political views. Let's face it, the folks at National Media aren't going to be sympathetic to her tree-hugging, 'takes a village to raise a child,' universal-health-care politics."

"So you think Luther Read has changed his mind about the sale?' asked Lucy.

"That's what I hear—and the family's not too happy about it, especially Junior. He's wanted to cash out for years. Of course, it's good news for the lesbian daughter; she gets to keep her feminazi rag, and Luther's brother Harold keeps his lock on the Manchester *Republican*."

Lucy's ears were burning. She didn't like hearing people she admired spoken of so crudely, especially Catherine. The others seemed unfazed by his attitude, however.

"Can't blame Junior," said Herb philosophically. "You can't make any money in newspapers anymore."

While the conversation turned to the sorry state of the news industry, Lucy fell silent, remembering the scene she'd witnessed earlier. Had Junior and Luther been arguing about the sale to National Media? What had Luther said? Something about pouring out his lifeblood for forty years? Something like that. From what she was hearing, Junior was the odd man out. The others were probably relieved the sale was off. Especially Catherine. Lucy wondered if she really was a lesbian, or if the guy with glasses thought the word was an insult.

Almost everyone was seated by now, filling all the tables except for number twenty, right next to twenty-one, where Lucy and Ted were sitting. The buzzing in the room quieted and there was an expectant hush, almost as if word had been received that the president's helicopter had landed outside. Only this time the awaited guest was Luther Read, the Newspaperman of the Year.

When he finally appeared in the doorway, followed by an entourage, there was a spontaneous outburst of applause. Many people got to their feet and greeted him as he passed, shaking hands and slapping him on the back. Several women embraced him, giving him air kisses.

"This could take all night," grumbled Herb. "When are they gonna start serving the food?"

"Honestly, Herb," said Harriet, rolling her eyes. "Can't you think of anything except your stomach?"

"It's been, what, seven hours since lunch. My ulcer's acting up."

"Well, take one of your pills and hush; here they come."

"He's not the goddamn king of the world," said Herb, as his wife popped out of her seat and reached for Luther's hand.

"Harriet! And Herb! Nice to see you!" boomed Luther. "Great to see you all."

Behind him, Junior and Catherine wore the bemused expressions of second-fiddle players, watching their father in action.

"We'd better get to our table, Dad. They're starting to serve. And we don't want to hold things up."

"Right, right. I just want to say hi to all my friends. Do I see Ted Stillings over there? The Rupert Murdoch of Tinker's Cove?"

Ted laughed at the joke, standing up and reaching across the table to take first Luther's hand and then Junior's. While they were exchanging congratulations, Catherine greeted Lucy.

"What was that all about?" asked Ted, when the Reads moved on to their table.

"What do you mean?"

"I didn't know you're friends with Catherine Read, that's all."

"I just met her today, at one of the panels," said Lucy. "We had lunch together."

"I heard she's head-hunting," said the glum woman. "Little Miss Perfect can't keep staff. People are quitting right and left."

Ted gave her a sharp look.

"Who's that couple?" asked Lucy, eager to change the subject. "The man who's about Luther's age and the woman who looks like Ivana Trump?"

She was especially curious about the man because he was sitting next to Sam Syrjala, of all people, and apparently sharing a joke with him. She would never have expected someone like Syrjala to be seated at the Reads' table, much less acting as if he belonged there.

Harriet chuckled merrily. "Ivana Trump, that's good," she said, as the waiter set a fruit cup in front of her.

"Harold Read, publisher of the Manchester *Republican*, and his wife," said Ted. "What's her name?"

"Inez," said the glum woman. "But it ought to be Imelda, if anybody's counting shoes."

"Like Imelda Marcos?" asked Lucy. "The wife of the deposed president of the Philippines?"

The glum woman screwed up her face, as if she'd like to say more.

"So let me get this. Harold is Luther's brother and he publishes that conservative New Hampshire paper, the *Republican*?"

"And the *Republican* is that conservative—" continued Lucy.

"Reactionary," said the glum woman, sounding like a teacher correcting a student.

" 'Course, that'll all change if National Media takes over," predicted Herb. "It'll be as bleached and bland as Wonder bread, and heavy on the feel-good features." He snorted. "It's enough to make you puke. I for one hope Luther does tell those bastards to keep their money." He paused, registering the fact that everyone at the table had their fruit cup except him. "Where the hell's my fruit salad?"

"The waiter ran out," said Harriet. "Look, he's bringing it now."

Conversation died down throughout the banquet room as the stuffed chicken breasts were served, and Lucy's table was no exception, apart from the occasional complaint from Herb.

"How come they don't cook vegetables anymore?" he grumbled, chasing a piece of carrot with his fork.

"They're crisp-tender," said Harriet. "That's so they keep the vitamins."

"Fit for goats, that's what it is," said Herb, shoving the vegetables aside and concentrating on his chicken. "And the portions are so small. There's not enough food here to feed my two-year-old grandson."

Lucy had no complaints about her dinner. Anything was fine with her as long as she didn't have to cook it. She was thoroughly enjoying her chicken and rice pilaf and assorted spring vegetables.

The waiters had begun to clear away the entrees and were pouring coffee when Lucy noticed a flurry of activity at the Reads' table. Luther was apparently having an allergic reaction of some kind. He was sneezing uncontrollably, coughing, and wiping his eyes. Harold handed him a handkerchief and he seemed better for a moment or two; then the sneezing and coughing started again. Aware that he was drawing attention, Luther covered his mouth and nose with the handkerchief and hurried out of the room, reaching into his jacket pocket as he went. He was obviously headed for the privacy of the men's room, where he intended to treat himself with an inhaler or other allergy medication.

Lucy was just finishing her dessert—a thin wedge of very rich chocolate cake sitting in a pool of raspberry sauce—when a man stepped to the microphone in the front of the room and asked for silence. The program, he said, was going to begin in a few minutes, as soon as the waiters finished clearing.

Hearing this news, Junior got to his feet and left the hall, presumably in search of his father. It was only a moment or two later that he returned in some agitation.

"We need an ambulance," Lucy heard him say to the man in charge of the program. "My father's collapsed."

Several people hurried out of the room, along with several members of the Read party, including Harold. Catherine, Monica, and Inez remained at the table with Syrjala, trying unsuccessfully not to look anxious.

People from the other tables, however, began drifting to the door, curious to see what was going on. That brought the emcee back to the microphone.

"Please stay in your seats," he said. "We're going to start the program with a short film, a biography of Luther Read."

Before the film could be started, however, the rumors began to spread from table to table. Luther Read was dead of a drug overdose. Luther Read had suffered a heart attack and was at this very moment being rushed to Boston Medical in critical condition. No, it was Mass General, and it wasn't a heart attack, it was a stroke, and he was completely paralyzed on his left side.

As the rumors swirled around them, Monica sat quietly, clutching Inez's hand. Sam Syrjala polished off his drink and signaled the waiter for another, then leaned toward Inez and began bending her ear. Catherine looked miserable and very alone with her father's and Junior's empty chairs on either side of her. Then Junior returned, looking very serious, and the room fell silent. Everyone watched as he hurried to the table. There, he bent down to Monica and shook his head from side to side sadly.

Lucy couldn't hear a word, but the little drama was as clear to her as if it had been onstage or in the movies. Monica's shocked expression as she struggled with the awful news; Junior's stricken yet controlled expression as he did what had to be done. He and Inez were leading Monica from the room when she suddenly halted, shaking her head.

"That's impossible," she was heard to say. "I gave him a fresh inhaler this morning. I saw him use it. It worked just fine this morning."

Then they were joined by Harold and Sam, who hustled them out the door, followed by Catherine. The lights were turned off and the film began to roll. It was eerie, thought Lucy, watching the images of Luther Read flicking across the screen. Maybe he was dead or maybe he was fighting for his life, but in the darkened room he was an enormous, living presence.

Then the film ended. The final image of Luther Read's smiling face had hardly faded when the announcement came.

"Luther Read, our Newspaperman of the Year, is dead."

That was incredible enough, but an even more shocking announcement followed.

"Remain in your seats, please, as the police will be collecting information from everyone."

Chapter Seven

Tuesday morning, when Lucy awoke in her light-filled room, there was a brief moment when she felt relaxed and refreshed, as if everything were right with the world. Then, as if a dark cloud had covered the sun, she remembered that something was very wrong indeed. Luther Read had been murdered and there was little doubt that the murderer was someone very close to him.

She glanced at the clock and stumbled into the bathroom, astonished to see it was well past nine. At home she was always up well before six and even on weekends rarely managed to sleep in past seven. Of course, she remembered as she groped for her toothbrush, she hadn't gotten to bed until after two this morning. The police had worked their way methodically through the banquet room, saving those seated near the Reads' table for last.

Not that anyone at her table had been able to tell Detective Paul Sullivan of the Boston Police Department very much.

"The Reads seemed happy enough," volunteered Herb.

"And why wouldn't they? They've got it all: money, prestige, and power."

"It was a celebration," offered Harriet. "Luther was being honored as Newspaperman of the Year. The whole family seemed to be enjoying themselves."

"No signs of discord? Nothing at all?" persisted Sullivan.

He was a stocky fellow in his early thirties, dressed casually in a polo shirt and khaki pants, who looked as if he took fitness seriously and worked out regularly. He also had a frank, pleasant face and reacted enthusiastically to every bit of information, almost as if it were a gift.

Lucy struggled with her conscience, debating whether she should tell the detective what she had seen before the banquet. It wasn't her business to tell, she felt. True, she had witnessed a disagreement, but family members often argued, and it was difficult for an outsider to understand what was really going on, especially one who simply blundered into a private gathering. She certainly wouldn't want some passerby who happened upon a squabble like Bill and Toby's fight over the shed tattling about her family. Plus, she had a reporter's instinct to hoard information in hopes of eventually developing a well-balanced—and exclusive—story.

"You were only sitting a few feet from the victim," said the detective, looking each of them in the eye in turn. "What did you see?"

His eyes moved from Ted to the New Hampshire couple, whom Lucy knew now as Arthur and Mildred, to the man with eyeglasses, Jim Prince, and his two younger colleagues, Kevin and Steve. The heavyset, glum Sylvia simpered flirtatiously when he turned to her, and Harriet gave him a motherly smile. Herb crossed his arms defensively across his chest and harrumphed. Then it was Lucy's turn to squirm uncomfortably under his penetrating gaze.

"I don't think this means anything at all," she began,

"but I opened the wrong door, looking for the banquet. The Reads were having some sort of private cocktail party."

"Figures," fumed Herb. "Too good to mingle with the hoi polloi on the mezzanine like everybody else."

"Shhh," hissed Harriet.

"Did something happen at this party?" asked Sullivan.

"I don't think you should attach too much importance to it," said Lucy, thinking once again of Bill's harsh words to Toby just before she left home. "Family members say things they don't mean."

"I understand that," said Sullivan. "Why don't you tell me what you heard and let me decide if it's important or not."

Everyone at the table was looking at Lucy.

"I don't remember exactly, but Junior and Luther were arguing. Junior's voice was angry, and Luther said something about pouring his lifeblood into the company for forty years. Something like that. That's all I remember."

"That fits in with what I heard," said Jim, shoving his glasses back up his nose. "I heard that Luther changed his mind, and the sale to National Media is off."

"Well, he was a fool if he decided not to sell," said Herb. "There'll never get another offer like this one. Now's the time to sell. The newspaper business is going to the dogs."

"You're right about that," said Arthur. "But Luther never was much of a businessman. His focus was always on the news side of things."

"Give me a break," said Jim. "If you ask me, Pioneer Press is strictly amateur hour. It's one crusade after another. They have no idea what balanced, fair reporting means."

Kevin and Steve nodded their agreement, much to Lucy's surprise. Until now she had thought everyone admired Luther.

The detective also looked puzzled. "Wasn't this guy Newspaperman of the Year?"

"He's been campaigning for it for years," said Sylvia, rolling her eyes and leaning heavily on the table. "The hospitality suite. The committees. The giveaways."

"She's right," said Ted. "Newspaperman of the Year isn't like the Pulitzer prize, which is awarded for excellence in journalism. It's more of a reward for helping the organization, the Northeast Newspaper Association. It's kind of a payback for going to a lot of meetings, stuff like that."

"Luther should have gotten it a few years ago, when he was NNA president," said Arthur, "but he made people so mad when he claimed thousands of dollars in expenses that they gave it to somebody else. Hildebrand, I think."

"No, it was Halvorsen," said Mildred, correcting her husband.

"The very next year he started the hospitality suite. I remember that well enough." Arthur smiled. "Free food and booze. I thought I'd died and gone to heaven. I mean, you have to understand the nature of the newspaper business to appreciate it. Strictly low budget. Until Luther you were lucky to get a free pen at this shindig."

"It worked," said Mildred. "Just like the unpopular kid who brings cupcakes for the whole class and gets elected to the student council."

"The papers still suck," said Jim. "Especially the Northampton *News*. It's nothing but a mouthpiece for alternative lifestyles. What a rag."

"Gay rights," said Kevin.

"Civil unions," added Steve.

"At least it's a liberal viewpoint," countered Sylvia. "If you ask me, the *Republican* is a lot worse. Harold's practically nominated Ronald Reagan for sainthood."

"I don't think Reagan is even Catholic," said Mildred, looking worried.

"I was just making a point," said Sylvia.

"Don't worry, dear," said Arthur, patting his wife's hand. "Eleanor will make sure Saint Peter doesn't let him in."

"I think we're getting off the track here," said Sullivan, consulting his notebook. "There was apparently some sort of disagreement between Luther and his son, Junior, just before the banquet. Did any of you notice anything like that during the banquet?"

"He came in here like he was the Duke of Earl or something," said Herb with a snort. "People were falling all over themselves to greet him."

Lucy nodded, remembering. She wondered how much of the enthusiastic welcome Luther had received had been genuine. Were people truly happy to congratulate him or had they merely been going through the motions, caught up in the moment?

"Luther and Junior both greeted me," said Ted. "There didn't seem to be any tension between them that I noticed."

"Me, either," said Herb.

"Everyone seemed to be behaving," said Harriet. "Even Sam Syrjala."

"Sam Syrjala?" asked the detective, writing the name down. "Who's he? Is he usually a problem?"

Sylvia snorted. "You could say that. He's the editor, and I mean that in the loosest possible sense, of Pioneer's Hartford paper, the *Gazette.*"

"Sam has a bit of a drinking problem," said Mildred.

"He's a lush," said Jim.

"He's a member of the family?" asked Sullivan.

"Practically," said Arthur. "He and Harold are old buddies."

The detective made another note, then looked up.

"Okay, the Read party make their entrance, they greet people, then they sit down. They're at the next table. Did you notice anything unusual?"

"Everything was fine until he started sneezing," said Lucy. "I thought it was some sort of allergic attack that was triggering an asthmatic reaction—my daughter has asthma, so I know the symptoms. It seemed like he was trying to downplay it, kind of denying it was happening, which is what people tend to do in that situation, especially if they're in public. The coughing and wheezing got worse and he finally left the room, holding a handkerchief over his face. I figured he was going out to take his medicine. Once you take it, it's very quick-acting."

"Luther left the room by himself?"

Ted and several others nodded.

"Junior eventually followed him out of the room, and when he came back he said his father had collapsed." Lucy's voice broke, as she remembered Junior's expression, outwardly calm and collected but betrayed by his eyes, which darted around the room frantically seeking help. "I guess the inhaler didn't work."

"I heard Monica Underwood say something about giving him a fresh one that morning," said Mildred. "It must have been defective."

"Or somebody made sure it didn't work," said Jim. "Somebody who had a lot to lose if Luther got his way and the sale didn't go through."

"There's no need to jump to conclusions," cautioned Sullivan. "I'm just looking for facts, folks."

By then Lucy was exhausted, but the questioning had gone on for hours, covering every detail, until they were all bleary-eyed. And although the police were eager to gather every bit of information they could, they were not willing to share it, especially with these assembled members of the press. In fact, frequent warnings were issued that the investigation was in its early stages and all information was privileged and confidential. Any leaks would be prosecuted as impeding an investigation. The hundreds of journalists at the convention, who had witnessed one of the biggest news stories of the year, were unable to report on it.

Hearing her phone ring, Lucy hurried out of the bathroom to answer it. It was Ted.

"Lucy, I've got a little job for you. Phyllis is going to call tradespeople and neighbors in town and get quotes about Luther Read and e-mail them to me here. But I need you to work them into a story. A kind of remembrance piece. I figured you could do it at lunchtime."

"Aren't we under some sort of gag order?"

"This is America, remember. There's such a thing as the First Amendment."

"There's also something called 'contempt of court' and 'impeding an official investigation,'" retorted Lucy, who'd often been threatened with those very terms by police in the course of investigating local crimes in Tinker's Cove.

"We're not going to write about the banquet or anything like that," said Ted. "Just a straight obit and this little bit of local reaction. I'll expect you at my room around noon."

Lucy was still figuring out what to wear when the phone rang again.

"Yeah," she said, figuring it was Ted.

"I guess you woke up on the wrong side of the bed this morning," responded Phyllis.

"Sorry. I thought you were Ted."

"I'm innocent on that score, but I do have some bad news for you."

Lucy sat down on the edge of the bed, half-in and half-out of her shirt, expecting the worst. The house had burned down with the whole family trapped inside. Bill had strangled Toby. Toby had strangled Bill. Elizabeth had totaled the Subaru and was on life support: doctors were hovering, waiting to claim her organs for transplant surgery.

"Mrs. Pratt called and asked me to tell you that Kudo got into her chicken run again."

Relief flooded Lucy. "Is that all?"

"She says she's had it and she's going to call the animal-control officer."

"Did you tell her I'd pay damages?"

"Of course. But she says a couple of dollars per chicken doesn't compensate for all the trouble she went to raise them, not to mention the eggs she's not getting."

"She's right. I don't blame her a bit." Lucy sighed. "The kids are so irresponsible. The dog's supposed to be in the house or on his run, but they let him loose."

"I'm just passing along the message. Do you want her phone number?"

"Sure." Lucy jotted it down. "How's it going with the quotes?"

"I'll get right on it," promised Phyllis.

Lucy had the beginnings of a headache when she hung up. She never should have agreed to come to the convention. She missed her family; she even missed Phyllis. And she had a bad feeling about the situation at home. The dog was running wild; what else was going on? Why had Bill been so evasive when they talked on the phone last night?

The headache was full-blown when she got down to the coffee shop, intending to buy something to take along to the morning workshop, since she was running late. The mere sight of the doughnuts ranged behind the counter and the greasy smell of eggs and sausage made her queasy, so she settled for a cup of black coffee and the morning papers.

The city's two dailies were not members of the NNA, which was comprised of smaller, regional papers, and hadn't been represented at the convention. They were free to give Luther Read's death front-page coverage.

But they hadn't, she discovered, as she quickly flipped through the papers while waiting in line to pay. The tabloid *Herald* had devoted its front page to a corrupt city official, and the *Globe* had placed the story inside, on the Metro section front. Murder was apparently too commonplace in the big city to attract much notice.

Poor Luther, thought Lucy, as she headed back to the hotel. Even in death he was only a big fish in a small pond. Still, the *Globe* had given the story twenty inches, and she wished she had time to read every word. Maybe, she thought hopefully, the panel would start late. The hotel lobby certainly seemed deserted, with none of its usual hustle and bustle, as if people were still recovering from last night's extraordinary events.

She had reached the stairs and was poised to go down to the meeting room when she hesitated, wondering if the panels had been canceled. When she got to the meeting room, however, she found a handful of tired-looking people, most of them clutching cups of coffee. She joined them, sipping from her own extra-large cup and reading the *Globe* story while she waited for the panel to start.

Not that it told her anything she didn't know. Luther's death was under investigation, but few facts were known, reported Brad McAbee. The remainder of the story was devoted to an account of Luther's career and the News-paperman of the Year award he would have received. Lucy got the impression that the story had originally been written to announce the award and a few lead paragraphs had been added after news of his death broke.

Lucy turned to the *Herald*, which was definitely the more lively of the city's two papers. Lucy chuckled over the front page, where enormous black letters proclaimed *CAUGHT* over a photo of a city official cavorting with

lobbyists and scantily clad women on the deck of a cabin
cruiser named *Bad Company*. She was flipping through
the rest of the paper when another photograph caught
her eye. *In town for the Northeast Newspaper Association
conference, Northampton* News *publisher Catherine Read and
partner Heloise Randall danced the night away Sunday at
Cambridge's famed girl bar the Coven,* read the cutline. The
photo showed Catherine, in a slinky halter top, gyrating
opposite a tall, statuesque blond. They both seemed to
be having a great time.

Interesting, thought Lucy, turning her attention to
the panel. It was on Internet reporting, and had been
one of the first she had chosen when she filled out her
conference registration form weeks ago in Tinker's
Cove. She knew the value of the Internet to a small-town
reporter like herself and was eager to learn more ways
to take advantage of it. So far she'd mostly used it to get
statistics from state agencies. If she wanted to know how
many cars were registered in town, or how many pounds
of lobster had been landed over the past five years, or
how many people were collecting social security, she
could have the answer in a matter of minutes instead of
the days it used to take to track down that information
by telephone. The right person always seemed to be on
vacation, or taking lunch, or in a meeting.

Lucy knew she'd only scratched the surface, however. There was lots more information available, if only
she knew how to access it. When the panelists got started,
however, it soon became clear that they were talking
about a different Internet than the one she had dab-
bled in. All three speakers had been spending way too
much time in virtual reality, and had no idea how to re-
late to ordinary people. So they talked to each other,
tossing around terms that nobody understood and making jokes that nobody got. She was longing for them to
announce a break, when Sam Syrjala staggered into the

room, dropped his briefcase on a chair, and headed for the podium.

"The newspaper business sure ain't what it used to be," he proclaimed as he lurched down the aisle between the seats. Observing his unsteady progress, Lucy was pretty sure he was drunk. Again. At ten in the morning.

Sam reached the podium and hugged it, causing consternation among the panelists, who didn't seem to know what to do about this interloper.

"Used to be we called 'em like we saw 'em. . . ." He shook his head slowly, as if it were a fragile container holding something precious. "Not anymore. Now if the cops arrest a black, we gotta ask if it's racial profiling. If you're writing about a woman, you gotta choose your words carefully: it's single mother, not unmarried. There's no more illegitimate kids, for God's sake. Did you know that?"

He stared blearily at the audience, challenging someone, anyone, to respond.

"It's true," he continued when no one spoke up. "Don't ask me how, but even though these kids' mothers never bothered to get married, the little bastards, they're not illegitimate."

He let go of the podium and threw out his arms for emphasis, swaying crazily.

"PC, political correctness, is gonna be the death of newspapers." He held up a finger and waggled it in front of his eyes. "See if it isn't," he said, and rested his head on the podium.

There was a buzz among the astonished audience members, and two of the panelists began an anxious, whispered conversation.

"Maybe we'd better get him up to his room," suggested one man, who was sitting in the front row.

"Good idea," said a second.

They each took a side, lifting Syrjala's arms over their shoulders and dragging him from the room.

One of the computer experts was speaking, apologizing for the interruption, when Lucy noticed Syrjala's briefcase, still propped on the chair where he had dropped it.

"Oh," she exclaimed, jumping to her feet. "They forgot his briefcase. I'll take it to him."

She was gone before anyone could object. It was only when she was safe in her room with the door closed behind her that she stopped to wonder what she was doing. Had she simply seized an excuse to leave the boring workshop, or did she hope to find evidence of some sort?

She set the briefcase—a battered leather model, the old-fashioned kind with accordion sides and a leather flap with a brass catch that held it closed—on the desk and sat down on the foot of the bed to think.

What did she hope to find? What did she think was inside? Papers, probably just papers. That's what briefcases usually held. Company reports, maybe, from Pioneer Press Group. Financial statements, budgets, memos, all of which could shed light on the company and maybe even provide a motive for Luther Read's murder. Sam and Harold were buddies, after all, and neither man agreed with Luther's liberal approach. Harold was a dyed-in-the-wool New Hampshire conservative and Sam, well, whatever his politics were, they appeared to be pretty reactionary.

Even more interesting, thought Lucy, both men would have had reason to oppose the sale of Pioneer Press Group to National Media. Sam, who clearly had a drinking problem, would most certainly be fired by the new owners. And Harold didn't want to lose control of his newspaper, which gave him a powerful voice in national politics vis-à-vis the New Hampshire primary.

Rumor was that the sale was off, but Lucy didn't know if that was true. And even if it was, the two men might have worried that Luther would again change his mind. Had the two men teamed up to murder Luther, fearing he was becoming too unpredictable? Had they conspired with each other, coming up with the plan to trigger Luther's asthma? If she opened the briefcase, would she find a full inhaler inside?

Lucy looked at the briefcase. It wasn't even locked; the flap was loose. It wasn't really violating his privacy to look inside; Syrjala had left it unattended. Why, in his condition, he might have dropped it and spilled the contents for anyone to see.

Maybe that was what she should do, thought Lucy. Just kind of knock it off the desk and see if anything spilled out.

No, she decided, if she was going to do it she might as well do it thoroughly. She spread the two sides apart and peered into the briefcase.

It was empty. No papers, no books, nothing, except for the side pocket, where she found a pint bottle of bourbon with about an inch remaining in the bottom.

Lucy suddenly felt very foolish. The man was an alcoholic; he had to stash his booze somewhere. What better place than a briefcase? Especially at a conference where most everyone was carrying one. She picked up the phone and asked to be connected to his room.

" 'Lo!"

"Mr. Syrjala?"

"Yuh."

"I have your briefcase. You left it in the conference room."

There was silence; then Sam spoke. "Who are you?"

"Lucy Stone."

"With Ted? From Maine?"

"That's me," said Lucy, surprised that he knew who she was.

"Well, uh, could you bring it to my room? I'm not feeling so well."

Lucy considered. This could be an opportunity to ask a few questions. Syrjala was drunk; he might also be loose-lipped.

"What's your room number?"

Lucy jotted it down on the notepad thoughtfully provided by the hotel and hung up. Then, before she could change her mind, she took the elevator down to the fifth floor, where she ran straight into Harold. Once again she was struck by the family resemblance. He looked like a shorter, stockier Luther. Where Luther had been relaxed and open, however, his brother was all business.

"I'm Harold Read," he said, sticking out his hand. "Sam told me you've got something of his."

"I'm Lucy Stone," she said, taking his hand. "He left his briefcase downstairs."

Harold didn't let her go, but held on to her hand, squeezing her fingers painfully.

Lucy's eyes widened. "What do you think—"

"You were on the down elevator."

His grip softened, and Lucy pulled her hand away.

"So what? I had to go to my room to call him and find out his room number."

"Or maybe you're some sort of snoop." Harold's eyes were flat and accusatory.

"I'm doing the man a favor," said Lucy, meeting his stare as she handed over the briefcase. She didn't know where she found the nerve, but she wasn't going to admit anything to this horrible man. Certainly not that she had searched the briefcase.

"Maybe," admitted Harold, holding the briefcase with two hands. "Of course you are." He paused. "We're all pretty upset. I didn't mean to be rude." He glanced at the door to Syrjala's room. "Sam's not really up for company. He's taking my brother's death very hard."

That was one interpretation of Sam's behavior, but

not one Lucy necessarily agreed with. She wasn't about to argue, however. She just wanted to get away.

Harold pushed the elevator call button and waited with her.

"I expect you'll want to get back to the panel. Internet reporting, isn't it?"

"Yes."

"Interesting subject. So much potential."

"Absolutely."

The elevator doors opened.

"Have a good day," said Harold.

"Thanks," said Lucy.

But as the door closed and the elevator descended, Lucy wondered what was going on. Harold must have been in the room with Syrjala when she called, and had gone out in the hallway to meet her. Did he want to hide Syrjala's condition from her? That hardly explained his hostile behavior, accusing her of snooping.

She had been snooping, of course. She was a reporter; it was part of her job. And Syrjala knew who she was. He'd been at the panel yesterday when she'd bragged about all the big stories she'd broken. He might even know about the prize she'd won.

Even so, Harold had been very aggressive. Trying to scare her off, perhaps? But why? What did he have to hide? The more she thought about it, the odder it seemed. Why did the Reads tolerate Syrjala's behavior in the first place? The man was a legendary drunk. Catherine didn't like him; she'd told Lucy as much. Even if he and Harold went way back, as people said, Sam's behavior would certainly seem to strain the bonds of friendship.

Things weren't adding up, and Lucy wanted to know why, but she'd have to wait. First she had to write that remembrance piece for Ted.

Chapter Eight

"**H**ey, aren't you supposed to be at a workshop?" demanded Ted when he answered Lucy's knock.

"Trust me. This is a better use of my time," replied Lucy, marching past him and plunking herself down in a chair.

Ted's room was a mess. The bed wasn't made, a wet towel was on the floor outside the bathroom, and rumpled clothes and papers were strewn everywhere. Half of a pizza remained in an open box perched on top of the TV. Lucy investigated. It was mushroom. She took a piece and bit into it.

"I wouldn't recommend that," cautioned Ted. "It's from last night."

"I didn't have any breakfast," said Lucy, chewing. "It's not bad."

"Have you seen that bumper sticker? 'Sex is like pizza. Even when it's bad, it's good.' "

As soon as he'd said it, Ted blushed furiously. Head bent, he started flipping though a pile of papers. When he found the one he wanted he cleared his throat and handed it to her.

"These are the quotes Phyllis got."

Lucy knew he hadn't meant anything. The words had popped out before he realized he was alone in a hotel room with a female employee. She took the page and skimmed it.

"Popular guy. Not a negative quote in the bunch."

"It's a small-town rule: Never speak ill of the dead until the estate has paid the outstanding bills."

"Did Luther owe a lot of money?"

"The richer they are, the slower they are to pay. You know the dry cleaner cut off the Winships last summer? They ran up a bill in the thousands."

Lucy knew it was true. The wealthy summer people with their enormous "cottages" on Smith Heights Road all had charge accounts with local merchants. Although they often complained, most of the shopkeepers tolerated slow payments because they didn't want to lose the business.

"Are you sure we can do this?" she asked, as she started clicking away on the laptop computer. "I don't want to go to jail for contempt or anything."

"All we're doing is reporting the fact that Luther Read, prominent summer resident, died at a newspaper conference in Boston, and providing some local reaction. We're not going to do anything about the investigation, we're not going to include any firsthand reports, we're not going to speculate. Just the facts, ma'am."

"Okay, okay. I guess reporting the fact that he liked to go fishing for striped bass isn't going to impede the investigation."

She was working on a quote from the commodore of the yacht club, where Luther kept his boat. He also liked to buy fresh corn at the farmstand and lobsters from the lobster pound, and occasionally went to church on Sunday. He had a decent handicap in golf, but preferred tennis, which he played regularly with Fred Ames, the president of the Tinker's Cove Five Cents Savings Bank. He collected decoys.

"This is fascinating stuff," said Lucy, yawning ostentatiously. "Somehow I don't think his tennis partner killed him. You want to take a look at this before I send it?"

Lucy got up to stretch while Ted read the story on the little screen. When he finished he e-mailed it to Phyllis, back in the *Pennysaver* office in Tinker's Cove.

"I'm sure Luther was a really nice guy," began Lucy, "but there's something weird about Pioneer Press."

"They're making money and the rest of us are struggling?"

"Well, yeah," said Lucy. "And everybody's all nicey-nice but somehow it's all surface. I had lunch with Catherine yesterday and she seemed very guarded. Very careful about what she said."

Ted laughed. "Just because she didn't bare her soul in response to your probing questions doesn't mean she's guarded. She's probably just a private person."

"A private person who goes out dancing half-naked with her same-sex partner."

"That's something else entirely. Everybody lets their hair down sometime."

"Or maybe Luther didn't approve of her lifestyle and she killed him after enduring years of insults and abuse."

"You've got some imagination."

"Or what about Harold, the brother? They have very different views, after all. Luther was pretty liberal and Harold's conservative. Maybe he wants to get control of the entire chain."

"People don't generally kill their brothers because of political convictions," said Ted.

"I guess you never heard of the Civil War," said Lucy.

"Point taken," said Ted. "But I'd put my money on Harold's wife, Inez. The dragon lady. Remember, the female of the species is deadlier than the male."

"Then I guess we have to consider Monica Underwood."

"What possible motive could she have?" asked Ted.

"Could be anything, I suppose. He called her by his late wife's name in a moment of passion. He threatened to print her real age. He was fooling around with another woman. He picked his teeth, or his nose. He had a—"

"I get the idea," said Ted, cutting her off. "Intimacy breeds contempt. The love/hate thing. A woman scorned. But it was early in the relationship, wasn't it? There really wasn't time for that sort of contempt to grow. That sort of thing takes years to get to the breaking point." He scratched his head. "But if you're going to consider Catherine, why not Junior? Fathers and sons. The king must die; long live the king."

"Nope. I can't go there. My daughter is working for that man, taking care of his little boy. Elizabeth is not working for a murderer and that's that."

"So much for rational deduction," said Ted.

"I never said I was rational," retorted Lucy. "I rely on intuition. And my intuition tells me it's Sam Syrjala."

"And why is that?"

"That whole thing is screwy. The guy's a drunk. Anybody else would fire him, but they treat him like he's a member of the family. It's as if he's got something on them, you know? A big secret."

"But why would he kill Luther? Wouldn't it be the other way 'round? Besides, Syrjala stayed behind at the table. He wasn't with Luther when he died."

"But Harold was," said Lucy thoughtfully.

"And so were a lot of other people, including Junior."

"I haven't worked it all out yet," admitted Lucy.

"And you're not going to," said Ted in a warning tone. "This has been a lot of fun, but I hope you don't think you're going to launch your own little investigation.

You're here for the newspaper conference, to polish your reportorial skills."

Lucy sat primly on her chair, hands folded and ankles together. "I know, Ted."

"Boston is a big, mean city. You're not in Tinker's Cove anymore, you know?" He turned and picked up the ringing phone. "Hello."

Whoever was on the other end wasn't giving him much of a chance to reply, but Ted was listening intently and his expression was grave. When he mentioned Toby's name, Lucy's antennae went up.

"I guess that's best for now," he finally said. "I wish I were there so you didn't have to deal with this alone."

When he hung up, Lucy pounced.

"What's going on?" she demanded.

"That was Pam. . . ."

"And?"

"Toby and Adam went out drinking at the Bilge last night. They got pretty loaded but they managed to drive back to our place, where they slept it off. Pam said it's a miracle the cops didn't catch them."

Lucy felt as if she'd been punched in the stomach. She was hurt and sick and angry, all at once. It was bad enough that Toby had felt it necessary to go drinking, even though he was underage, but doing it with her boss's son was completely outrageous. She couldn't stand it. She had to get out of that room; she had to get away from Ted.

"I need some lunch," she said, picking up her purse and heading for the door.

Chapter Nine

A member of the hotel's cleaning staff was vacuuming the hallway when Lucy exited Ted's room. She smiled and said good morning, but Lucy brushed past without acknowledging her, stopping only when confronted with the closed elevator doors. She stabbed the call button furiously.

When the elevator arrived, Lucy instinctively pressed the button for her floor, but when the doors opened she decided she didn't want to go to her room. Too small. Too confining. She wanted to move, to work off some of this emotion. She hit the button for the lobby and soon found herself marching along the sidewalk.

How could Toby do something like this? How could he be so stupid? What if he'd been arrested? The days when the cops and courts winked at youthful indiscretion were long past. Now it was zero tolerance. He would have spent the night in jail and been hauled into court in the morning, where he would have certainly lost his driver's license and would probably have been put on probation, too. Compounding his offense, of course, was the fact that he'd involved Ted's son, Adam.

Not only did he have no regard for his own future, but he didn't care much about how his behavior affected others, not even his own mother.

"Hey, lady. Watch it!"

Recalled from her thoughts, Lucy realized she'd been about to step in front of traffic. She waited for the light to change and crossed the street, resuming her train of thought when she was safely on the other side.

Toby might have escaped the law, but there was no way he was going to escape his father. Bill would be furious with him. There was no way he wouldn't find out. Toby didn't sleep at home and Bill would want to know why. It wasn't as if he could hide his condition; he'd be reeking of alcohol when he showed up for work. If he showed up for work. And if he didn't show up, Bill would be angry about that.

This was terrible. A real family crisis, and she wasn't there. Things seemed to be going to the dogs without her. Dogs. Kudo running loose. Toby out of control. Maybe she should leave the conference and go home. These things wouldn't happen if she were home.

Lucy stopped in her tracks and laughed at herself. What was she thinking? These things happened when she was home, too. The day she left the dog got into Mrs. Pratt's chickens, and Bill and Toby had a big fight. What did she think she could do? Toby wasn't the first kid who sowed some wild oats. Kudo wasn't the only dog who ever killed a chicken. Bill wasn't unique; plenty of fathers blew their tops now and then.

She could worry about them, but it wouldn't change anything. She looked around. It was a beautiful day; she was in the middle of Boston. On Newbury Street, in fact. Maybe it was time to stop and smell the roses that were arranged on the sidewalk in front of a florist's shop. Or check out the goodies displayed in the store windows.

The shops were dazzling: art galleries, jewelers, furniture stores, and exclusive European designer boutiques like Armani, Longchamps, and Rodier. Lucy strolled along, taking in the shop windows and the displays that oftentimes spilled right out onto the sidewalk, and admiring the other pedestrians, some of whom were elegantly dressed in designer clothes. Others were seated at outdoor café tables, engaged in lively conversations or simply sitting and watching the passing parade.

As she passed one café Lucy got a whiff of something delicious and she suddenly realized how hungry she was. She decided to try the very next restaurant and soon found herself in a Vietnamese place, where she was quickly seated at a tiny table, next to some people who had huge bowls of noodle soup.

"I'll have what they're having," she told the waiter. He brought her chicken soup along with fresh mint leaves and other herbs to mix in. The scent of the mint was released when she tore the leaves and dropped them in the broth, and she inhaled deeply, feeling her tense muscles relax when she exhaled. She wasn't used to handling the large, squarish Chinese-style spoon or the chopsticks, and it took all her concentration to catch the slippery noodles and to eat her soup without slurping.

When she finished she noticed some people being served coffee in glass cups, with a layer of milk at the bottom. She asked for one when the waiter came to remove her bowl, and sat back against the wall, enjoying the sense of well-being that followed a satisfying meal. The coffee came and she stirred it, discovering the creamy layer on the bottom was thick condensed milk. The coffee was delicious; she'd never had anything like it before. When she paid her bill, she realized she'd had an adventure as well as a meal.

Back on the sidewalk, she checked her watch and discovered she had just enough time to get back to the hotel for the afternoon workshop: "Why Don't They Teach

Grammar Anymore? Copyeditors to the Rescue!" New-
bury Street beckoned, but the call of duty was stronger.
Lucy began walking back to the hotel, pausing at the
Armani boutique for one last look at the window.

She was admiring a beautifully cut jacket when she
recognized Inez Read leaving the store with several
shopping bags dangling from her arms. Maybe she
needed something to wear to the funeral, thought Lucy,
watching as a uniformed chauffeur hurried to assist
her. In moments the packages were stowed in the trunk
and Inez was seated in the back and whisked away.

Must be nice, thought Lucy. Imagine never having to
wrestle bags and bags of groceries into the car, never
having to worry about prices and whether you could afford something or not. And never having to fill up the
gas tank yourself. Just leave the driving to the chauffeur.
Wow. Kind of like being the queen of England or something.

Lucy's steps grew slower. The queen of England was
reportedly the richest woman in the world. That kind of
lifestyle took a lot of money. Even if Inez didn't have to
maintain Buckingham Palace, her expenses had to be
enormous. Just how much money were the Reads pulling
out of Pioneer Press Group? And how could they do it
when all the other newspapers were struggling to sur-
vive?

Lucy stopped and dug in her purse for the little map
of Boston the hotel had provided. Just as she thought,
she wasn't far from the Boston Public Library. The choice
was clear: grammar lessons from nitpicky copyeditors or
the opportunity to practice her Internet skills at the library researching Pioneer Press. The copyeditors never
had a chance.

The Boston Public Library, with its cavernous ceiling and massive staircase, was a far cry from its cozy

cousin in Tinker's Cove. The guard was helpful, however, and she soon found the reference department. A librarian there not only directed her to one of the newer computers—"Some of these older machines are awfully slow"—but gave her some helpful tips on the best search engines. She was soon clicking her way through pages and pages of information.

Some of it—like the fact that Pioneer Press Group was a chain of small- and mid-size newspapers located in the Northeast—she already knew. Of more interest was the company's corporate structure, especially who actually owned it and who had the power to make decisions.

Luther Senior, she was not surprised to learn, had been a major stockholder, with 25 percent of the shares, and was also the CEO. Harold, his younger brother, held a similar number of shares and was chief financial officer. Junior and Catherine together held another quarter; the remaining shares were held by a long list of stockholders including individuals, banks, and corporations. What this meant, Lucy concluded, was that Luther had not had free rein to do whatever he wanted with the corporation. Any big change, like a sale, would require agreement with other stockholders. Getting that agreement would require discussion, and discussion often led to arguments, especially in a family. Heated arguments, like the one she'd witnessed. If only she knew what it was about.

Of course, everything had changed now that Luther was dead. Lucy wanted to know who would inherit his shares, and found Luther had made no secret of his intentions. He'd been honored recently at a fund-raising roast, and when it was his turn to speak, he'd responded to Junior's mildly humorous speech by joking that Junior could have been a lot funnier but didn't want to risk being disinherited. Then he'd turned serious and said how gratifying it was to know that his son would carry on the business that he'd built.

Lucy paused, scratching her head. Did this mean that he'd left all his shares to Junior? That would give him more stock than anyone else, but was still just short of the fifty-one percent needed to make decisions single-handedly. But what about Catherine? Didn't she inherit anything? Perhaps Luther hadn't been quite as open-minded as he'd claimed and had been unhappy about Catherine's lifestyle choices.

Rather more surprising to Lucy was the discovery that the Pioneer Press Group was in deep financial trouble. Despite the lavish hospitality-suite spreads and the private cocktail parties and the carefully cultivated aura of success, the chain was steadily losing money. The proof was in the reorganizations and layoffs that followed every fourth quarter. Lucy wondered how long this pattern could continue without major cutbacks or even filing for Chapter 11 protection. Some of the papers appeared to be profitable, like Catherine's Northampton *News* and Harold's *Republican,* but the larger-city papers, Junior's Hartford *Gazette* and the Lowell *Times,* for example, were facing hard times.

Considering the situation, she couldn't understand why Luther had decided against National Media's offer to buy the chain, if he had. The company was leaking capital and the sale was the only lifeboat in sight. Making it even more appealing was National Media's promise not to close any of the papers, but to increase profitability by "streamlining and eliminating duplication of effort." Lucy took this to mean job cuts in departments like features, sports, business, and advertising. A single features department, for example, could provide material for all the papers, and a consolidated ad department could sell to regional, as well as local, customers.

Lucy was the first to admit she didn't know much about business, but the National Media deal sure looked good to her. Some people would lose their jobs, but there would be no jobs at all if the chain went out of business.

Plus, the individual papers would continue to serve local communities. The sale seemed like the most responsible choice, and she found it hard to believe that someone with Luther's commitment to news would throw it away and risk his reputation and his family's fortune because of a woman. Even a woman with Monica Underwood's undeniable charisma.

Of course, admitted Lucy, it wouldn't be the first time a man had made a bad decision because of a woman, and maintaining control of the papers would certainly allow him to help advance her political career. Ideally, newspapers were supposed to be impartial and to present the truth, but her experience as a reporter had shown her how easy it was to give a twist to a story simply by choosing what quotes to include, what details to highlight, what adjectives to use. Knowing Luther's relationship with Monica, reporters and editors would behoove themselves to choose their words carefully when writing about her or the issues she favored.

When her eyes would no longer focus and her hand was stiff from clicking the mouse, Lucy finally decided she'd gotten enough information. She stretched after she logged off but she still felt stiff as she went back outside. Pausing on the library steps to consult her map, she decided Boylston Street was the most direct route to the hotel.

Her little map also informed her that the European-style square populated with many pigeons opposite the library was Copley Square, and the Romanesque-style church was the famous Trinity Church, where generations of Boston Brahmins had worshiped under Henry Hobson Richardson's soaring gilt ceilings and John LaFarge's stained-glass windows. She stepped inside and stood for a moment in the lobby, listening as the organist rehearsed and breathing in the old-church smell of candles and flowers. It was too late in the day for a tour, however, so she went on her way, past the controversial Saint-Gaudens's statue of Phillips Brooks, the legendary nineteenth-century minister of the church, with Jesus standing behind him, imparting his divine blessing. Even today, she decided, it seemed a bit presumptuous.

She continued on past the tall John Hancock Building, with its reflective glass walls, and made steady progress until the gilt-swan sign of the Women's Educational and Industrial Union caught her eye. Inside she found a fascinating mix of antiques, relatively reasonably priced designer clothing and accessories, and a display of unique Father's Day cards that were much more appealing than the mass-produced ones at the drugstore. She found one that was just right for Bill and bought it, resolving to head straight back to the hotel.

It was there that she literally bumped into Ted in the lobby.

"Lucy! There you are! I didn't see you at the workshop and I was worried about you. I called your room but there was no answer. Are you okay?"

"I'm fine now," she said. "I did some sight-seeing."

"Instead of the Copyeditor's Revenge?" asked Ted, eyes twinkling.

"I'm afraid so," admitted Lucy as they walked together to the elevators.

They were standing there together, waiting, when the doors opened and a knot of men issued from the elevator, moving together and forcing everyone out of their way. This was certainly no group of conventioneers casually heading out for drinks before dinner, she realized, recognizing Detective Sullivan. These were police officers hustling someone out of the building. That someone was Junior Read.

"I don't believe it," said Ted under his breath, following them.

Lucy went too, unable to believe what she was seeing. They stood on the sidewalk, watching as one of the officers placed a hand on Junior's head, preventing him from bumping it on the roof of the cruiser at the same time he was firmly shoved inside. Lucy caught a glimpse of his face, white and pale with shock behind the grimy window. He looked like a drowning man. Then the door slammed and the cruiser peeled away, followed by a second, unmarked car.

For a moment neither Lucy nor Ted spoke. Lucy was simply trying to absorb what she had seen. Junior was under arrest. The police were going to charge him with murdering his father. Where had they gotten the idea he could do such a thing? she wondered. Anybody who had seen them together, who had seen the regard they so obviously had for each other, would know Junior could never do such a thing. It was absurd. Impossible. Crazy.

"This is a story," said Ted, taking her elbow. "We've got to get to work."

Lucy nodded and allowed herself to be steered back into the hotel. She was halfway through the revolving door when the thought hit her: she was the one who had seen Junior and Luther fighting before the banquet. She was the one who had told Detective Sullivan. Overcome with guilt, she grabbed Ted's arm and faced him.

"It's because of me," she said. "Junior was arrested because of me!"

Chapter Ten

"**D**on't flatter yourself, Lucy," said Ted. "The cops didn't arrest Junior because of anything you said. They arrested him because they've got a case against him."

Lucy watched miserably as the police cars turned the corner and vanished, carrying Junior off to jail. The lockup in Tinker's Cove was grim enough; she could only imagine what the cells in Boston were like.

"But I'm the one who told Sullivan about the fight."

Ted wrapped an arm around her shoulder and led her back inside the hotel.

"People don't get arrested for murder because they had a disagreement," he said. "Trust me, they wouldn't take someone with Junior's clout without a really solid case. Face it, he was there when his father died. That would automatically make him a prime suspect. He was on the scene; he had opportunity."

"And means," admitted Lucy reluctantly. "He would have known about his father's asthma and could have substituted an empty canister in his emergency inhaler." She chewed her lip. "But what about motive?"

They had paused by one of the furniture arrangements in the lobby, and were half standing, half sitting, leaning against the back of a sofa.

"I don't know for sure, but I have a good idea," said Ted. "He stopped by the office last summer with what he called an 'interesting proposal.' He wanted to get out of the newspaper business and start a lifestyle magazine. He wanted to call it *Maine Living*, and he wanted me to invest in it."

"Did you?"

"No. For one thing, I don't have that kind of money. For another, I thought it was a crazy idea." Ted scratched his chin, chuckling. "I mean, there're simply not enough year-round people with disposable income to support something like that in Maine, and I told him so. I ribbed him some about it; I used to send him e-mails with suggestions for stories. *'When Your Family's Had Enough: 101 Ways to Cook Moose.' 'Fun in the Muck: Don't Let Mud Season Stop You.'* And then there was my favorite: *'Flannel à la Mode: New Ways to Wear Your Favorite Shirt.'* "

"Very funny, Ted," scoffed Lucy. "But how is this a motive?"

"Junior came up with a better idea: a Connecticut lifestyle magazine." He paused. "In case you didn't know, Connecticut has one of the highest per capita incomes in the country. There's a huge market there for the right magazine, but it would take a lot of capital to get started."

"Which the National Media sale would provide."

"Right. But if Luther had decided against it, or even to postpone it—"

"You think he's guilty!" accused Lucy, her voice rising.

"No, I don't. I've known Junior for a long time and I don't believe he could kill anyone, much less his father. But I think the police could see this as a motive." He glanced at the door. "I think I'll head over to police headquarters and see what I can find out. While I'm doing that, maybe you could call his wife and see if she's got anything to say."

Lucy was horrified. She didn't want to be the one to deliver the bad news to Angela.

"Are you crazy? We're under a gag order, remember?"

"Not anymore," said Ted, grinning broadly. "They've made an arrest. They can't say we're impeding an investigation, can they? The investigation's over." Ted started for the door, then turned. "If you get anything, leave a message on my phone. Okay?"

Lucy nodded glumly, watching him stride off.

The lobby was no place to make the call. It was too public and full of nosy journalists who wouldn't think twice about listening in. They'd think it was their duty, in fact. Rather than risk being overheard she decided to make the call from the privacy of her room. But even when she was safely inside the chained and bolted door, she hesitated.

This was the part of her job that she could never get used to. She hated intruding on anyone's private grief, yet she often found herself calling people who were reeling in shock from the death of a loved one. People who'd lost their house and all their belongings in a fire, or folks who'd seen a hurricane destroy the business they'd worked a lifetime to build.

Sometimes, she admitted, people were eager to talk. Glad to have someone who would listen. But others snarled insults—she'd been called everything from a ghoul to a filthy buzzard—or simply hung up. Lucy fingered the phone, doubting that she'd get very far with Angela. She took a deep breath and dialed.

A familiar voice answered.

"Elizabeth!" she exclaimed.

"Mom!" Elizabeth didn't question why her mother had called; she assumed it was to hear news from home. She plunged right in. "You'll never believe what happened! Dad fired Toby! He didn't come home last night, and when he showed up this morning they had a big fight and Dad told him he's got to find a new job by Friday or he gets kicked out of the house."

"I thought something like that might have happened," said Lucy. "Pam called Ted and said Toby spent last night there." She decided not to mention the drinking. "How's everything else?"

"Okay, I guess. Sara and Zoe are real pains, I've got to tell you. They missed the bus yesterday and I had to drive them to school. I think they did it on purpose so they wouldn't have to ride the bus. They'd much rather have me chauffeur them around."

Lucy knew the feeling. "What about the dog? I got a call from Mrs. Pratt. He got into her chickens again."

"The dog? I haven't seen much of him lately."

Lucy was beginning to feel dizzy. "That's exactly the problem, Elizabeth. You've got to keep track of him. Make sure he's in the house or on his run. He can't run loose."

"Right, Mom. I've been pretty busy with this job, you know." Elizabeth expelled a huge sigh. "I'm bored to death, Mom. Why didn't you tell me this job stinks? It's like I'm a slave or something. Angela doesn't do a thing. I have to do absolutely everything for Trevor: feed him and play with him and even wipe his bottom when he goes poopy."

Trust Elizabeth to view the world from her own perspective, thought Lucy.

"Well, that's what you get paid for," she said.

"And when I take him over to the club—you won't believe this, Mom—I'm not supposed to mingle with the members! That's what Angela actually said. 'Mingling with the club members is discouraged.' Instead, I'm supposed to stay right by the kiddie pool with the other au pairs. I mean, it's like we're servants or something."

Lucy didn't quite know how to answer this. No matter, Elizabeth was rattling on.

"The other girls are really nice, though. There's Emmanuelle—she's from France and has the cutest clothes—and Sonia from Italy and Katerina from Sweden or someplace where everyone is blond and tall and beautiful. We're very international, which is kind of fun because we're teaching each other swear words in different languages. But I don't know if I'm going to be taking Trevor to the club much anymore, because there's been a death in the family. It's his grandfather, but I don't think he knows about it yet. Or maybe he's too young to understand. I'm not supposed to say anything about it; I'm just supposed to keep him busy."

When she paused for breath Lucy seized the opportunity. "You know, I really need to talk to Angela. Is she around?"

"Uh, no, Mom. She got a call a little while ago and had to leave. I'm supposed to stay until she gets back, even if I have to sleep over."

Lucy wondered if Angela had heard about Junior's arrest. "Who called?"

"I dunno. She doesn't talk to me, except to give orders about Trevor. She's on the phone all the time, though. I mean, today I had to track her down in her office—you know I'm not supposed to bother her when she's working in there?—but there was nothing to give Trevor for lunch and I didn't know what to do. She was complaining to a friend, I think. Saying how everything's on hold now. I think she was talking about this magazine she wants to start, *Connecticut Country Life*. She's got pages and covers tacked up all around the office; it's a big deal to her."

Lucy had a sinking feeling. If Angela had been pressuring Junior about the magazine it would have given him an even stronger motive for killing his father. The prosecution could argue that he was afraid of disappointing his wife.

"She's not upset about Luther?"

"Oh, yeah. Like I said, she's been calling lawyers and family members."

Suddenly Lucy felt very sorry for the little boy who had lost his grandfather, whose father had just been arrested, and whose mother was too busy for him.

"Trevor's going to need some extra-special attention," she advised Elizabeth. "He may not know what has happened, but he knows something is wrong."

"You know, Mom, Trevor already misses his dad. He's always asking when he's coming home."

Lucy felt a visceral stab of pain. "Really?"

"Yeah. There's pictures of the two of them all over the house. Trevor loves to look at them. I mean, you can't walk by some of them without him stopping to tell me all about them. 'We went fishing,' he'll say. 'That's Dad and me at the ball game.' "

Lucy swallowed hard, trying to get rid of the lump in her throat.

"He sounds like a really good dad."

"I think so, Mom. Angela asked me to help him make a Father's Day present, so we've been collecting seashells for a picture frame."

"That's really nice." Lucy suddenly felt tired. "I've got to go," she said.

"Wait, Mom. There's just one more thing. If Toby doesn't get a job and Dad throws him out of the house, can I have his room? Please? It's just awful sharing with Sara and Zoe. I mean, I have no privacy at all."

Lucy was once again feeling a familiar burning sensation in her chest. "We'll see," she said, firmly pressing the end button. She immediately picked up the hotel phone and dialed Ted's room number, leaving a message that she hadn't been able to contact Angela.

She was off the hook for the moment, but Ted would be disappointed. He wouldn't give up, either. Sooner or later she'd have to talk to Angela.

Chapter Eleven

It was dinnertime, according to the clock, but Lucy didn't have any appetite. She had heartburn. She reached for her purse and began searching for the roll of antacid mints she'd bought at the hotel gift shop. When she finally found them she popped two in her mouth and let herself fall back onto the bed, legs dangling over the side, waiting for them to work.

It must be the odd meals she was eating at the convention, she decided. At home she had three square meals every day, but here she'd been skipping meals and gnawing on stale pizza and eating strange, exotic foods in Vietnamese restaurants. Not to mention those jumbo-sized coffees every morning. No wonder she had heartburn. No wonder she couldn't seem to handle these long-distance calls.

It was one disaster after another. Lucy shook her head. It was so like Elizabeth to try to capitalize on her brother's disgrace. She could imagine only too well how angry Bill must have been with Toby, and she didn't blame him one bit. Toby was behaving irresponsibly, breaking the law. They couldn't tolerate this sort of behavior. It was bad enough that Toby was running wild, but Lucy suspected he was breaking his father's heart. Not that Bill would admit it, but he had been awfully pleased when Toby had suggested working with him and learning restoration carpentry. Now it seemed that Toby had been less interested in learning his father's craft than in coming up with an excuse to get out of going back to college.

Lucy remembered Toby as a cute little towheaded tyke, just like Trevor. When Toby was a boy he had adored his father. His favorite toys had been a set of plastic carpenter's tools. Bill had given him a nail apron, a giveaway from the local lumberyard, and for months Toby never went anywhere without his "tool belt." Instead of watching *Mr. Rogers' Neighborhood* on TV with Elizabeth, he waited anxiously by the window every night for Bill to come home. No sooner would the red pickup turn into the driveway than Toby would be out the door, running to greet his father.

How times change, thought Lucy. These days Toby was probably working very hard to avoid his father. Unlike poor little Trevor, who was eagerly awaiting his father's return. Learning that Junior was a devoted dad, who was adored by his son, made Lucy feel absolutely awful. Maybe Ted was right that she'd had nothing to do with Junior's arrest, but she still felt guilty. She'd implicated an innocent man. Junior hadn't killed Luther; Lucy was sure of it. It was impossible. She'd seen him with Luther herself and had been struck by their obvious affection for each other; she'd even wished that Toby and Bill's relationship were more like theirs.

No, she decided, the police must have the wrong man. From what she'd seen at the banquet last night there was a whole tableful of Reads who had the means and opportunity to commit murder. She didn't know which one it was, but she was determined to find out. It was the least she could do. After all, she had to assuage her own guilt. She couldn't be the one who kept Junior from spending Father's Day with his son.

The only problem was, she admitted to herself as she sat up, she didn't have the foggiest idea where to begin. Moping in her room sure wasn't going to help. What she needed was some exercise, something to get the blood flowing, the neurons firing, and the synapses snapping. She needed a workout, but first she had one more chore. She had to call Mrs. Pratt and convince her not to insist on the dog hearing.

She didn't blame the woman one bit, she told herself as she dialed. She had every right to do it. But Kudo had already narrowly escaped with his life from a previous hearing when he belonged to Curt Nolan, and there was no guarantee he'd be so lucky a second time. She knew that the board of selectmen took a dim view of repeat offenders.

"Hi," she began, when Mrs. Pratt answered the phone. "This is Lucy Stone. I heard Kudo got into your chicken coop again."

"Well, it's about time you called."

"I only just heard," lied Lucy. "I'm out of town. In Boston."

Mrs. Pratt sniffed. "Well, if you ask me, you've got no business running off to the city and leaving that dog unattended."

Lucy felt her hackles rise.

"I didn't have any choice. It's part of my job."

"Well, in my day women stayed home and took care of their families, including their dogs. There was none of this gallivanting around."

Lucy counted to ten. She'd love nothing better than to tell Mrs. Pratt exactly what she thought of her outmoded views, but she knew it would be counterproductive. "The reason I'm calling," she said, "is to tell you how sorry I am and to ask if you'd reconsider your request for a dog hearing. Kudo's already had one hearing, you see, and

I'm afraid this time they'll order him destroyed. He's not really a bad dog, you know; he's a family pet and we all love him. I can promise you that once I get home he'll be under lock and key and he won't get out."

Lucy thought it sounded pretty good. Mrs. Pratt didn't agree.

"Absolutely not. That dog is out of control, and frankly I don't care what happens to him."

"I'm sure we can work something out," pleaded Lucy.

"You're a day late and a dollar short, Lucy Stone. I'll see you at the hearing. Good-bye."

"Good-bye to you, too," shouted Lucy, but Mrs. Pratt wasn't listening. She'd hung up. So much for trying to get along with her neighbors. So much for tolerance. So much for animal rights.

Lucy stomped around the room, looking for her exercise clothes. When she found them she ripped off her clothes, tossing them on the floor, and pulled on her T-shirt and shorts. She jammed her feet into her sneakers, pulling the laces so tight that one of them snapped.

She wanted to scream and howl; she wanted to throw the sneaker against the wall. But she didn't. She sat on the bed and took a few deep breaths. Then she tied the broken ends of the lace back together and put the shoe back on. When she had it laced up she tucked her key card in her pocket and left the room, making sure the door was locked behind her.

In the gym she hopped onto a stationary bike and started pedaling as fast as she could, but that didn't last very long. A TV set above her head was playing the local news, and her pace slowed as she became interested in the report, wondering if they had the story about Junior's arrest. It was hard to tell. If they'd started the newscast with the story, she would have missed it. She was trying to figure out how much lead time a TV news report required when Morgan Dodd greeted her.

Morgan was dressed in a skintight Lycra workout outfit that bared her skinny little middle and actually bagged on her nonexistent bottom. She was so thin, in fact, that Lucy wondered why she was killing herself on the treadmill that way. The treadmill was just a warm-up for Morgan; after ten minutes she abandoned it for the StairMaster.

Lucy was amazed at Morgan's energy; she was already starting to feel winded on the bicycle, where the speedometer indicated she was going three miles per hour. It must be broken, she decided, pedaling steadily. Morgan soon joined her, climbing up on the adjacent bike. She was sweating profusely, but wasn't the least bit out of breath.

"Congratulations," said Morgan, wiping her face with a towel. "I saw your series won first place."

"It did?" This was news to Lucy. "How do you know?"

"Didn't you hear the announcement? They've got all the winning stories up on display in the mezzanine. You can pick up your award at the registration desk"

"I'll have to stop by," said Lucy. "How did you do?"

"Second. I'm hot on your heels." Morgan grinned. "Did you see the Boston papers this morning? Not very good coverage of Luther Read's death, do you think?"

"Not very good," agreed Lucy. "Of course, it was pretty late last night and they were working on deadline."

"I tell you, the *Globe* needs me," said Morgan. "Sooner or later they're gonna realize it."

Lucy found herself smiling at the girl reporter's chutzpah and wondered if she knew about Junior's arrest. Not that she was about to volunteer any information to a competitor.

"How come they need you? What do you know that they don't?"

"A lot," said Morgan. "Because I'm pretty close with the cops working the case."

Lucy was intrigued. "Really?" she asked.

"Yeah." Morgan pedaled on in silence for a few minutes, and Lucy could see her muscles working underneath her tanned skin. "I know where they hang out, get coffee and stuff, you know. The doughnuts. So I was there first thing this morning."

"These guys were willing to talk to you about an ongoing case?" Lucy couldn't believe it.

"Not exactly," admitted Morgan with a shrug. "It's a small place. You hear things."

"You can't use hearsay," said Lucy, recalling her libel workshop.

"I can if I get it confirmed," said Morgan.

"But then they'll know you were eavesdropping and they'll start watching what they say when you're around. Not a good long-term strategy." Lucy's legs were aching, but she didn't want to stop pedaling before she found out what Morgan knew. "So what did you learn?" she asked.

"Well, from what I heard, it's just a matter of time before they arrest Junior."

"You're right!" exclaimed Lucy. "They did it just about an hour ago. I saw the cops take him through the lobby."

Morgan smiled smugly. "Pretty fast, don't you think? I mean, they didn't have time to run any tests on the physical evidence, but they went ahead anyway."

"That's true," said Lucy, who hadn't really thought about it.

"Well, it's because he was fingered by a disgruntled employee—that fat editor from the interviewing workshop, Sam Syrjala. The cops said he really hates Junior. They said he said that Junior was born with a silver pica pole in his hand." She shrugged. "The guy's got a way with words."

"I'm surprised the cops knew what a pica pole is,"

said Lucy. The poles, specialized rulers used to measure column length, were rarely used anymore, now that newspaper pages were designed on computers.

"They didn't," said Morgan. "But they had some interesting ideas."

Lucy chuckled, thinking ruefully that if they were on real bicycles, Morgan would be miles ahead of her by now. "Did they say what Junior's motive was?"

"I wondered the same thing," said Morgan. "I called some of my contacts but they told me they're still developing the case."

Lucy was beginning to doubt that Morgan had a future at the *Globe*. Not if she couldn't tell when the police were stonewalling.

"This place where the cops hang out, is it around here?" asked Lucy, dismounting from her bike and leaning casually against it.

"Wouldn't you like to know," said Morgan, pedaling even harder than before.

"Maybe we can work out something," said Lucy, in a speculative tone. "I can give you some background on the Read family—they have a summer place in my town— and you can help me develop some police contacts."

Morgan slowed her pace. "Two prizewinning reporters. We'd make a pretty good team. Let me think about it, okay?"

"Sure," said Lucy. "You know where to find me."

She started to leave, then paused, wondering why Morgan was staying at the hotel. The gym was open only to guests, she knew, but Morgan worked for a suburban paper. If she lived nearby, her paper would hardly provide hotel accommodations.

"Are you staying here at the Park Plaza?" she asked.

"No." Morgan shook her head. "My boss is a real cheapskate. I'm driving to Riverside and taking the T in every day."

"So how'd you get in the gym?'

"I just signed in. Nobody checks."

"They might. What room did you put down?"

"Yours. I figured it's probably big enough for two. Right?'

"Wrong," said Lucy, laughing. "It's hardly big enough for me."

When Lucy opened the door to her room, she didn't mind its modest size at all. The best part of staying in a hotel, she decided, was leaving the unmade bed and dirty towels and coming back to find everything fresh and neat. Except, of course, for the little pile of dirty clothes she'd left on the floor. She flopped down on the smooth comforter, the one she hadn't had to wrestle into submission that morning, and kicked off her sneakers, enjoying the fact that all she had to do was take a shower and find herself some supper.

She hauled herself to her feet, intending to take a nice, long shower, since the hot water never seemed to run out at the hotel, unlike at home. She was passing the desk when something caught her eye. It was her notebook, flipped open.

Lucy stopped in her tracks. Why was her notebook open? She hadn't taken it out of her bag. Or had she? She stood in place, trying to remember her actions when she'd called the Read house to talk to Angela. She'd sat on the bed. She remembered that much. But had she taken her notebook out and then, when she hadn't been able to speak to Angela, put it on the desk? She didn't think so. She didn't remember doing it.

Of course, these days she often forgot things. Some mornings she couldn't remember if she'd brushed her teeth or taken her vitamin. The drive to work passed in a blur; she could rarely remember if the traffic light on Main Street had been green or red. And then there were those restless reading glasses—they seemingly wandered about the house of their own accord, turning up in the most unlikely places. So it was entirely possible she had put the notebook on the desk and forgotten all about it.

Considering the matter, Lucy decided she'd prefer it that way, because the alternative was that someone had entered her room while she was out and had rifled through her belongings. Who would do that? And why? The only explanation she could come up with was that someone with a guilty conscience—Luther's murderer?—had pegged her as a skilled investigative reporter, probably because she'd won first prize. But that was ridiculous. Lucy had no illusions about her abilities in that regard. Getting a story depended upon luck as much as anything, and she sure wasn't feeling lucky these days.

She decided to put it out of her mind and take that shower. But before she went in the bathroom, she made sure the lock was bolted and the safety chain was securely fastened.

Chapter Twelve

Things always looked brighter after a good night's sleep. It was true, Lucy decided when she woke on Wednesday morning. Nothing had changed overnight except for her mood. She felt refreshed and ready to face whatever the day brought. Take Toby, for example. He was a decent kid at heart. No doubt he'd learn from his mistakes. And Kudo. She'd covered plenty of dog hearings and she was confident that if she came prepared with proof that Kudo was now housed in a proper kennel, with a fenced run, the selectmen would be satisfied and wouldn't take action against the dog.

Energized by these encouraging thoughts, Lucy leaped from bed and stretched, then threw open the drapes, revealing the dreary view. Not so dreary after all; sunlight was angling down, bathing part of the brick wall in a golden glow. It was going to be a good day, she decided, practicing the power of positive thinking.

She was still humming with optimism when she entered the coffee shop and ran smack-dab into the last person she'd expected to see. It was Catherine Read, looking crisp and professional as ever. Lucy knew it was wrong to judge people and that everyone reacted differently to death, but she would have expected Catherine to be in seclusion with her family. Unless, of course, some decision had been made to get out in public to show the family had confidence in Junior's innocence. Whatever it was, it was darned awkward.

"Hi," she said, getting in line behind Catherine. It would be rude not to acknowledge the woman, after all.

"Hi, Lucy," replied Catherine, managing a small, tight smile.

"I'm so sorry about your father." Lucy didn't know what else to say. "And your brother."

"You know," said Catherine, handing over a couple of dollars and accepting a cardboard cup and a grossly oversize muffin, "I don't think I've absorbed it yet."

She waited for Lucy and they sat down together at a table. Lucy eyed her muffin skeptically. "They say it's blueberry, but these seem more like little bits of blue gum or something."

"Not like the blueberries that grow wild in Tinker's Cove," said Catherine. "Gosh, I'd love to be there now."

"This must be awful for you."

"It's bad enough losing Dad in a tragic accident, but now that they've arrested Junior . . ." She paused and plucked a piece of muffin, keeping her head down. "It's ridiculous, of course. The whole family is behind him one hundred percent, and we've got the lawyers on it. We're hoping he can get the charges dropped so he won't have to go to trial."

"Can I quote you on that?" asked Lucy. "I tried to reach Angela last night but she wasn't home."

"You just missed her. She was here last night, kicking up a huge fuss and calling lawyers and anybody else she could think of, including Ted Kennedy, but I'm happy to say she left for Tinker's Cove first thing this morning."

"Does she have a cell phone?" inquired Lucy.

"Do me a favor," said Catherine, leaning toward Lucy. "Don't bother Angela. She's having a difficult time right now. I'll be happy to give you a statement on behalf of the family."

"That's very kind of you," said Lucy, pulling out her notebook.

Catherine took a moment to collect her thoughts, then spoke slowly so Lucy could get it all down. "My entire family believes the Boston Police Department has made a terrible mistake in arresting my brother and charging him with murdering his father. We know Junior is innocent and we're confident that he will eventually be exonerated, but these accusations have caused our family a great deal of additional sorrow." She paused. "How's that?"

"Fine."

"Not too strong?"

"Not at all." Lucy chewed her muffin. "They were awfully quick to arrest him. Do you know why?"

Catherine blinked rapidly, as if considering how to react. "This is off the record, but in my opinion it's absolutely ridiculous!" she finally exclaimed indignantly. "Talk about a rush to judgment!"

Catherine had reduced her muffin to a pile of crumbs and was picking up one bit and then another, but not taking a single bite.

"Okay, so there was a full inhaler canister in his room, but that doesn't mean anything. We've all got inhalers—asthma and allergies run in our family. For me it's dust and mold. Junior can't handle tree pollen. Dad, rest his soul, couldn't be anywhere near a cat. But we all take the same medications—it's no wonder the canisters got mixed up. Dad probably put his down and Junior picked it up, thinking it was his. Who can tell one Proventil from another?"

"Your father was allergic to cats?" asked Lucy. "There are no cats here."

"He's *most* allergic to cats, but he's allergic to lots of other stuff, too. You never know what's going to set you off. Sometimes I can drink orange juice; sometimes I can't." She paused. "I didn't think I'd risk it today, considering everything."

"Good call," agreed Lucy. "My daughter has asthma. Like you say, sometimes the pollen count is high and she's fine; other days it's low but she runs into trouble anyway."

"Then you understand what it's like. I hope Junior's doing okay in jail. You can just imagine the conditions: mildew, dust mites—I can't deal with it. Angela took his medicine over, but we don't know if they'll let him have it." She examined a lump of muffin, then put it down.

"I'm sorry. I shouldn't be venting like this, inflicting my feelings on you." She shook her head ruefully. "I'm on the organizing committee, you know. I'm supposed to be running the conference, but I don't know whether I'm coming or going." She furrowed her brow. "How's it going, by the way?"

"Great," said Lucy, making her voice sound enthusiastic. "Terrific workshops. Fabulous. I've learned a lot."

"I'm so glad." Catherine sounded relieved. "Have you heard anything about the judging? We made some changes, you know, to try to make it fairer."

Where was this conversation going? wondered Lucy. If she were in Catherine's place she would hardly have been thinking about rule changes.

"I can only speak for myself, but I don't think it could be any fairer," she said. "Of course, I could be biased, since I won a first place."

"Congratulations!" Catherine paused. "You know that job offer's still good." She stood up. "Thanks for listening. I've got to run."

Lucy watched her leave, chewing thoughtfully on the last bit of her muffin. Definitely not blueberries, she decided, but some artificial substance designed to simulate blueberries. Real blueberries wouldn't keep very well; the muffins might spoil before they could be sold.

Maybe something similar was going on at Pioneer Press, thought Lucy. Maybe the Reads were putting on a good appearance, pretending all was fine with the company, so they could unload it on National Media. Or maybe Pioneer wasn't in such rocky financial shape as she thought. After all, Inez could hardly go on shopping sprees at Armani, and Catherine couldn't hire new staff if the company was almost bankrupt, could they?

Was it one of those phony corporate bookkeeping scams she'd heard so much about lately? Were they deliberately fiddling with the figures for some reason? To avoid paying taxes? To make the company more attractive to a buyer? Was that what Sam Syrjala had on them?

As her mind leaped from one idea to another, Lucy realized she'd had the same confused sensation after her lunch with Catherine on Monday. Only this time Catherine had taken great pains to connect with her emotionally and win her sympathy. Had it been genuine, or had she been deliberately manipulating her? It was as if Catherine had a list of ideas that she wanted to convey, almost like a government official who had a list of talking points to cover.

For one thing, Lucy didn't buy her insistence that Luther's death had been an accident. Catherine was too experienced a journalist to believe that the police would make a mistake like that. They might have arrested the wrong person, and Lucy happened to think they had, but they never would have announced it was a homicide if there was the least possibility it was an accidental death.

She'd also refused to give Lucy Angela's cell phone number, which guaranteed Angela would be incommunicado until after Lucy's deadline at noon today. Was that intentional, or just coincidence?

As for the bit about the conference, Lucy thought it

was more proof that Catherine was busily erecting barriers to protect herself from her true emotions. Instead of grieving for her father or worrying about Junior, she was focusing on the conference as something manageable and controllable.

Okay, maybe she was sounding like a psychologist, but she was beginning to think that Catherine might have built up quite a few resentments against her father over the years. There was the issue of her sexuality and whether that was the reason Luther had left all of his Pioneer Press shares to Junior. And what about Monica? Perhaps Catherine didn't see her as a worthy successor to her late mother. Maybe she even feared losing her father's affection when he became involved with Monica. Especially if his relationship with Monica was the reason he'd decided against selling the chain. Catherine had as much to gain from the sale as Junior, maybe more. She was clearly one of the stars of the company with her profitable paper, and National Media would certainly want to keep her. For Catherine, the giant conglomerate would certainly offer her more opportunities for advancement than she would have had in the small, family-owned Pioneer Press.

Lucy popped the last of her muffin into her mouth. It may have been fake, but it did taste a lot like blueberries. The imitation blueberries somehow tasted more like blueberries than the real thing, which were sometimes bland, or acidic instead of sweet. And maybe she was overreacting. She'd like to think so, she admitted to herself, but it was hard to overlook the fact that Catherine had plenty of reasons for wishing her father dead.

Lucy still had a few minutes before her workshop, so she refilled her coffee cup and sat back down at the sticky Formica table, pulling her cell phone from her purse. She dialed Ted's room.

"I'll start with the bad news," she said when he answered. "I couldn't get Angela."

"Damn."

"But there's good news. I did get a nice quote from Catherine."

She read it off so Ted could get it down.

"Good work, Lucy. That fills the hole in my story nicely."

Lucy knew he was speaking literally. He had probably written the story about Junior's arrest last night when he got back from police headquarters, leaving a space for reaction from the family. Now that the story was finished, he could e-mail it to Phyllis, who was putting the paper together for the noon deadline.

"Well, Catherine's a pro," replied Lucy. "She knew what we wanted."

"It sounds like you two are getting pretty buddy-buddy."

"Hardly. She's all smoke and mirrors, believe me. She was trying to tell me that the cops have made a terrible mistake and Luther's death was really an accident."

"It's called denial, Lucy." Ted's voice was gentle. "Who can blame her?"

"Well, if my father were murdered I'd want to know who did it." Lucy paused. "Heck, I'm just a casual acquaintance and I want to know who did it. Did you get anything interesting from the cops last night?"

"Lucy, listen to me. You're not investigating this murder; you're attending a conference. Don't you have a workshop this morning?"

Lucy checked her watch. It was time to get moving or she'd be late.

"I'm practically there," she told Ted.

Chapter Thirteen

New England weather is remarkably unreliable, but every now and then the meteorological forces cooperate to produce a perfectly brilliant day at least once every June. It was just such a morning when Lucy left the coffee shop: the sun was shining in a cloudless blue sky, the air was fresh, and a gentle breeze ruffled her hair. It seemed horribly unfair that Ted expected her to spend such a morning in a windowless subterranean meeting room.

In a small act of rebellion she decided to delay the inevitable by walking around the block to the entrance on the other side of the hotel. The top-hatted doorman was too busy to hold open the door for her and when she went inside she found quite a crowd of people standing by the valet parking window. They were all waiting for their cars to be brought from the garage, and some of them seemed to be growing impatient. Harold Read, she noticed, was among them.

"Who ever heard of a hotel that doesn't have a garage, that has to park the cars out in who-knows-where!"

Inez nervously plucked something from her beige,

tailored silk sleeve. "Take it easy," she murmured. "People will hear."

Intrigued by this family drama, Lucy slowed her pace.

"I don't care if they do hear. We've been waiting for half an hour. Where the hell is the car? Out in Dorchester?"

"I'd like to send that cat of yours to Dorchester," declared Inez, holding out her arms for his inspection. "Look at this. My new suit is covered with cat hair."

Hearing the word *cat*, Lucy decided to stick around. She found a spot against the marble wall and joined the group waiting for their cars.

"One or two hairs, that's all," said Harold. "It's not Fluffy's fault. Cats shed, especially in summer." He tapped his foot. "Fluffy could have that car here faster than these idiots."

"Calm down. You're just going to raise your blood pressure," said Inez, brushing at her sleeve.

She was perched on stiletto heels and her hips were encased in a short, tight skirt that matched her jacket. Lucy couldn't imagine a more uncomfortable outfit. Inez was clearly a woman who put a premium on her appearance. The shoes, Lucy guessed, probably cost at least three hundred dollars; the suit must have set Harold back a couple of thousand. And then there was the hair, nails, and makeup, plus a generous sprinkling of jewelry. Inez was definitely high-maintenance and surely required frequent visits to the beauty salon, masseuse, and gym. It all seemed rather expensive for a man whose business was losing money.

"Tell me about it," fumed Harold. "I know you don't like Fluffy much, Inez, but you've got to admit she has a calming influence. All she has to do is sit in your lap and start purring and it's better than a scotch and soda."

"How would you know?" asked Inez. "You always have the scotch and soda, too."

"I could use one now," said Harold, pulling out a handkerchief and wiping his brow. "Maybe I should talk to that guy again. Make sure he hasn't forgotten us."

"The car's here," said Inez, pointing with a coral-tipped and bejeweled finger.

"So it is," said Harold, stuffing the handkerchief in his pocket and taking his wife by the elbow.

In his haste, he missed the pocket and the handkerchief fluttered to the marble floor. Lucy quickly scooped it up and followed them outside to return it. She never got a chance.

"You've wrecked my car!" shouted Harold, grabbing the valet driver by the scruff of his neck and pointing to a ding on the door of his gold Lexus. "You're gonna pay!"

The driver tried to wriggle out of his grasp, all the while offering a rapid-fire explanation in a foreign language. A language Harold definitely didn't understand.

"Can't you speak English? This is America, God damn it." He gave the driver a shake and yelled, *"We speak English!"*

The manager hurried out of his booth, and Harold, distracted, let the driver go. He remained in place, gesturing with his arms and repeating his staccato explanation to the manager.

"He says it was like that; he didn't do anything."

"Are you calling me a liar?" demanded Harold.

"No, no, no," insisted the manager. "But it is a small dent. Very small. You may not have noticed it until now."

"I would have noticed," growled Harold. "I'm calling the police! I want to file a report!" His face was beet red, and Inez was trying to soothe his temper by patting his arm. He shook her off and planted himself in front of the manager, shoving his face out and jabbing the man's chest with his finger.

This was definitely not the time to return the hand-

kerchief, especially since it was past time for her workshop. She'd mail it to him, or give it to Catherine. She
certainly didn't want to get involved in this scene, even
though it made for fascinating drama. She reluctantly
pulled herself away, stepping into a pool of sunlight.
The handkerchief, she saw, was sparkling. When she held
it closer to examine it, she sneezed. Cat hair. Inez wasn't
the only one covered with cat hair—the handkerchief
was full of it.

"Dad, rest his soul, couldn't be anywhere near a cat."
That's what Catherine had said. But it seemed likely
that Luther had been exposed to cat hair the night he
died. Lucy remembered seeing Luther leaving the banquet room with a handkerchief over his face. Was it his
handkerchief, or had Harold given him one of his? A
handkerchief, if it was anything like this one, that was
full of cat hair. And cat hair, Lucy knew, was one of the
most powerful allergens. It could linger in carpets and
furniture long after the cat was gone, even remaining in
houses for years after the cat owners moved out.

What could Harold have been thinking when he
handed Luther his handkerchief? wondered Lucy. What
indeed? Had he simply not realized that the handkerchief would exacerbate Luther's symptoms? Or had he
done it deliberately, knowing full well that Luther's inhaler was empty because he'd switched it? Murder by
cat hair—could such a thing even be possible?

Lucy was debating whether she should call Detective
Sullivan when she arrived at the workshop. She took a
seat in the back and reached for her notebook, realizing she didn't have the foggiest idea which workshop
she was attending. A huge sense of guilt accompanied
this realization; she had to admit she really wasn't getting as much out of the conference as she could. She'd
been too distracted by the murder, not to mention worrying about the situation at home. Ted wouldn't approve; she knew he'd be furious if he knew.

She resolved to mend her ways and pay attention from now on. She cleared her mind and focused on the speaker at the front of the room, a thirtyish fellow with wire-rimmed glasses dressed in a blue Oxford-cloth shirt and khaki pants.

"First off," he said, "you have to recognize the fact that the cops are only going to tell you what they want you to know. Take, for example, the murder of the priest in Roxbury a few months ago. The man who was charged with the killing was very popular in the community, a coach and teacher. They wanted to let enough information out so there wouldn't be a public outcry that they'd arrested the wrong man, but they couldn't risk prejudicing a jury, either. They had to walk a very fine line in that case."

"Or that kid who murdered the lady next door," offered the second panelist, a heavyset woman with bangs and oversize glasses. Her nameplate identified her as Eileen Rivers, a name Lucy recognized from her byline in *Boston* magazine. "He looked like a choirboy. Hell, he *was* a choirboy. Big for his age, though. There was a lot of sympathy for that kid." She paused. "He stabbed that poor woman forty-seven times or something."

Ed Murphy, the third panelist, looked like he'd been around for a while and had seen it all.

"It affects how we cover crimes, too. We didn't run the little psychopath's picture on the front page at the *Herald*—the powers that be decided it would upset the little old ladies who go to Mass every day." He scratched his chin. "Thank God for DNA or that kid woulda walked. Public sentiment was so strong, the jury never could've convicted him. Not if they wanted to live to tell about it."

Lucy was enthralled, leaning forward eagerly to hear every word. This was the workshop she'd been most excited about attending: "The Police Beat: Cooperating with and Getting Cooperation from Police and Other

Local Officials." She'd really been looking forward to it, especially considering that her own relations with the police in Tinker's Cove weren't especially good. She had only one friend on the force, Barney Culpepper, and she suspected even he found her a nuisance more often than not.

"Given the fact that the police are naturally going to be stingy with info, we have to figure out some ways to get them to be more forthcoming. Any ideas?"

It was the first panelist, looking for input from the class. He was also acting as moderator and was standing in front of the table where the others were seated. Lucy couldn't see his nameplate and wondered who he was.

Only one hand was up, and Lucy was not surprised to see it belonged to Morgan Dodd. The girl reporter was so eager to talk that she didn't wait for the moderator to recognize her.

"Well, I always find that one hand washes the other, you know. I think I can say I have a pretty good relationship with the Framingham police, and that's because I give them a lot of coverage for Neighborhood Watch and the annual bike auction. It really pays off when we have a big story."

"Framingham's not Boston," said Eileen, exchanging glances with Ed.

The moderator, however, nodded encouragingly at Morgan.

"It's always good to do all that you can to develop good relations with the police," he said, "but it can be dangerous to rely on them too much. If you can get information from somebody else—witnesses, family members, whoever—then you've got some firepower. If they know you're going to print it anyway, sometimes they'll be more forthcoming."

"Isn't that blackmail?" Lucy was surprised to hear her own voice.

The moderator stared at her, as if affronted, then smiled slowly.

"Any ideas on that?" he asked.

Hands shot up around the room. Soon a lively discussion was under way, which inevitably turned to Luther Read's murder.

"I was a little surprised at the local coverage, especially the *Globe*," said Lucy. "I guess murder isn't front-page news in Boston."

Everyone fell silent and Lucy knew immediately that she'd said the wrong thing.

"That was my story," said the moderator. "I'm Brad McAbee."

"Oops," said Lucy, and everyone laughed. "I didn't know that—I came a little late."

"No problem. You're right, of course. I don't know if there's a lot of pressure from the chamber of commerce or what, but it's now company policy to put violent crimes on the Metro page, unless it's someone very important."

"Luther Read wasn't important enough?"

"He probably was, actually, but he got himself killed late on Sunday night. There's no way they'd change the front page except for the president . . . maybe."

Everybody laughed again, recognizing the truth of what he was saying. The cry to stop the presses was heard a lot more frequently in movies than pressrooms because of the enormous expense involved.

"But what about Tuesday's paper? There wasn't much in that either. Are the police being especially close-mouthed?" asked Lucy.

"You could say that," said Brad. "And I haven't been able to follow my own advice of developing alternate sources. His family's talking but it's all spin. They're in the business so they know the danger of talking freely to reporters."

There were knowing chuckles from around the room.

"Part of the problem is that he got killed here, at the convention. If he'd died at home, I could talk to the neighbors. But here, I don't know who knew him and who has an ax to grind. I could find out, if I had plenty of time, but my editor isn't going to budget much time for this story." Brad shrugged. "How about you guys helping me out—anybody got any theories? Have the cops got the right guy?"

That was the very question Lucy wanted to ask. The only person who raised a hand to answer was Morgan.

"I got it from a very reliable, *official* informant that they have 'every confidence' that they'll get a conviction." She nodded knowingly. "Figure it out. It had to be somebody close to him, somebody in the family, who could switch the asthma medication."

Eileen and Ed were exchanging glances, as if they'd never heard anything so stupid in their lives.

"You're young and obviously new to the business, but you can take my word for it that a lot of people at this convention know Luther Read has asthma," said Ed. "It's common knowledge."

Instead of being insulted, Morgan nodded like a good student.

"Don't forget, the cause of death hasn't been officially determined," cautioned Brad.

Lucy pricked up her ears.

"You mean it might have been something else?" asked Morgan.

"I have my doubts about the asthma theory," said someone else. "How could the killer know he'd have an attack in the first place?"

"The murderer could have introduced an asthma trigger," offered Lucy, thinking of the handkerchief. "If the murderer knew he was allergic to cat hair, for example . . ."

This was met with titters from the group.

"Cat hair! That's a good one," scoffed Morgan.

"How could the killer be sure he would have a severe enough attack to kill him?"

"Maybe time wasn't important. Maybe the murderer was willing to try again if it didn't work this time," speculated Lucy, defending her theory.

"Again, that would seem to point to someone in the family, someone who knew there would be other opportunities," said Brad.

"My sources in the BPD say Junior had it all: motive, means, and opportunity," said Morgan. "Do you think this is just some sort of smoke screen?"

"Oldest trick in the book," said Ed.

"The surer they are, the more likely it is that they're wrong," said Eileen. "Remember that drive-by, when the little kid was killed in his bed? Bullet went right through his little beating heart."

Lucy was horrified, but from the cool reaction of the others she judged the shooting must be old news.

"Yeah," said Brad. "They got a conviction on that one, and it wasn't until some jailhouse snitch started talking that they realized they'd put the wrong guy away for twenty to life."

"The bad news for Junior Read is that this case isn't sensational enough to generate much interest, not enough gore," observed Ed. "Remember the female torso in the Dumpster? Now, that was a story. And who could forget the weirdo who dropped the radio in the tub while his mother was taking a bath?"

"It wasn't the radio that was so fascinating," said Eileen. "It was the fact that he ate her for dinner afterward."

Everybody groaned.

"And on that note," said Brad, checking his watch, "we'll break for lunch. *Bon appetit!*"

Lucy was gathering her things together when Morgan approached her.

"What did you think of the panel?" she asked.

"Pretty interesting, but I'm sure glad I cover crime in Tinker's Cove instead of Boston."

Morgan grinned. "No cannibalism cases?"

"Not so far," said Lucy.

"You do seem to have some pretty interesting neighbors, though. Why don't we have lunch together and you can tell me all about Junior Read?"

Lucy smiled. "So you're beginning to think he might be innocent?"

Morgan shrugged. "Who knows? But I'm looking for a story, and it'd be a lot more interesting read if the cops have the wrong guy, right?"

"Right," agreed Lucy.

"So what do you say? Can I interest you in some lunch? My treat."

The very idea of food made Lucy queasy. Besides, she was still stinging from Morgan's put-down of her cat-hair theory and didn't want to share her inside information about the Read family.

"Thanks, but I'm not very hungry. I think I need some fresh air."

"Well, catch you later," said Morgan, taking off down the hall after Brad.

Lucy shook her head. That girl was certainly determined to break a big story and didn't mind stepping on a few toes to get it. She'd better be careful, thought Lucy, because such tactics could backfire.

Lucy climbed up the stairs slowly, considering her options. She could take a walk, but the concrete sidewalks and busy streets weren't appealing. What she really wanted, what she longed for, was a patch of green where she could soak up some sun. At home she was surrounded by grass and trees and flowers, but here in the city they were in short supply, most often confined to decorative planters. She wanted to surround herself with growing things; she wanted to escape the constant roar of traffic and the smell of exhaust.

She asked the doorman for directions to the nearest park and he instructed her to follow Arlington Street to the Public Garden. She soon found herself standing on the corner of Arlington and Boylston, waiting for a red light to stop the constant stream of traffic so she could cross to the park on the opposite side. Once she was safely inside the ornate wrought-iron fence, however, the sound of traffic receded and she inhaled the fresh scent of newly cut grass. She followed a winding path bordering a pretty pond and discovered a delightful little bridge. She paused at the railing, amazed at the unexpected yet familiar sight of water in the city. Not water fit for swimming, admitted Lucy, staring at the green, murky surface, but people could pay a small fee and cruise aboard the quaint swan boats. These ungainly watercraft wouldn't do very well in Maine waters, she decided. They were little more than flat platforms for rows of seats, propelled by human pedal power. The driver sat in the rear, hidden between the molded halves of a large swan shape.

It was as if she'd seen this pond before, she thought, racking her brain. It finally came to her as she watched a little brown duck following one of the swan boats: it was the pond in Robert McCloskey's *Make Way for Ducklings*, a book she'd read hundreds of times to the kids.

The boat rides were a popular attraction, and many families were waiting in line. Lucy found a seat on a nearby bench and sat down, enjoying the slight breeze that blew across the water and watching the little children waiting with their parents. The very littlest were in strollers or backpacks, but the three- and four-year-olds were usually held firmly by the hand. That didn't stop them from jumping up and down, or stooping to examine the ground, or even attempting to pull each other's hair. That was what one little freckle-faced boy was doing, yanking at his sister's braids.

Siblings, thought Lucy, fingering the handkerchief she had tucked into her pocket. She couldn't help thinking that Harold, Luther's brother, was a far likelier murderer than Junior, his son. Having refereed countless squabbles among her own children, Lucy had no illusions about the power of sibling rivalry. Take Elizabeth, for example. She wouldn't hesitate to kill Toby, if she could be sure of getting his room.

Impulsively, Lucy reached for the cell phone in her purse, then dug around until she found Detective Sullivan's card. She dialed, only to be flooded with doubts when she heard his voice.

"This is Lucy Stone—you interviewed me Monday night."

"I remember," said Sullivan. "What's up?"

"I don't know if anything's really up," she replied, "but I thought I'd better call. I know this probably sounds foolish, but it's better to speak up and be wrong than to be quiet and watch an innocent man be convicted, right?"

"Uh, right."

Lucy studied the handkerchief. It was definitely covered with glistening white cat hair.

She took a deep breath.

"I happened to see Harold Read drop a handkerchief and I picked it up." She paused. "It's absolutely covered with cat hair."

There was a long silence. Finally Sullivan spoke.

"Cat hair?"

"Yeah. Luther Read died because of an asthma attack, right? Well, cat hair is a very common allergen. In fact, I happen to know that he was extremely allergic to cats. His daughter told me so." Lucy paused to catch her breath. "So do you want the handkerchief? What should I do with it?"

"Give it back to Mr. Read, I guess."

Lucy was stunned. "But it's evidence!"

"I don't think so," said Sullivan. "I appreciate your call, but we're following a different line of investigation."

"What do you mean? Wasn't asthma the cause of death?"

"Thank you for your concern," said Sullivan. "Have a nice day."

So much for trying to be a good citizen, thought Lucy, watching in fascination as the freckle-faced boy gave a particularly vicious yank and his sister reacted by pummeling his chest. The parents, unaware of their son's misbehavior, were scolding the little girl.

The father, a bearded fellow who also had a bouncing toddler in a backpack, reminded her of Bill. He also had toted all the kids, in turn, in the backpack.

The memory made her smile. Bill hadn't been much for changing diapers or coping with upset stomachs, but he'd been great at soothing colicky babies and could cajole a cranky two-year-old out of a temper tantrum. Somehow he'd always known when she had reached the end of her rope and came to the rescue. She wanted to get him something wonderful for Father's Day; the only problem was, she wasn't sure what it was. She'd know it when she saw it, she decided, wishing that she had time to go shopping. She didn't, she realized; she had just enough time to buy herself an ice-cream pop and get back to the hotel for her afternoon panel.

Chapter Fourteen

Three hours later, when the "Keeping Features Fresh" panel ended, Lucy was more convinced than ever that there were no new feature stories. They had all been written. Even worse, they'd all been written by her: the heartwarming reunion with long-lost relatives or pets, the lucky discovery of a priceless antique carelessly used for a humble purpose, and the always popular struggle of one courageous individual or family to overcome a cruel and debilitating disease—or the variation in which a courageous individual or family battles to raise money for an experimental but potentially lifesaving procedure that was not covered by medical insurance.

It was enough to make you a cynical sob sister, thought Lucy, as she closed her unused notebook and dropped her pen into her purse. In fact, one of the panelists had been an extreme example of what happened to a features editor who had lost all interest in human-interest stories. Lucy recognized her from the registration line, where she'd admired her shoes. Today she was wearing a different, equally fascinating pair. Her name was Carole Rose, and Lucy was interested to discover that she worked for the Pioneer Press Group's Hartford paper, one of the papers published by Junior and edited by Sam Syrjala.

"That was very interesting," said Lucy, approaching Carole when the panel was over and introducing herself.

"I saw you yawning, you know," said Carole, a trim, fiftyish woman dressed in a tailored pantsuit and sporting oversize eyeglasses with black rims. "Not that I blame you. I could hardly keep myself awake."

"How about a reviving cup of tea at the Swan Court?" suggested Lucy.

"How about a stiff drink at the Whiskey Bar?" countered Carole.

It seemed a little early to Lucy, but she really wanted to talk to Carole. She was sure to have some insight into Junior's role in the company and his relationship with Sam Syrjala, the *Gazette* editor who had given the police evidence incriminating him.

"Sure," she said. "I hear it's one of the trendiest bars in Boston."

"Honey, I don't care if it's trendy or not as long as they don't water the booze."

Lucy treated this as a joke and laughed, but she had a feeling Carole was absolutely serious. She struggled to keep up as Carole hurried through the lobby and into the candlelit lounge, where low banquettes were arranged around cube-shaped tables. It took Lucy's eyes a few moments to adjust to the darkness—all natural light was carefully excluded and the walls and furniture appeared to be black—and she stumbled as they sat down. Fortunately, the bar was virtually empty and no one saw her gaffe, not even Carole, who was busy lighting a cigarette.

"What can I get you ladies?" inquired a waiter, speaking down to them from a lofty height. It wasn't just the fact that he was quite tall and the banquettes were very low; Lucy was pretty sure he considered himself a superior being.

"Double martini," growled Carole.

"White wine for me," said Lucy.

"Which white wine would that be?" inquired the waiter.

"The house white."

"We don't have a house wine," he said, looking down his nose. "Perhaps you'd like to peruse the wine list."

The waiter handed her a menu that was larger than the Tinker's Cove phone book. She flipped it open and scanned the prices, looking for the cheapest. Whatever she chose, she'd have to make it last. She certainly couldn't afford a second at these prices.

"The California pinot grigio," she told him.

The waiter sighed and snatched the menu, as if to suggest that such a magnificent array of choices had been wasted on her. He vanished, presumably to get their drinks, and Lucy looked around. Her vision had cleared but she still couldn't make out much. It was like being in a cozy cave.

"This is very chic, and practical, too," she said, resisting the urge to open the blinds and let the June sunlight stream in. "After all, black doesn't show the dirt."

"Sounds like a feature story to me," said Carole, inhaling slowly and deeply on her cigarette. "Bar decor for the home."

Lucy smiled. "How come you're in features? You don't seem to have your heart in it, if you know what I mean."

Carole snorted, expelling a cloud of swirling smoke. "That's a good question—it's the question I ask myself all the time." She glanced around the empty lounge. "Where the hell is that waiter?"

"Pressing the grapes," said Lucy.

Carole cocked an eyebrow and looked at Lucy.

"You're not quite the sweet young thing I took you for."

"Not sweet, not young," said Lucy. "But I don't mind admitting I feel a little bit like Dorothy when she woke up in Oz with Toto. I'm definitely not in Tinker's Cove anymore."

"Tinker's Cove?" Carole squinted and blew smoke through her nostrils. "Isn't that where the late, lamented Luther Read had a summer home?"

Lucy nodded, watching as the waiter set down their glasses. "Junior's family is there now. . . ."

"Without Junior." Carole raised her glass. "I'll drink to that," she said, and took a healthy swallow.

Lucy took a sip of wine. "You're not a fan of Junior's?"

"You could say that." Carole promptly drained her glass and signaled the waiter for another. "And I'm not the only one. You can bet there was a collective sigh of relief across the board from everyone at Pioneer when they heard Luther was gone and Junior was in jail."

"Really? I'm surprised. They're real popular in Tinker's Cove."

"It's nothing personal." She leaned forward and stubbed out her cigarette in the ashtray. "God, I've heard them use that phrase enough times. 'It's nothing personal but there's a two-percent cap on raises this year.' 'It's nothing personal but you're only allowed six sick days under the company policy.' " She paused to light up. "It's nothing personal, don't get me wrong. Luther and Junior are great guys. But now that Luther's gone to meet his maker and Junior's facing murder charges, I don't think anybody at Pioneer Press will be shedding any tears."

"I guess the employees were in favor of the National Media sale, then."

"Not exactly. A lot of people would have lost their jobs. There was even one of those time-management guys sniffing around the office a week or so ago."

Lucy had finished her first glass of wine, so she asked for another when the waiter brought Carole's second double martini. Now that she was comfortably ensconced in the luxurious lounge, sticking to her budget no longer seemed a high priority.

"Better bring me one, too," said Carole. "Save yourself a trip."

"I heard rumors that the sale was on hold before Luther's death," said Lucy. "Something about Monica Underwood wanting a platform for her views . . ."

Carole shook her head. "Luther was first and foremost a businessman. Anybody who thought different soon found they were wrong. Take Harold, for example. He loves that paper of his, gets to spout all his wacky right-wing politics, but Luther was determined to sell it out from under him. Do you think Luther would let him keep it? No way. It was all or nothin' with Luther."

"How would that work? Would he have to buy it?" The wheels were turning in Lucy's head. If Harold had wanted more independence and more autonomy, and Luther had refused to allow it, it could have been a motive for murder.

"I don't know the details, but Sam told me that Harold was pretty upset about the whole thing." She lifted her empty glass. "Here's to friendship."

"So Sam and Harold are buddies?"

"They go way back," said Carole. "Sam's first job was working for Harold at the *Republican.*"

No wonder Syrjala had been seated with the Read family at the banquet, thought Lucy, taking a moment to digest this information. He was buddy-buddy with Harold. Was that why he told the police about Junior? Was he trying to protect Harold? Or was it simply jealousy of Junior's privileged position in the company? She wanted to ask Carole, but it didn't look as if she was going to get any more information from her.

She was sprawled on the banquette, nodding along to the music. Spotting the waiter approaching with their drinks, she gave a lopsided smile.

"This is a nice place," she said, lifting her fresh drink. "I like it here."

"Me, too," said Lucy.

Carole knocked back most of her drink, then rose unsteadily to her feet. "Where do you think they keep the ladies' room?"

"Let's find it together," suggested Lucy.

The waiter pointed them to a larger, similarly decorated room, where loud music was pounding even though there was no one to hear it, and down a curving staircase. They found themselves in a black hall, empty except for two curtains, pink and blue, that billowed from two identical doorways. Lucy made an intuitive leap.

"I say we go with the pink."

She steered Carole inside and gasped in amazement at the illuminated pink Lucite sink that seemed to float in the darkness. Everything else was painted black, even the ceiling tile.

"That's cool," she said.

"If you say so," said Carole, heading for a stall.

They were standing in front of the mirror, refreshing their lipstick, when Lucy noticed one of Carole's simple pearl earrings was missing. Not that Carole minded.

"I probably forgot to put it on this morning," she said. "Or maybe I only took one off last night." The idea struck her as hilarious, and she laughed all the way up the stairs.

Back in the lounge, Lucy declined Carole's invitation to have another drink and tried to settle her bill. Carole refused her offer and insisted on paying. "Expense account," she said, winking. "It's not like Sam's gonna ask any questions."

After the quiet, dim bar the lobby seemed very bright and loud as Lucy crossed it and stood waiting for the elevator. When the doors opened she stepped inside, only to feel it shudder beneath her as it lurched upward. She felt a bit woozy and realized she'd been drinking on a virtually empty stomach, since all she'd had to eat since breakfast was an ice-cream bar.

When she got to her room she rinsed her face and drank a glass of water and immediately felt better. So good, in fact, that she decided to call home. She was dying to tell Bill about the illuminated Lucite sink in the ladies' room, but Zoe picked up on the first ring.

"It's Mom, honey. How are you doing?"

"You sound funny, Mom."

"I'm just tired," said Lucy. "Do you miss me?"

"Yes! Daddy's not a good cook. We've had pizza every night—*with* pepperoni. I *hate* pepperoni."

"You can pick them off, you know."

"I can still taste it, Mom. Yuck!"

Lucy had heard this complaint before.

"Only a few more days of school left—tomorrow and Friday, right?"

"Mom! You know what? I'm not getting the perfect-attendance award, and it's all Elizabeth's fault because I've been late three days in a row!"

Zoe's voice quavered with outrage.

"Really?" Lucy couldn't believe it. She knew the school wouldn't take away the award unless Zoe had been very late indeed.

"What time did you get there today?"

"Nine o'clock!"

That was more than an hour late.

"Wasn't Elizabeth late for work?"

"She says she doesn't care because she hates her job."

"If she keeps on being late she might get fired."

"I hope she does!"

"Zoe, that's not very nice. I'm surprised at you."

"Elizabeth's mean. Sara says so, too."

"Did Sara have a fight with Elizabeth?"

"Elizabeth told Sara she has to feed Kudo, and Sara says it's not fair because she's already doing the dishes and Dad makes her take out the garbage. Plus she didn't get to go horseback riding yesterday. . . ."

Zoe was turning into a mother lode of information that was definitely worth mining. "Did Kudo run away?" she asked.

"A long time ago. He's back now. He's right here. Want to talk to him?"

"No, honey. Just give him a doggy cookie for me."

Lucy heard a thud as Zoe dropped the phone and then the clink of the cover on the canister of dog treats.

"Mom?" Zoe was back on the line. "I didn't get to go to ballet because Dad was working late because Toby quit."

She was about to ask if Toby had found a new job when she heard Zoe squeal in protest.

"Mom?" Sara had taken the phone from her younger sister.

"Hi, honey. How's it going?"

"Elizabeth is the biggest pig in the world and I hate her."

"Zoe told me all about it," said Lucy. "Don't you have any good news?"

"Let me think." There was a long silence, and Lucy imagined she could hear the clock running on her call like a taxi meter. "Oh, I know! Sara and I are making a spectacular surprise for Dad for Father's Day."

"That's great," exclaimed Lucy. Then she had a dreadful thought. "You're not using power tools or anything dangerous, are you?"

"No, Mom. Just glue and scissors, but it's terrific, all the same. He'll love it."

"That's great. I really miss you guys, but I'll be home soon."

"We miss you, too, Mom."

Lucy felt a little weepy when she said good-bye.

Probably a mix of too much wine, anxiety, and general longing for her girls. The cure was distraction, so she flicked on the TV, intending to watch the evening news. What she got, however, was the title frame for the Alfred Hitchcock film *Notorious*.

Enthralled, she sat at the foot of the bed as the credits rolled. Ingrid Bergman. Cary Grant. Claude Rains. It was one of her favorite films and she knew she wouldn't be able to turn it off. She'd have to watch, and she definitely needed some nourishment.

Oh, well. She sighed, reaching for the room-service menu. Throwing caution to the wind, she decided to splurge. After all, the Trask Trust was covering her expenses. She hadn't even paid for her drinks at the bar; Carole had refused her money. She hadn't spent a cent of her own money so far, except for a couple of dollars for Bill's Father's Day card. A girl had to do what a girl had to do and it looked as if this girl's immediate future included chicken Caesar salad, chocolate cake, and Cary Grant.

Chapter Fifteen

"**M**y, my, don't you look bright and perky this morning."

Lucy was sitting in the coffee shop, savoring her morning coffee and reading the *Herald*. She smiled at Carole, who she had to admit looked better than she would have expected, considering the number of double martinis she'd downed the day before. Her crisp, starched white shirt gave her a fresh appearance, and the short skirt she was wearing showed her legs to advantage, tipped with a pair of sexy, killer heels.

"I had a wonderful time last night."

"A man? Did you meet a man?" Carole sat down in the opposite chair and put down her coffee. "Someone here at the convention? Tell me all about it."

Now that she looked closer, Lucy could see that Carole was wearing rather a lot of skillfully applied makeup.

"The handsomest man I've ever seen," said Lucy with a sigh. "Sophisticated, urbane, a real knight in shining armor."

"He couldn't be in the newspaper business then," said Carole, unsnapping the lid on her coffee with a slightly trembling hand. "How'd you meet him?" Her eyes fell on Lucy's left hand. "Hey, aren't you married?"

Lucy tried very hard and almost succeeded in pulling off a world-weary shrug.

"There's nothing the matter with a little extracurricular activity—so long as my husband doesn't find out."

Carole's eyes widened. "Somehow I didn't take you for that kind of girl."

Lucy couldn't contain herself any longer and burst out laughing. "It was Cary Grant. I spent last night in my room—alone—watching *Notorious.*"

"You really had me going," said Carole, taking a swallow of coffee. "But I was suspicious. He sounded too good to be true." She sighed. "Believe me, I know from experience."

"I've been married for a very long time," said Lucy. "I can't imagine what it's like to be unattached and dating."

"After my last relationship ended I decided to swear off men forever."

Lucy smiled sympathetically. "That bad?"

Carole shook her head and pulled out her cigarettes, then realized the shop didn't allow smoking.

"Damn." She fingered the cigarette, then held it to her nose and inhaled deeply before replacing it in the pack. "I'm such a fool. I really thought I had something going with this guy. I mean, we were together for years. Then one day he meets somebody else and it's all over. Bye-bye. *Adios. Sayonara,* baby."

"That stinks."

"Tell me about it."

"You'll find somebody else."

"At my age? With my responsibilities?"

"Do you have kids?" Lucy was surprised.

"No. It's my dad. He was injured in a pressroom accident and needs a lot of care." Carole drained her coffee cup and set it down with a click. "Very expensive care."

"Doesn't he get disability benefits?"

"Oh, sure. The lawyers and human resources people were at his bedside the minute he was out of surgery with a big, fat offer. He was only too happy to take it, but it turned out to be a lot less than he needed."

"And he signed away any future claims?"

"How'd you guess? It was a condition of receiving the money."

"Who did he work for?"

"Pioneer Press."

Lucy nodded. She was beginning to understand why the Read family wasn't very popular with the employees at Pioneer Press. Not that they were any different from management at many companies these days.

"It's pretty late," Carole finally said. "I'd better go."

Lucy lingered at the table for a few minutes to finish her coffee. When she entered the hotel lobby her hand was immediately grasped and shaken energetically by a round-faced man sporting a *Shrubsole for Senate* button on the lapel of his rather tight suit jacket.

"I'm Dick Shrubsole, and I'm running for the U.S. Senate from Vermont. I'm going to be here in the hotel all day, and my press secretary here will be glad to sign you up for an interview."

He indicated a tiny, very serious-looking woman who was clutching a clipboard.

"I have openings at one, two, and three-fifteen," she offered, peering hopefully through her horn-rimmed glasses.

"I'm from Maine," said Lucy. "I don't think you want to waste any of that precious time on me."

"Mr. Shrubsole is attracting a lot of interest nation-wide," said the girl, blinking rapidly. "They're filling up fast," she said, "but right now I can probably squeeze you in whenever you'd like."

Lucy suspected he wasn't generating quite as much interest among the journalists at the convention as he hoped, but she was intrigued by the opportunity to interview the challenger for Monica Underwood's seat in the Senate.

"When did you say those openings were?" she asked.

She was reaching for her day planner when Ted appeared at her side and steered her toward the stairs.

"We'll get back to you," he called over his shoulder, but Shrubsole and his companion had already cornered a couple of other NNA conferees, clearly identifiable by their badges.

"What's going on?" asked Lucy. "That might've been interesting."

"Trust me, he's not gonna tell you anything he doesn't say at the publishers' breakfast this morning. It'll be a waste of time. All he wants is a puff piece, anyway." He stopped and turned, fixing a beady eye on Shrubsole. "I'm no fan of Monica Underwood's, believe me, but this is in really bad taste."

"I don't understand."

"Traditionally, all the regional candidates for the fall elections are invited to the breakfast. It's a chance to meet and greet the publishers and shmooze over some Nova salmon and eggs Benedict. It's usually pretty interesting."

"So Shrubsole's here for the breakfast and he's making himself available for interviews. What's the matter with that?"

"It's taking advantage, because Monica Underwood had to cancel. She can't be doing any campaigning while she's supposed to be in mourning, can she?"

"Oohh," drawled Lucy, as the light dawned. "What a weasel."

Ted shrugged. "He's a politician. That's the way they are. But we don't have to let them get away with it."

Lucy noticed they were blocking the stairway and stepped aside to allow a group of conferees to descend to the downstairs meeting room. "I guess I'd better get going. I don't want to miss anything," she said.

Ted nodded his approval. "What's the topic this morning?"

"All your secrets will be revealed," said Lucy. "It's the 'Editors' Roundtable: What Do Editors Really Want?' "

"Don't let me keep you," said Ted. "I'll expect a full report later."

Lucy waggled her fingers in a little wave as she started down the stairs. She was pretty sure she knew what Ted wanted—interesting stories and lots of them—but she thought it would be advantageous to discover if his requirements were industry-wide standards or merely quirks. Was it really a universal rule that you couldn't begin a story with a name, for example? And what about his insistence on including ages? Lucy didn't see that it mattered, and the people she interviewed often resented it.

She was surprised when she took her seat and noticed Jim Prince was one of the panelists. She remembered him from the banquet as rather brash and outspoken. He seemed an odd choice, considering his fellow panelists: two tiny, wizened ladies with their hair twisted into tight buns and wearing identical blouses with Peter Pan collars.

"Let's get started," said Jim, fixing his eyes on a group engaged in a noisy conversation in the back of the room.

They quieted down immediately.

"As most of you know, I'm the editor-in-chief of the New Bedford *Standard Times.*"

Lucy knew that New Bedford was a gritty old industrial city in Massachusetts that had fallen on hard times when fishing declined and manufacturers abandoned the city's old brick mills in search of cheaper labor in Mexico and Asia. No wonder Prince was such a tough guy, she thought as he introduced his fellow panelists.

"Ada Crabtree is a journalism professor at my alma mater, Boston University, where she is the adviser to the student paper. Her sister, Amanda, is editor of the highly regarded, indeed legendary Nantucket *Gam,* a paper that includes the White House and numerous members of Congress on its subscription list."

One of the ladies, the one with the circle pin placed front and center between the two edges of her collar, gave a tiny nod. "Thank you so much for that extremely kind introduction, Jim," she said. "Of course, I always knew you'd go far in the newspaper business."

Lucy was amused to see him grow a little red around the collar.

"I wouldn't be quite so proud, if I were you, Ada," Amanda sniffed. "Sometimes Mr. Prince stoops a bit low. I fear he meets his readers on their own level, when he ought to strive to raise them to a higher understanding of the issues."

"Not all of us have the sort of readership you do, dear Amanda," replied Ada. "New Bedford is hardly Nantucket, even if they were both whaling ports in the nineteenth century."

"Then, of course, there was that awful business with the Borden woman," admitted Amanda. "The city has never been the same since."

"That was Fall River," said Jim. "Lizzie Borden lived in Fall River."

"I'm quite sure you're mistaken," insisted Amanda.

"On the contrary," snapped Ada. "I'm sure we can rely on Jim's knowledge of the history of New Bedford."

"Shall we get started?" he said, clearing his throat. "I suggest we start with assigned stories and, if we have time, move on to enterprise reporting."

Lucy opened her notebook, but as the morning wore on she made very few notes. Jim, she soon learned, was an overbearing editor who kept his reporters on a tight leash. The Crabtree sisters didn't live up to their star

billing, either. As editors they encouraged solid reporting and welcomed diverse points of view, but their real
passion was grammar. Over the years they'd developed a
few pet peeves, and they were determined to use the
panel to express their views on the sloppy use of semi-
colons, the inappropriate use of adjectives, and what
Ada termed a deplorable tendency to unnecessary cap-
italization.

Lucy found her mind wandering, back to her own
girls in Tinker's Cove. She'd always assumed they would
stop squabbling as they grew older, but the example of
the Crabtree sisters wasn't encouraging. Ada and Amanda
were well into their sixties and they were still bickering
with each other.

As an only child, Lucy had always envied her friends
who had brothers and sisters. Her parents saw themselves as partners in an ongoing love story, and she had
often felt excluded from the affection they showered
on each other. What she hadn't realized, however, was
the level of competition between brothers and sisters
for their parents' attention. Her parents hadn't had
much attention to spare, but what little there was had
been all hers. She hadn't had to share it.

Lucy wondered about Catherine's role in the Read
family. She was more successful than Junior, but that
didn't seem to impress her father. Luther seemed to
save all his affection for Junior, choosing him as his heir
over Catherine. That would have been hard enough to
bear, but Lucy suspected that Luther's affection for
Monica might have been a worse blow to Catherine.

After all, recalled Lucy, Lizzie Borden supposedly
reached for that ax because she didn't get along with
her stepmother. Maybe Catherine didn't get along with
Monica; maybe she resented her arrival on the scene.
Maybe instead of giving her father forty whacks she'd
handed him an empty inhaler. Lucy didn't like thinking
of Catherine as the murderer, but she had to admit it

was a possibility. She had the means; she had opportunity and perhaps a motive.

It was becoming clear even to the Crabtree sisters that they were losing their audience, so it came as a relief to everyone in the room when Jim announced a brief break. Lucy got up to stretch and headed for the ladies' room. There was a line, so she decided to go up to her room, and when she got there she saw that she had a phone message. She sat for a minute, staring at the rosy little message light. An emergency at home? Probably. Fearing the worst, she pushed the button.

To her surprise, she heard Monica Underwood's smooth, well-modulated voice.

"This is Monica Underwood. I believe we met on Sunday night, in happier times. I would appreciate it if you'd give me a call, Lucy."

Lucy copied down the number and dialed, quickly, before she had a chance to change her mind. She never knew what to say to someone who was grieving anyway, and she was intimidated by Monica's position as a senator. If she waited, she knew she'd never make the call.

Monica herself answered the phone.

"I got your message," began Lucy.

"Thank you so much for getting back to me so promptly," cooed Monica, who apparently knew the Rule of Twelve: Your first twelve words should always include a thank-you.

"You're very welcome," replied Lucy. "I'm sorry for your loss. Luther was a wonderful man and will be greatly missed."

"A great voice has been silenced," said Monica. "A staunch advocate for the free exchange of ideas and a champion of First Amendment rights."

Lucy found herself questioning Monica's motive for calling her. "Is there something I can do for you?" she asked.

"I'm so glad you asked," began Monica. "My contacts

have told me that Dick Shrubsole is at the conference for the publishers' breakfast. Is that true?"

"I saw him myself this morning," said Lucy.

"Are you aware, Lucy, that there is a vast right-wing conspiracy in this country that is trying to do away with our most precious freedoms?"

"I have heard that suggestion before," said Lucy, hedging.

"Well, then you'll understand that what I am about to tell you is not motivated by any personal considerations whatsoever, but only by my great love for my country."

"Okay." Lucy could hardly wait to hear what she had to say.

"When we met on Sunday night, I believe Luther introduced you as a top-notch investigative reporter. He had great regard for you. That's why I've decided to call you with this information."

"I appreciate your faith in me."

"I do have faith in you, Lucy. I have every confidence that you will use this information appropriately. There can be no indication that you got this information from me, do you understand?"

"I'll consider it off the record," said Lucy. "I'm listening."

"Well, I've been thinking about who might have had a motive to kill Luther, and one name keeps popping up. I thought perhaps you could investigate. It would be a big story."

"Who is it?" Lucy had a feeling she knew the answer.

"Dick Shrubsole, that's who."

"As part of this right-wing conspiracy?"

"I see we're on the same wavelength here."

Same planet, yes. Same wavelength? Lucy didn't think so.

"Well, thanks for the information," said Lucy. "I really have to go."

"But you will follow up on this?"

"Sure," said Lucy, crumpling up the piece of notepaper and tossing it in the wastebasket. "I'm filing it away for future reference."

Chapter Sixteen

Coming to the conference had definitely been a mistake, thought Lucy. She had expected an inspiring exchange of ideas, challenging seminars, and an opportunity to grow professionally, but instead she was discovering the seamy side of human nature. She couldn't believe Monica Underwood, a woman she had admired for years, would behave like this. Completely disillusioned, Lucy sat on her bed.

She would have been better off staying home, where she belonged. She wasn't honing her skills, she wasn't getting much out of these sorry excuses for panels at all. Instead of wasting her time here she could be home in Tinker's Cove, covering local news and, most important, taking care of her family. Keeping Toby out of trouble. Making sure the girls stayed on schedule, getting them to school and activities on time. Attending the awards ceremony.

Now poor Zoe wasn't going to get her perfect-attendance award, and it was her fault for going to the conference. And instead of giving Elizabeth the support she needed in a job that had suddenly become extremely challenging, she had left her to manage completely on her own. It wasn't fair. Instead of simply providing child care for a typical three-year-old, Elizabeth was in the middle of a family tragedy.

Lucy wanted to go home, but she knew it wasn't an option. The Trask Foundation expected a report on how the grant money had been spent, and Ted could hardly tell them the recipient had quit the conference early because she was homesick. Lucy knew she had to stick it out, but she was darned if she was going back to that "Editors' Roundtable" to listen to those two old maids natter on about dangling participles, whatever those were. She needed a break, something distracting, and she knew where to get it. She'd always heard about the fabulous bargains at Filene's Basement, and here she was in Boston. It was the perfect opportunity.

The doorman's directions were simple enough: walk around the Common toward the statehouse, easily identifiable by its gold dome, cross Tremont Street at the traffic light by the Park Street T stop, and walk down Temple Street to Filene's.

The walk took only a few minutes, and Lucy found herself in the Downtown Crossing shopping area, where the streets were closed to automobile traffic and pedestrians could wander easily among the stores and peddler's carts. There was even an outdoor café, and a group of colorfully garbed Andean musicians were playing flute music.

Filene's was an enormous department store that took up an entire block. Lucy entered through the nearest door and found herself in the men's department; from the prices she knew this was definitely not the basement. A clerk directed her to the escalator and she descended to the fabled bargain hunter's paradise.

A rather dingy paradise, she discovered, that was strictly a bare-bones operation. No attempt had been made to pretty things up. Clothes and shoes and handbags were piled in battered wooden bins beneath hand-lettered signs announcing the price-reduction policy: after an item had been on the floor for two weeks it was reduced by 25 percent, after three weeks the discount increased to 50 percent, and an item that lingered for four weeks was reduced in price by 75 percent. After that, it was donated to charity.

From the way the shoppers were pawing through the merchandise, checking the price tags for dates, Lucy suspected a four-week reduction was extremely rare. She had never seen such determined shoppers. Mostly women, they were intent on bargains and didn't bother to waste time in the dressing room, preferring instead to try things on in the aisles. And no wonder, she realized as she made her way to the children's department; much of the merchandise was from top designers. There was even, she was surprised to see, a fur department. This was off-price shopping on a whole new scale, she decided, resolving to tell her friend Sue Finch, an inveterate shopper, all about it.

On impulse, she pulled her cell phone from her bag and dialed the familiar number.

"You'll never guess where I am," she crowed.

"I know you're in Boston," began Sue.

"Filene's Basement!"

"Tell me all about it. What have you bought?"

"Nothing yet. But it's wonderful. They have furs and designer handbags and"—Lucy's eyes fell on the sign for the shoe department—"oh, my God, shoes!"

"What kind of shoes?"

"I'm not sure." Lucy wound her way past the racks of toiletries and socks. "I'm on my way. I'm almost there." She stopped at a rack and picked up a pair of strappy, high-heeled pink sandals. "Manolo Blahnik. I've heard of those. These are Ferragamos. And these"—she picked up a pair of red flats—"these are called Mootsie Tootsies."

"Those Manolo Blahniks sound like they're straight out of *Vogue* magazine. I hope you're trying them on."

"I don't think so," said Lucy. "They have ridiculously high heels. I'd never be able to walk in them."

"Oh, Lucy," said Sue with a little sigh. "What do the Ferragamos look like?"

"Preppy. Turquoise with little bows."

"How much?"

"Sixty bucks! Too expensive."

"Not for Ferragamos. Give them a try."

"Ouch!"

"They always have the narrow ones there. Anything else?"

"The Mootsie Tootsies are cute, but they're red."

"How do they feel?"

"Great. They're really cute. Toe cleavage."

"Sexy."

"But they're red! Where would I wear red?"

"Red's the new beige."

"What?"

"I read it in a magazine. Buy them!"

"They're almost thirty dollars."

"That's cheap."

"I don't know," said Lucy, admiring her feet in the pretty little shoes. "You can get shoes for fifteen dollars at the outlet mall."

"Boat shoes in colors that don't match." Sue snorted. "Sandals that buckle on the inside because they sewed the straps on backward."

"You're right. I'm going to get them. I have to have them. I can't live without them."

"Thatta girl! Don't come home without them."

"I won't." Lucy paused. "So how's everything at home? Has my house burned down or anything?"

"So far, so good. I called to see if they needed anything and talked to Bill. He said everything's fine. And I saw Elizabeth the other day."

"She's certainly got her hands full, taking care of that little boy with everything that's going on."

"She looked fine, from what I could see, and I could see almost all of her."

Lucy was suspicious. "What do you mean?"

"She was wearing an itsy-bitsy string bikini."

"You saw her at the beach?"

"No. In the middle of Main Street. Sitting in a Jeep with her boyfriend."

"Jeep? Boyfriend?"

"Oops. I thought you knew. A very handsome lad. Muscular. With the cutest little tattoo on his shoulder."

"Tattoo?"

"Yeah. Some Oriental hieroglyphic. Very striking."

"I spoke to her the other day. I can't believe she didn't mention him. And she shouldn't be riding around town with practically nothing on. Was her seat belt fastened?"

"Sorry, Lucy. I was looking at her companion and I didn't notice."

"You're a dirty old woman."

"He's very attractive and I'm merely human." Sue sighed. "So how's the conference?"

Lucy didn't want to go into it. "Intense."

"Give me a call when you get home. I want to see those shoes."

Well, that was interesting, thought Lucy as she slid her cell phone into her bag. It was tempting to think that Sue, who loved to gossip, was exaggerating, but somehow she doubted it. Elizabeth had always been a bit of an exhibitionist, who delighted in shocking her conservative parents. She'd have to ask her about the bikini the next time she called home, resolved Lucy, firmly relegating her daughter's behavior to a corner of her mind. She had more important things to do right now.

It didn't take long to find a cute swimsuit for Zoe and designer T-shirts with prominent logos for Sara and

Elizabeth. Toby was also easy; she found an assortment of boxer shorts printed with the New England Patriots football team logo. But search as she might in the men's department she couldn't find anything for Bill.

It wasn't that the selection was poor; there were shirts and pants and ties and shoes galore, but nothing that she thought he would really like. Nothing special. Nothing that spoke to her, insisting it was the perfect present for Bill Stone.

She paid for all her purchases with a hundred-dollar bill, amazed to discover she had snagged a few pairs of boxers that qualified for the 50-percent markdown. She left the store, feeling enormously proud of herself for being so thrifty—and pleased that she'd splurged on the stylish shoes—and decided to try Charles Street, where she'd heard there were a lot of antique shops. Maybe she could find a Father's Day gift there.

She had no idea where Charles Street was, exactly, but she remembered seeing an information booth on the Common. There she learned that all she had to do was walk up to the corner by the statehouse and proceed along Park and then down Beacon Street to Charles.

"Don't forget to look at the Shaw Memorial," advised the helpful woman inside the booth. "It's opposite the statehouse and you can't miss it."

Lucy chugged up the rather steep hill to the corner and joined the knot of people standing in front of the memorial, which was a large bronze bas-relief by Saint-Gaudens commemorating the heroic 54th Infantry regiment. Comprised entirely of blacks and led by Colonel Robert Gould Shaw, the regiment's bravery in the Civil War inspired the motion picture *Glory*.

Lucy stood a moment, studying the lifelike faces of the soldiers, all so young and determined, marching off to their deaths. She hated war memorials and the thought of so many precious lives lost. It was always for a worthy cause, always an enormous waste. There had to be other ways of working out differences that didn't require human sacrifice.

Turning away she walked along Beacon Street which was lined with nineteenth-century row houses that overlooked the Common. She tried to peek inside the windows as she walked by and occasionally caught a glimpse of a chandelier, or a bit of fringe on a silk curtain. Some of the windows had a decidedly lavender tint and she wondered if it had once been the fashion to look out on a purple-tinted world.

She turned at the corner of Charles Street and poked along, looking into windows. It was a remarkably countrified street for a big city; it looked a bit like Main Street in Tinker's Cove with trees and a variety of stores. Here, of course, there were apartments above the store fronts and Lucy wondered what it would be like to live in one.

Passing an antique store with its door propped open to reveal an inviting interior, Lucy ventured in. A young woman greeted her pleasantly, telling her to ask if she needed help, and returned to her computer.

Lucy wandered about and discovered that the shop was much larger than she thought, with five or six rooms. In the farthest from the front and smallest room she found an assortment of old tools. Just the sort of thing Bill loved. A little ruler caught her eye; it was obviously handmade and had a movable stop and a sharp scribe that could be used to mark a board to a certain width for cutting. When she checked the price tag and discovered she could afford it she promptly bought it, confident that Bill would be thrilled with it.

Her packages were light and she was enjoying herself, so she continued down the street, window-shopping and looking for someplace to get a bite to eat. A little sandwich shop sold mostly takeout, but had a few stools lined up underneath a shelf in the front window. She bought a turkey rollup and perched there, contentedly munching her sandwich and watching people walk by. All sorts of people: an old lady with a small fur ball of a dog, a distinguished man in a beautifully tailored business suit, college kids in scruffy clothes with backpacks, and young mothers pushing strollers. She saw more people in the fifteen minutes it took her to eat her sandwich than she saw in a week in Tinker's Cove.

After eating she didn't have much energy, so she decided to go back to the Common, where she could find a bench in a sunny spot and rest a bit, maybe even read a newspaper. When she reached the Common she discovered that a lot of people had the same idea. There were plenty of benches, however, and she soon found a seat.

Unfolding her *Globe,* she ignored the front page and went to the Metro section, looking for news about the murder. The story was small and below the fold, but the headline immediately caught her eye: *Publisher's Death Ruled Poison.*

According to Brad McAbee, whose byline was on the story, the medical examiner had found that cyanide, not asthma, caused Luther Read's death.

Lucy was stunned. Yet she realized she shouldn't really be so shocked. McAbee had cautioned everyone at the workshop to wait for the medical examiner's report. He must have known then that the report would contain some surprises.

So much for her handkerchief theory, thought Lucy. No wonder Sullivan had given her the brush-off. He was probably still laughing. She read on, wondering what this new development meant for Junior. Would the police continue to charge him with the murder?

Indeed they would, said the district attorney. *We remain confident that all charges against Luther Read, Junior, will stand,* he said. *Read had ready access to cyanide, which is used in photographic processes.*

And so did a lot of other people, thought Lucy. Cyanide

was a dark-room staple, easily available to anyone who worked at a newspaper. She remembered how relieved Ted had been when he got rid of the tiny dark room at the *Pennysaver*. It had been expensive and there had been a lot of red tape, but it had been worth it in the end. "Now I don't have to worry about those damned chemicals," he'd said.

In fact, as she recalled, he'd had to get a special permit from the state and town health departments just to dispose of the chemicals. He'd also had to use a special waste-handling company that specialized in hazardous materials.

Lucy suspected that Ted was the exception, taking the time and trouble to get rid of the dark room properly. Most publishers probably didn't bother, even after switching to digital cameras that produced images on the computer. They just shut the door on the no-longer-needed facilities and forgot about them, leaving the cyanide and other chemicals in place. Why go looking for trouble? they'd reason. Let the EPA and OSHA and the health department in the place and you never knew what they'd find. Talk about opening a can of worms.

Lucy wasn't sure who she imagined was speaking these words. Perhaps Harold Read? Or maybe Sam Syrjala? Neither one would welcome any sort of outside intervention in their business; they would resent workplace rules and regulations as imposing on their personal freedom.

And if the police were still considering Junior their prime suspect, she didn't see why Harold and Syrjala couldn't remain hers. Especially, she realized, with a sensation like a brick dropping through her interior, since Syrjala carried a bottle in his briefcase. Had it really been bourbon? She should have sniffed it when she had the chance. Cyanide, as she knew from her habit of reading mysteries, smelled like bitter almonds.

Suddenly energized, Lucy decided to head back to the hotel to track down Ted. She wanted to know what he made of this new development.

She gathered up her packages and began walking briskly along the pathway. A bit too briskly, perhaps, because she forgot to take the turn that would lead her to the corner of Tremont and Boylston. Instead she once again found herself at the crosswalk leading to the Public Garden.

Quite a crowd of people had gathered, waiting for the long light to change. Lucy didn't like to be crowded and she felt uneasy, especially since traffic was whizzing by so closely. A single misstep or a stumble could have terrible consequences, since there was no way the driver could stop in time. She hoped parents were holding tight to their children, and took a step backward herself. She had the oddest feeling, as if someone were watching her.

Trying not to be too obvious, she bent down as if to adjust her shoe and took a quick look over her shoulder. She almost jumped out of her skin when she spotted Sam Syrjala.

The light finally changed and she walked across, reminding herself to be calm. She was imagining things. Why would Sam follow her? How could he possibly know she suspected him?

Because, she told herself, he knew she'd won a prize for investigative reporting. Because he knew she lived in Tinker's Cove, where Luther's death and Junior's arrest would be big news. Because he was guilty and he wanted to protect himself from a snooping reporter.

There was a way to figure out if she was being followed, she reasoned. She could vary her pace or step off the beaten path and observe what he did. Emboldened, she marched toward the bridge, then took an abrupt left, pausing at a trash barrel and making a show of emptying her pockets. Syrjala, she saw, had also stopped, ostensibly to read the label on a very large tree. It was taking him a very long time to read two words, even if they were in Latin.

Moving quite slowly she strolled along the path that ran along the bank of the pond. It wasn't crowded, but there were plenty of people around. They were taking their time, not using the Public Garden as a shortcut but lingering to enjoy its beauty. The path eventually brought her around to the gate, and she knew she had to come up with a plan to get rid of him. She was safe enough in the park, but she didn't want him following her down the long, empty blocks and alleys around the hotel. She stood on the curb, waiting once again for a break in traffic, and spotted her solution: the Four Seasons Hotel. She'd duck into the hotel and wait him out in the lobby. If he followed her inside, she would complain to the doorman. If he loitered outside, waiting for her to emerge, the doorman would certainly send him on his way.

The stream of cars finally dwindled, and she dashed across the street with a handful of pedestrians and ducked under the hotel's porte cochere. The doorman greeted her with a smile and she sashayed inside. Surely nothing terrible could happen here, she thought, taking in the luxurious furnishings, the bowl of Granny Smith apples, and the vases of fresh flowers.

The lobby was much smaller than the Park Plaza's, it could almost be taken for someone's large living room. Someone with exquisite taste, she decided, perching on a sofa and angling herself so she could see out the window. Sure enough, moments later she saw Syrjala walk by, scowling.

As soon as he passed she felt a huge sense of relief and let out a big sigh. He'd really spooked her, she realized as the tension left her body.

"Can I get you something?" It was one of the bellmen, bending over her with a look of concern.

"No, thank you," she said. "I'm just catching my breath."

"Very well," he said. "Take as long as you need."

"I'm feeling better already," said Lucy, getting to her feet. "Thank you."

Back on the street, Lucy saw no sign of Syrjala. She started back to her hotel, passing the windows of the restaurant at the Four Seasons. Several tables were set in the window, she noticed, offering passersby a glimpse of the leisured, privileged world inside. What would it be like, wondered Lucy, to be one of the well-dressed people sitting at a window table, sipping tea and nibbling on lobster salad, unconcerned about paying the check?

Not quite as carefree as she imagined, she discovered, judging from the couple in the second window. They certainly weren't enjoying themselves; they were having a hell of an argument. It was so obvious, even through the glass, that people on the sidewalk were pausing to watch the little drama.

"It's better than TV," said one woman.

Lucy nodded in agreement and continued on her way, looking back one last time. Her jaw dropped when she recognized the couple: it was Inez and Harold Read. She stopped in her tracks, gaping at them, only to catch Harold's eye. Embarrassed at her rudeness she hurried on, but his expression stayed with her. If looks could kill, she'd be a dead woman.

Chapter Seventeen

Gasping for breath, Lucy collapsed onto the nearest sofa when she reached the safety of the Park Plaza lobby. She'd been so unnerved by Harold's stare that she had practically run all the way back to her hotel. She was sprawled there with shopping bags strewn all around when Ted saw her.

"You know," he said slowly, "I never actually saw someone shop until she dropped."

Lucy wasn't sure if she was in trouble or not. She knew Ted expected her to take the conference seriously, but he was smiling. Sort of.

"This isn't quite what it looks like," she said.

"Let me guess," he said, moving a shopping bag aside and sitting beside her. "This was research for a feature story?"

"I was shopping. I admit it," said Lucy, feeling rather warm. "But only after I went to the 'Editors' Roundtable.' It was a dud. So I did the only sensible thing I could think of—I sought shop therapy."

"Well, I guess it's all right then." He paused. "Did you see the morning papers?"

"You mean about the cyanide?"

"Yeah. You know, I really can't see Junior doing something like that. When they thought it was the asthma, I could almost buy into it. The argument, a momentary flare of anger, some confusion about inhalers . . ." He shrugged. "Maybe if you stretched it you'd have a case for voluntary manslaughter. But not cyanide. Whoever did this planned ahead; it was calculated, cold-blooded murder." He shook his head. "They've got the wrong guy."

"Sam Syrjala keeps a bottle in his briefcase."

"How do you know that?"

"I saw it."

"It's probably booze."

"Or he's not quite the drunk everybody thinks he is."

Ted looked at her. "You think he's faking."

"I don't know." Lucy remembered the way Harold had looked at her through the window and shivered. "I do think Harold's got a guilty conscience about something, and I think Sam knows what it is. Some kind of corporate fraud. Just look at his lifestyle—designer clothes for Inez, a chauffeur—at the same time Pioneer Press is losing money. And they are losing money, even if they don't admit it. There have been layoffs the past few years. Cutbacks in employee benefits."

"How do you know all this stuff?" demanded Ted. "You're supposed to be attending workshops, not conducting your own investigation."

"I got most of it at workshops, talking to people," said Lucy. "But if there were some sort of financial skulduggery going on . . ."

"And Luther discovered it," speculated Ted.

"Well, it would be an awfully strong motive. . . ."

"And it would explain why he backed out of the National Media sale," said Ted.

"But how can we find out for sure?" asked Lucy. "Pioneer is a privately owned company. They don't even have to make their annual report public."

"Didn't you say Luther played tennis with the bank president?"

"Yeah. In fact, I wouldn't be surprised if the Tinker's Cove Five Cents Savings Bank has invested in Pioneer Press."

"Neither would I." Ted scratched his chin. "I think I'll give Fred Ames a call. He's probably got those annual reports neatly filed away."

"Meanwhile, kemosabe, what's happening with Junior?"

"Nothing. There's a bail hearing this afternoon, so I guess he'll be getting out of jail soon, but the DA is convinced he's got the right man and wants to take it to trial. He's making lots of noise about no plea bargains."

"Junior wouldn't cop a plea."

"You seem awfully sure," said Ted.

"Aren't you?"

"I'm keeping an open mind. And an open line with his wife. I want to get an interview for Thursday's paper."

"His lawyer probably won't let him talk."

"We'll see," said Ted, getting to his feet. "Listen, a bunch of us are going out to eat tonight at Durgin Park. Want to come?"

Durgin Park, Lucy discovered, was a venerable institution where the patrons did not get their own tables, but sat instead at long communal tables covered with snowy white cloths. The group from the convention was so large, however, that it didn't matter, because they took up an entire table anyway. They were also noisy enough for the whole restaurant.

"So where're you merrymakers from?" asked the waitress, pulling her pencil from her unnaturally red hair. Like all the waitresses, she was a heavyset woman who was getting on in years. She dropped her Rs, speaking with a broad Boston accent.

"New Hampshire!" proclaimed Fred Easton, Ted's longtime friend, who published the Franconia *Mountain News,* a weekly much like the *Pennysaver.*

"Live free or die!" exclaimed Bob Hunsaker, who also published a weekly. His proclamation of the state motto was greeted with rousing cheers by the rest of the group, except for Ted.

"Remember Maine!" he yelled, inspiring a chorus of boos.

"Sam Adams all 'round?" It wasn't so much a question as a statement of fact.

"Sure," agreed Fred.

"Have you got any light beer?" asked Lucy.

"Not for you, honey. You're too skinny as is."

"Well, I never," began Lucy, staring at the waitress's back as she crossed the room.

"The waitresses here are known for their rudeness," said Bob. "It's one of the things that makes the place so popular."

It didn't make much sense to Lucy, but she figured she was just going along for the ride. She opened her menu.

The waitress returned, easily carrying an overloaded tray filled with beers for the entire group. As soon as she'd finished distributing them she opened her pad, licked her pencil, and asked, "What'll you have? We'll start with the lady."

"I'll begin with salad."

"Don't recommend it."

Lucy figured arguing wouldn't do any good. "Okay. How about chowder?"

"Good."

Lucy felt as if she'd answered the question correctly. Buoyed with confidence, she ventured to choose an entrée. "Broiled scrod."

Wrong. No buzzers went off; no red lights flashed.

The waitress simply overrode her choice. "Most people have the prime rib. Do you want beans?"

"Green?"

"Baked."

"I'll pass."

"You've gotta try the beans," said Bob, assisted by a chorus of encouragement from the others.

"This is Boston, the land of the bean and the cod," said Fred, and everybody cheered.

"What'll you tell the kids when they ask if you had Boston baked beans?" asked Ted.

Such an eventuality seemed extremely remote to Lucy, but she didn't want to be a party pooper. "Okay," she said.

"And for dessert?"

"Just coffee."

"No way!" exclaimed Fred. "She's got to try the Indian pudding."

"Can't miss the Indian pudding," agreed Bob. "It's the house specialty. Baked all day in a brick oven."

"You'll want that à la mode, right?"

Lucy sighed. "Sure."

The waitress moved on to Ted and Lucy took a sip of her beer. It was delicious, but filling. She vowed she'd sip slowly and make it last.

"Another round?"

The group cheered noisily.

It wasn't until the group was well into their second round of drinks that their high spirits began to subside and the conversation grew more serious.

"Who ever thought Luther Read would end up like this?" mused Fred. "Him, of all people. The man who had everything. I figured he'd grab the cash and live to a ripe old age, mummifying himself on some Arizona golf course."

"I guess Junior had different plans for him," said Bob.

"I don't buy it," said a man with a crew cut whose name Lucy hadn't been able to catch. "He's too smart. He'd know he'd never get away with it. I think he was framed."

Lucy nodded in agreement.

"If he did it, he must've known he was taking an awful risk," said Fred.

"A stupid risk," said Bob. "If he'd just let nature take its course he would have inherited his father's shares. Now it'll probably all go to Harold."

"What do you mean?" asked Lucy. "I thought he left everything to Junior."

"He can't benefit from a crime," said Fred. "The chain will go to Harold, unless by some miracle Junior manages to get off."

"Harold doesn't seem very happy about it," said Lucy, wondering if his grim demeanor was an act.

"He lost his brother. . . ."

"It's a big responsibility. Plus, the chain's not in good shape."

"What would you do if you were in his shoes?"

"Me?" The guy with the crew cut scratched his head. "For starters, I'd sell off the losers and keep the money-makers, try to grow them."

"I heard he's considering launching a chain of weeklies. . . ."

"That'd be a smart move," said Fred. "All it would cost him is the paper and ink, since he's already got the writers and editors, and he'd pick up plenty of advertisers who can't afford the dailies."

"It'd be the end of independent weeklies in New Hampshire," said Bob.

The group fell silent, considering his grim prediction.

"Why so glum?" asked the waitress, arriving with the chowder. "Another round?"

"Another round!" said Fred.

Everybody cheered.

Lucy was glassy-eyed when she finally got back to her room, where she immediately unbuckled her belt and unbuttoned her slacks. She had never in her life eaten— or drunk—so much. The chowder and beer had pretty much filled her up, and she hadn't been prepared for Durgin Park's prime rib, which was two inches thick and so large that it hung over the sides of the plate. She'd left most of it, much to the derision of the waitress, but she still felt as if she might explode at any moment.

She really didn't know why she'd eaten the Indian pudding. She'd intended to have a taste, just a bite, but when she tasted the heady mix of corn meal and spices, a perfect foil for the cool, creamy vanilla ice cream, she'd been unable to resist eating the whole thing. Not that the waitress had been impressed. "Seconds, honey?" she'd asked.

Slowly, Lucy eased herself onto the bed and slipped off her shoes. Then she snaked her hand up her back and unhooked her bra. That felt better. She rubbed her taut tummy. She hated to admit it, but she felt great. Like a lioness who'd just finished off a tasty gazelle snack. All she wanted to do now was sleep. But first she had to call home. Sighing, she reached for the phone.

Bill answered.

"Hi."

"Long time, no hear. How's the convention?"

Lucy didn't like his tone of voice. It was casual. Too casual, considering everything that had been going on.

"The convention's fine and I'm fine," she snapped, "which is more than you can say."

"What do you mean?"

"Oh, come on. You fired Toby, the dog ran away, the girls are at each other's throats and Elizabeth's running around town practically naked with some guy with a tattoo. . . ."

"I don't know who you've been talking to, but it's not as bad as it sounds."

Lucy didn't want excuses.

"You've been lying to me! Why do you keep pretending everything's okay when it's not?"

"I didn't want you to worry."

"Don't you see? I worry more because I don't know what's really going on. Now, what are you going to do about Toby? You're not really going to kick him out of the house, are you?"

There was a long silence. When Bill spoke, his voice was dead serious.

"Listen, Lucy, you're not here and I am. I have to handle this my own way."

"Oh, Bill," she began, protesting, but Bill wasn't listening. He'd hung up.

Chapter Eighteen

Despite her tiredness, it took Lucy a long time to fall asleep. She stretched out between the clean sheets, alone in the dark room, and closed her eyes, but her usual defense system failed her. Instead of filtering out the sounds of people coming and going in the hallway, the thunk of the elevator and the sirens in the streets outside, she found herself straining to hear what was going on. What were the people outside her door talking about? Who was in the elevator? Were they ambulance or police sirens? Had she fastened the safety chain on her door?

Her mind wouldn't rest but went around and around, chasing scraps of thought, tattered sentences and fleeting expressions. Harold's stare: had it really been directed at her or had he turned away in anger from Inez? She had only a kaleidoscope of impressions about Inez: hair like straw, a Barbie-doll face, pretty but was anybody home? Pointy bloodred nails, sharp little teeth, spike heels.

Then there was Harold's cat. A fluffy white Persian, claws well hidden. It had a woman's face. Inez's face.

Suddenly the cat pounced on something, neatly pinning it with a single talon. The thing squirmed. It was Sam Syrjala, more concerned with recovering the bottle that was rolling away from him than with his own danger. The bottle spun around, and when it stopped it was pointing at Junior.

Who, me? mouthed Junior; then he smiled, revealing a shark's mouth full of triangular teeth. Luther and Junior were in the elevator, which had become a glass-sided aquarium. They were swimming back and forth, endlessly chasing each other like the sharks in the giant tank at the New England Aquarium. A diver was bringing them food, big slabs of raw fish in a net bag. The bag was empty but the sharks were still hungry, circling the diver. She tried to swim away, but she couldn't. The sharks were now Bill and Toby. They kept nudging the diver with their snouts, forcing her down. She was on the bottom of the tank, on her back, face upward with hair swirling loosely around her mask. The face in the mask was her own.

Then she was awake, caught in a tangle of sheets, breathing heavily and damp with perspiration. It took her a moment to remember that she wasn't home; she was in the Park Plaza hotel because she was attending the Northeast Newspaper Association conference. What time was it anyway? She looked at the clock. Only four. She could go back to sleep. Maybe.

Lucy was sitting in the coffee shop, mulling over her dream and wondering if it had any significance apart from indicating her own tangled emotions, when Morgan Dodd plunked herself down in the seat on the opposite side of the table.

"Big news," said Morgan.

Lucy doubted it, but she was willing to play along. "What?"

"Junior's out on bail."

"That's good."

Morgan narrowed her eyes. "I want to interview him."

"You and everybody else," said Lucy. "But his lawyer will never allow it. The most you can hope for is a carefully worded, prepared statement. He's probably 'eager to prove his innocence at the trial,' or maybe even 'willing to do everything he can to catch the real murderer, who is still at large.' They might even offer a reward, but maybe not, since PPG isn't doing all that well."

"Whoa, Sally. Maybe, just maybe, he'd appreciate an opportunity to talk to a sympathetic local reporter who'll give him a chance to tell his side of the story."

"What's that got to do with you?" asked Lucy.

"I was thinking I could go along with you, to set up the tape recorder or take a picture. Kind of be your assistant."

"I don't think so," said Lucy, amused. "Besides, why should I share my story with you? What's in it for me?"

Morgan smiled slyly. "I might be willing to share some information. I've been investigating on my own, you know, and I've uncovered some interesting facts."

Did she really have something, or was she bluffing? Lucy was trying to decide when Junior suddenly appeared beside her, in the flesh. He wasn't the hale and hearty fellow she remembered, but seemed diminished in size somehow. Almost fragile.

"Hi, stranger," she said softly. "How are you doing?"

"I'm Morgan Dodd." Morgan stood up and grabbed his hand, pumping it energetically. "With the Framingham *Trib.*"

"Nice to meet you."

"It must feel pretty good getting out of jail," continued Morgan.

"You bet." He grinned at Lucy. "I can't wait to get back to Tinker's Cove."

"Have you and your lawyer decided on a defense strategy?" Morgan asked.

Junior's eyes met Lucy's; then he turned to Morgan. "I can't comment on the case, except to say that I welcome the opportunity to prove my innocence, and I have complete faith in the American system of justice."

Lucy mouthed the words *I told you so* to Morgan.

"I'm awfully sorry about your father," said Lucy. "He's really going to be missed in Tinker's Cove. I often used to see him around town. He had a smile for everyone."

Lucy could see Morgan rolling her eyes behind Junior's back but ignored her, allowing Junior to clasp her hand.

"That means a lot to me, Lucy," said Junior, his voice thick with emotion.

"Will the funeral be in Tinker's Cove?"

"I don't know what's been decided." He shrugged. "I've been out of the loop. I just want to go home and take some time to absorb what's happened."

"That's understandable. I hope things work out for you." The enormity of his situation loomed ominously between them. "I really do," she added.

"Maybe you should consider granting some interviews to sympathetic reporters," said Morgan in a helpful tone of voice, as if the idea had just occurred to her. "Like Lucy. Or me."

"Thanks for the advice. Actually, I'm meeting with Ted tomorrow." Someone outside caught his eye. Lucy followed his glance and recognized his lawyer from his picture in the *Globe,* standing in the doorway with Catherine. "Well, I've got to go. I just wanted to say hi. See you around, Lucy."

As soon as he was out the door, Morgan grabbed Lucy's arm. "Who's this Ted?"

"My boss."

Morgan wasn't one to miss an opportunity. "Is he here at the convention? Can you point him out to me?"

"I think he's gone. He was leaving first thing today."

"Damn."

"Are you going to the workshop this morning?" asked Lucy, checking her watch.

"Are you kidding? This is the story of a lifetime and I intend to get it." She shook her head. "I mean, what's the point of all these workshops if you don't have anything to write about? The story's the important thing."

She had a point, Lucy supposed, but did she know what a dangerous game she was playing?

"You know," said Lucy slowly, recalling the frightening, toothy images of her dream, "if Junior isn't the murderer, that means there's somebody out there who doesn't want to be discovered. Somebody who's already killed once."

"Are you telling me to be careful?" Morgan was defiant. "Because if you are, I already have a mother, thank you very much."

Good point, thought Lucy. "Does your mother know what you're doing?"

Morgan didn't answer, but whirled around and strode out of the coffee shop. Lucy sighed and picked up her bag. She had a workshop to attend.

The creative writing workshop was better than she expected, and Lucy was both elated and depleted when it was over. She was too keyed up to consider returning to the confining meeting room for the afternoon session. Ted was gone; there was no one to chide her if she took some time for herself. She had always wanted to visit the famous Isabella Stewart Gardner Museum, and this was her chance.

The doorman advised taking the Green Line, and Lucy followed his directions, soon finding herself gazing at the museum's glass-enclosed courtyard, where live green plants and flowering orchids mingled with fragments of ancient Roman sculpture and mosaics.

The air was moist and heavy with the scent of earth and flowers.

A sign pointed the way to the café, and Lucy realized she was hungry. The tiny restaurant was crowded, so she followed the example of some others and purchased a bottled drink and a sandwich to eat outside in the sculpture garden. As she sat in the peaceful garden, she resolutely emptied her mind and concentrated on enjoying the moment. She studied the beads of moisture condensing on her bottle of iced tea, and concentrated on the chewy texture of the bread in her sandwich.

Refreshed by her little Zen exercise, she returned to the museum through the Chinese Gallery, pausing at John Singer Sargent's masterpiece *El Jaleo.* The subject was a flamenco dancer, famous in her day, and Sargent caught her in the midst of her dance with one arm cocked awkwardly and her head thrown back. It was full of life and light, and Lucy was saddened to think that Sargent would never lift another brush, the dancer would never again twitch her skirt, and the musicians and singers pictured in the background would be forever silent.

It was in this somber mood that she ascended the dark and dusty stairs to the second floor, where treasures collected by Mrs. Gardner were displayed in the rooms where she had once entertained the great and famous.

To Lucy's mind there was something quaint and old-fashioned about the museum. Mrs. Gardner had stipulated in her will that nothing could be changed after her death, so everything remained as it had been during her lifetime. No new acquisitions could be added, and signs marked the empty places where the paintings once hung that were stolen in an unsolved theft. Especially fragile works, like drawings and lace, were contained in wood-and-glass cases with removable velvet covers that kept out the light. *Lift to View Contents* was printed on labels sewn onto some of the covers.

It was hard to take it all in. The collection was so diverse, containing everything from Han Dynasty Chinese bears to gilded eighteenth-century sedan chairs to masterpieces by Rubens and Raphael. Sometimes Lucy could hardly make out a painting at all, due to the light pouring in from the courtyard; other times she would puzzle over a beautiful painting that caught her eye, looking in vain for a sign identifying the artist.

One painting in particular caught her eye. It featured a classically columned courtyard filled with a crowd of people gathered in great excitement around the body of a beautiful young woman. Lucy had no clue as to who the unfortunate beauty was, but she could clearly identify the raw emotions displayed by the mourners: shock, denial, pain, grief, and rage. In fact, she thought, the scene was eerily similar to the one she'd witnessed Monday night at the banquet, when Luther's death was announced. She wanted to know more about the painting, but there was no little plaque identifying it or the artist who created it.

Discouraged, Lucy wandered around the room, gazing at the other paintings but inevitably drawn to the windows overlooking the courtyard. She stood there for quite a while, simply enjoying the ordered beauty of the lush interior garden. When she finally turned to go, she was surprised to see Carole Rose standing in front of the painting that had so fascinated Lucy. Carole was absorbed in a guidebook, busily shifting her gaze from painting to book and back again.

"Hi," said Lucy. "Are you playing hooky too?"

Carole laughed. "You could say that."

"Isn't this a wonderful museum? But frustrating. A lot of the paintings aren't labeled, like this one. Would you mind telling me what it is?"

"It's a real eye-catcher, isn't it?" said Carole. "It's by Botticelli, *The Tragedy of Lucretia.*"

"Oh." Lucy studied the painting. "How did Lucretia come to die? Was she a martyred saint or something?"

"Sort of," said Carole, consulting the book. "Apparently she had a great reputation for virtue but was seduced by a villain who threatened to kill her if she didn't yield to him. The next day she confessed all to her husband and father and killed herself to save her reputation."

Lucy was stunned. "My word. No wonder everyone's so upset."

"Isn't that always the way? The stupid woman kills herself instead of going after the guy who seduced her. If you ask me, she should have stabbed him."

"If she had, they probably would have caught her and executed her anyway," said Lucy philosophically. "Women didn't have a lot of options in those days."

"Probably," agreed Carole. "But at least she would have had the satisfaction of getting revenge on the man who ruined her reputation."

"I guess she figured she could leave that part to her father and husband. By killing herself she pretty much guaranteed they'd go after him."

"This is exactly the kind of thinking that holds women back, even today," said Carole. "Women are still turning their anger on themselves instead of at the guy who done them wrong. She should've killed him." She paused. "How can she be sure her father and husband won't decide the guy's not so bad, and they all go out to the Coliseum together to watch the games and have a few flagons of mead?"

Lucy found herself laughing and enjoying herself as she and Carole worked their way through the rest of the museum. Carole kept up a lively commentary, spicing up the information from the guidebook with her own pithy observations. Lucy was sorry when they ran out of rooms to explore, and suggested they prolong the afternoon by having a cup of tea in the café.

"Sorry," said Carole. "I've got to get back. I've got a meeting in half an hour. Do you want to share a cab?"

"No, thanks," said Lucy. "I'm going to check out the gift shop." She paused. "If I don't see you again, thanks for a lovely afternoon."

"See you next year, right?"

Lucy was flipping through the postcards in the shop, looking for one of *The Tragedy of Lucretia.* What a story, she thought when she found it. Lucretia killed herself to save her reputation. Luther, too, had zealously protected his reputation when he was alive, but it would unravel fast now that he was dead. The Pioneer Press Group and the people connected with it would not come out of the trial unscathed; no one ever did. By the time the defense and prosecution attorneys had finished with them, reputations would be tarnished and family secrets would be laid bare.

Pioneer's reputation—and Luther's too—had acted as a shield, protecting everyone connected with the company from inspection and criticism. They were literally above reproach. Beneath that facade, however, there lurked a tangle of motives and emotions: greed, jealousy, ambition, resentment. And somewhere in that tangle lay the truth, the identity of Luther's killer.

It was time, Lucy decided, to do some more research. But this time she wasn't going to the library; she had another destination in mind. When she was finished, she intended to know more about them than they knew about themselves.

Chapter Nineteen

Lucy hailed a cab outside the museum and directed the driver to take her to the offices of the Boston *Herald*. She had absolutely no idea where the newspaper's headquarters were located, but the driver apparently did, because he merely nodded and pulled smoothly into traffic.

For a brief moment Lucy savored the picture of herself as a sophisticated city dweller, a woman with an important job who routinely hailed taxis to take her to gleaming office towers housing the movers and shakers who made things happen. Then reality set in and she wondered exactly what she thought she was doing. Before she could change her mind and order the driver to take her directly to the comfort of the Park Plaza Hotel, however, he was pulling up in front of a grimy office building that had clearly seen better days. It was definitely the *Herald*, according to the sign and the adjacent parking lot full of delivery trucks. She paid the fare and clambered out, shaking off a piece of blowing paper that had wrapped itself around her ankle.

Inside, Lucy stood at the reception counter and announced her intention to see Fran Rappaport, the gossip columnist responsible for the "Rap Sheet." A uniformed guard stood by the elevators, keeping an eye on her. The idea of a newspaper needing security was a novelty to Lucy; at home, the *Pennysaver* office was open to all and sundry.

"Do you have an appointment?" inquired the receptionist, a pleasantly plump woman with tightly coifed gray hair and a sprinkling of freckles on her nose.

"No, I'm afraid I don't." She leaned closer to the greasy sheet of Plexiglas that separated her from the receptionist. "I'm in town for the newspaper convention and thought I'd just take a chance and drop in on Fran, kind of spur of the moment, if you know what I mean."

Lucy was hoping to give the impression that she was an old friend of the columnist, but the receptionist wasn't impressed.

"Convention?" she asked, raising an eyebrow.

"The Northeast Newspaper Association—surely you've heard of it."

"No, I haven't." She shrugged. "But it doesn't matter. Ms. Rappaport's not in yet; she doesn't usually show up for an hour or two. You're welcome to leave a message."

Lucy blushed. She should have known that people working for a daily paper didn't keep nine-to-five hours. She looked at her watch, wondering if she should wait.

"A couple of hours?"

"I can't really say. It varies, depending on her schedule."

Lucy nodded and decided to try again later. She turned to go, figuring there must be a coffee shop or bar nearby where *Herald* staffers congregated and she could hang out for a while. She was standing on the curb, looking around, when a woman in dyed-blond hair and oversize glasses with black rims approached her.

"Are you looking for the Duck Tour, honey?"

Lucy had seen advertisements for the Duck Tour,

which took riders on a tour of points of interest via city streets and the Charles River in amphibious vehicles, actually refitted World War II landing craft.

"Uh, no," stammered Lucy, displeased that this sophisticated woman immediately took her for an out-of-towner. "I was hoping to talk to someone at the paper."

"Who?"

She gave the woman a second look. "Are you Fran Rappaport?"

"You recognized me!"

It wasn't quite the remarkable coincidence that Fran's delighted tone implied. The hairdo and glasses featured prominently in the little photo that accompanied her column and were as much a trademark as McDonald's golden arches.

"You're actually the person I wanted to talk to," said Lucy.

"Really! And you are?"

"Lucy Stone." When Fran didn't seem impressed, Lucy added, "From Tinker's Cove."

"Ah. Summer home of Junior Read, our slayer du jour."

"That's right," said Lucy. "And that's what I wanted to talk to you about."

"Well, come on up," said Fran, taking her by the elbow. "I love a nice cozy chat about the neighbors, don't you?"

"I'm so glad you dropped by," said Fran, indicating with a wave of her glossy purple-tipped fingers that Lucy should take the spare chair in her glass-walled office. It was one of a handful flanking one wall of the newsroom, which was otherwise filled with cubicles, about a quarter of which were presently occupied. "It's those little homey touches that my readers love. I mean, when Ben Affleck comes home, of course I have to write about how he's doing in rehab and who he's dating and is he still friends with Gwyneth, but what people really want to know"—she paused for emphasis, staring at Lucy through those glasses—"is whether his mom made him peanut butter and jelly for lunch or a BLT!"

"I don't really know what Junior eats for lunch," said Lucy, who was beginning to feel like a fly who'd walked into the spider's parlor.

Somehow she had to turn the tables, she decided, promising herself that no matter what happened she would not let the fact that Elizabeth worked for Junior Read slip out. That would be an unforgivable violation of her personal ethics, not to mention that she'd promised Junior that anything Elizabeth told her about the household would remain strictly off the record. This was strictly private information, and she would have to guard it like a state secret.

"Of course you don't know what he has for lunch," said Fran, chuckling. "That was just an example. But I suppose you know what his house is like, don't you?"

"Sure," agreed Lucy, enormously relieved. The Reads' house could be viewed by anyone, as it stood alone on a rock promontory high above the harbor on Smith Heights Road. "It's one of those old-fashioned seaside cottages. You know, big, shingled, with a porch, of course."

"And his family will be awaiting his return, now that he's out on bail?"

Danger! Danger! screamed a voice in Lucy's head. *Don't go there!*

"I assume so," she said, with a little shrug.

"The folks in town will be greeting him with open arms?"

Lucy chuckled. "Well, I don't think there'll be a parade or anything."

"He's not too popular in Tinker's Cove?"

"Oh, I didn't mean that," said Lucy, eager to clear up any misunderstanding. "He's well liked. It's just that . . ."

"Yes?"

"He has been charged with murdering his father, after all. People are going to reserve judgment, but there's always the possibility that he is guilty. You know?"

Fran nodded, tapping a pearly white tooth with a perfectly polished fingernail. Lucy noticed that her nail polish matched her lipstick. She was suddenly glad she was wearing her new shoes, and glanced at them.

"Cute shoes," gushed Fran. "I wish I could wear flats."

She was wearing a pair of stiletto heels with very pointed toes. Lucy couldn't imagine how she could even walk in them, much less chase after stories.

"I love your column," said Lucy. "That photo of Catherine Read caught my eye. . . ."

"Great photo, wasn't it?" exclaimed Fran. "Lesbian lovers! My readers eat that stuff up. They love to be outraged. The letters have absolutely been pouring in."

"I'll bet," said Lucy. She knew that newspapers loved to generate controversy and counted success by the number of readers who responded to a story. "I'm surprised you haven't written about Inez—she's pretty outrageous."

"Oh, I have, honey. She was the other woman, you know, in a very messy divorce."

"I didn't know," said Lucy.

"Oh, yes. But that's all ancient history. You can read all about it in the morgue. I'll take you down, but first . . . well, what do you think Junior will do when he gets home? The very first thing? Will he go for a sail in his boat? Watch the sunset from his porch? Gaze at a favorite painting?"

"I don't know," admitted Lucy, laughing. "I suppose he'll give his son a big hug. My daughter says Trevor really misses his dad."

"Mmm, interesting," cooed Fran, tapping away on her keyboard.

Lucy wished she could bite her tongue right off.

* * *

Later, as she sat in front of a computer terminal in the paper's morgue searching the archived files, Lucy decided she hadn't done too badly. She'd made it very clear to Fran that even though her daughter did work in the Read household, she could hardly be considered a reliable source of information. Furthermore, the only knowledge Lucy had of the family was hearsay, like the business about not paying their bills. She didn't really know if that was true or not. She personally had only the highest regard for Junior and absolutely believed he was innocent.

Besides, even if she had been a tad indiscreet, it was a small price to pay for access to the *Herald*'s archives. They were a gold mine of information, all carefully cataloged and indexed and accessible with a click of the mouse, unlike the morgue at the *Pennysaver*, which was little more than a cramped closet full of bound editions dating back to the mid nineteenth century and stacks of recent issues, generally muddled and out of sequence. The *Herald* also employed an obliging librarian, who helped Lucy find the information she wanted.

And the more information she found, the more convinced she became that Harold Read was behind Luther's murder. Most telling were the accounts of his divorce five years earlier from the first Mrs. Read.

Inez's predecessor, Louise, had stated under oath that Harold had been unfaithful and had both verbally and physically abused her. She even claimed that he had tried to poison her to save himself the expense of a divorce. This had happened, she claimed, when the couple was estranged but had both attended their eldest son's college graduation. Following a celebratory dinner, Harold had invited her to his hotel room to discuss some family matters and had mixed a drink for her, even though she had declined the offer. She was suspicious, she explained, "because he had never made a drink for me before in twenty years of married life but always yelled at me to make them for him."

Louise's refusal to join in a toast to their son had so infuriated Harold, she told the court, that he threw the drink across the room, breaking the glass. She had been unable to save any of the liquid for testing, but had managed to slip a shard of glass into her purse when he wasn't looking.

Laboratory analysis had been inconclusive, because the tiny amount of residue had not been adequate for testing.

"That doesn't prove a thing," she'd claimed, sniffling into a handkerchief. "I know what he was up to and I'm convinced I was lucky to escape with my life."

Lucy was somewhat skeptical of the story, because she knew parties in a divorce often tended to exaggerate their grievances; nevertheless it was interesting in light of Luther's death by poisoning.

The judge in the case hadn't been impressed and had acted in Harold's favor, reducing the size of the requested settlement. Lucy wasn't convinced the judge had been absolutely impartial, however, since Harold had noisily supported his nomination for the judgeship with several laudatory editorials, a tidbit she picked up from Fran's "Rap Sheet" column.

Inez's high-flying lifestyle hadn't gone unnoticed by Fran, either. Through the years there had been frequent mention of arrivals and departures on vacations to Europe and the Caribbean, galas and expensive parties hosted by Harold and Inez at their Château Marmite, which was reportedly a replica of a French palace built in the New Hampshire mountains, and stays in top Boston hotels to visit her favorite hairdresser, masseuse, aesthetician, and plastic surgeon.

Lucy jotted it all down in her notebook, but she was only too aware that it was probably a wasted effort. She had enough information for a story, but the chances that Ted would run it were slim indeed, and she didn't blame him. Harold Read would certainly slap the *Pennysaver* with a libel suit, and he had enough powerful friends that he had a good chance of winning. If justice prevailed and he lost, Ted would still have the expense of a trial that he could ill afford.

If she were home, thought Lucy, she might have been able to convince the police to look into her theory, but that was a very big *might*. Here in Boston, as she knew only too well, she'd be dismissed as a crackpot. If only there was some way to precipitate matters. She couldn't bring all the suspects together for a confrontational meeting like Hercule Poirot; she hadn't deduced a logical proof like Sherlock Holmes. All that she had was an unshakable belief in Junior's innocence and a serious suspicion about his uncle Harold.

"I don't know if you're interested in this," said the librarian, peering at a dense block of print on her computer screen. "It's a Read wedding announcement. The date is September twelfth."

"Thank you," said Lucy. "I really appreciate your help. And Fran's. Giving me access to the archives like this is fantastic."

The librarian shot her an odd look. "The archives are accessible to anyone with a computer," she said. "They're on the Internet."

"Really?" Lucy suddenly felt very stupid.

The librarian nodded. "BostonHerald-dot-com."

"But when I did research at the public library none of this stuff came up," said Lucy. "How come?"

"What you get depends on your search engine and what you ask it to search for," said the librarian. "Sometimes it can be pretty frustrating. A period, even, can make a big difference."

There was more to this information revolution than she'd realized, decided Lucy, pulling up the file. But when she scanned the names in bold black print she didn't

see any Reads. Discouraged, she started to scroll through
the text with tired eyes. There was something to be said
for the old microfiche system, she decided. At least it
had pictures. She was about to give up when the penny
dropped and she realized the identity of the bride,
Louise Randolph.

Louise! Harold's first wife! She quickly zoomed in on
the announcement, learning that the new Mrs. Alan K.
Hutchinson, the former Mrs. Harold Read, would be
living with her husband in Boston after returning from
their honeymoon in Hawaii. Louise had apparently re-
verted to her maiden name, Randolph, when she divorced Harold.

Since the wedding was in September and it was now
June, Lucy thought it safe to assume they had returned
from their honeymoon. She decided to give the former
Mrs. Read a call, on the off chance she'd like nothing
better than an opportunity to speak ill of her former
husband.

Chapter Twenty

Louise Hutchinson didn't take it the least bit amiss that Lucy wanted to question her about her ex-husband.

"You're an investigator, like in a book or something?" she asked, when Lucy explained the purpose of her phone call.

"Not exactly. I work for a newspaper. The Tinker's Cove *Pennysaver*."

"Oh, Tinker's Cove. That was the one good thing about being married to that worm. The summer visits. It was like going back in time. Picking blueberries. Clamming. I loved it."

Lucy was beginning to feel homesick. She could hardly wait until tomorrow, when she would catch the first bus out of Boston. And once she was home she'd straighten things out with Bill, get the kids back on track, and tackle the mountain of laundry that was no doubt waiting for her.

"That's why I need to talk to you tonight," she said. "I'm going back tomorrow."

"No problem," said Louise. "My husband is working tonight—he's a firefighter. I'd love some company."

She gave Lucy the address, which turned out to be a far cry from the living arrangements Lucy had come to expect of the Read family. Louise's home was no château; it wasn't a commodious Queen Anne cottage; it was a classic three-decker in Dorchester containing an apartment on each level. The Hutchinsons lived at the top, and Lucy was puffing a bit from climbing up two flights of stairs when she knocked on the thickly varnished brown door.

"Come on in," said Louise, a round-faced woman in her fifties with very curly hair who was wearing a brightly colored Hawaiian muumuu. A souvenir of her honeymoon, guessed Lucy.

Louise led her into a spacious, airy living room filled with comfortable, well-used furniture. A bay window was filled with a collection of thriving plants, including a few orchids.

"They're my passion, like Nero Wolfe. I'm reading one of his right now," said Louise, indicating a well-worn stack of books on a table next to a slipcovered wing chair. "I love reading mysteries; it's an addiction. Fortunately, I get them cheap at the used-book store." She rolled her eyes. "But what am I doing keeping you standing like this? Let's sit down. Would you like a cup of tea, like Miss Marple?"

"I would," said Lucy, hoping she'd add a plate of cookies. It had been a long time since she'd had anything to eat.

"How about a sandwich? That's what I usually have for supper when Al works nights."

"I'd love one," said Lucy, sinking gratefully onto the couch.

"Egg salad okay?"

The thought made Lucy's mouth water. "Fabulous."

"I'll be just a sec—or if you want, come on in the kitchen."

Lucy rose wearily and followed Louise into the kitchen, where she sat at a red Formica table next to the sparkling window. The windowsill, and the porch beyond, were filled with pots of geraniums and impatiens and other flowering plants; there were even pots of fresh herbs, and Louise snipped some parsley to add to the egg salad. In the distance, Lucy could see sparkling blue water and a steady stream of silvery jets coming and going from Logan International Airport.

When Lucy complimented her on the view, Louise dismissed it. "It's nothing like Tinker's Cove," she said, with a sigh. "The air in Tinker's Cove is something, you know. So fresh. That's what I miss the most, I guess. You know that smell when you dry the sheets and towels outside on a line, in the sunshine? I try here on the porch, but it's not the same. There's always that hint of diesel exhaust."

"So how long were you married to Harold?"

"Close to twenty-five years."

Louise set a plate loaded with a thick sandwich, a generous heap of potato chips, and a half a dill pickle in front of Lucy.

"This is delicious," said Lucy. "Lunch was a long time ago."

"I guess you newspaper people don't take time to eat," said Louise, taking the opposite seat. "The girl who was here earlier must have eaten an entire box of cookies."

Lucy had a feeling she knew who it was. "Someone was here earlier?"

"She was a cute little thing. Said she was from Framingham. Maureen—no, Morgan. That was it. Morgan Dodd."

"I know Morgan," said Lucy, feeling rather put out that Morgan had found Louise first. "What did she want to know?"

"Probably the same as you. She wanted to know about Harold and whether I think he could've killed his brother,

Luther." Louise picked up a chip. "I told her I wouldn't put it past him, not after what he tried to do to me."

"You really believe he tried to poison you?"

Louise's eyes were huge. "There is no doubt in my mind! That drink smelled funny. Bitter. He wanted to get rid of me, you see, and he didn't want to have to spend any money to do it. He needed it all for Inez."

"Tell me," began Lucy, "when you were married to Harold, did you enjoy a lavish lifestyle?"

Louise tipped back her head and roared in laughter. "Lavish! That's a scream, honey. He was the cheapest man I've ever known. I mean, I loved vacations in Tinker's Cove, but it was definitely a low-cost option. Staying with family. Free food, free lodging. Maybe he'd take everybody out for ice cream, something like that. Nobody could make the bull scream better than Harold, that's for sure."

"Was money tight?"

"Don't get me wrong. We did have a very nice house and nice cars and the kids went to private schools. There was money, a lot more than most people have." She glanced around her kitchen. "I know that now." She smiled. "And I know that money doesn't buy you happiness; that's for sure."

"But he wasn't taking you to lunch at the Four Seasons, or encouraging you to shop at Armani?" persisted Lucy.

"Uh, no. A nice outfit from Talbot's for a special occasion was about all I could expect, and it was better if I managed to buy it on sale."

"So what changed? Is the company suddenly making a lot more money?"

"I doubt it, but I don't really know. I'm no businesswoman."

Lucy decided to try a different tack.

"Do you know how he met Inez? Were you in the same social circle?"

"No, Inez would hardly fit in at the Sleepy Hollow

Country Club." She paused, clearing the dirty plates off the table and setting down a freshly baked pound cake. "As I understand it, she was with an accounting firm that was hired to do an audit." She lifted the knife and sliced a piece for Lucy. "I never saw it coming. I thought all he was interested in was her bookkeeping."

Maybe he was, thought Lucy, taking a bite of cake.

"Mmm," she moaned. "This is delicious."

"Sour cream," admitted Louise, with a rueful pat of her tummy. "Thank God for muumuus."

Lucy followed Louise's instructions and took the Red Line back to the hotel from a nearby T station, saving herself a large taxi fare. When the train pulled into Park Street she decided that rather than changing to the Green Line for a single stop she'd walk instead. It would give her a chance to organize her thoughts, which had been in a whirl since her conversation with Louise.

It was beginning to get dark, however, and she was nervous about walking alone through the shadows of Boston Common. She decided to skirt the park by walking along Tremont Street. At the corner of Boylston a brightly lit McDonald's beckoned; the evening had grown chilly and she had a sudden yearning for a cup of hot coffee.

She was sitting at a table, sipping her coffee, when she heard a familiar voice.

"Wow. Imagine meeting you here. Mind if I sit down?"

Surprised, Lucy choked on her coffee. All she could do was nod. Morgan took it for an invitation and sat down. Her tray, Lucy noticed, held a salad and a bottle of water. Clearly the antimuumuu diet.

"This is a hell of a way to spend your last night at the convention," said Morgan. "All alone in a fast-food joint."

"I haven't been here all night," said Lucy. "In fact, I was paying a visit to a very nice lady in Dorchester. I think you know her."

"Great minds think alike," said Morgan, nibbling on a piece of lettuce. "Did you have an interesting conversation?"

"If I did, do you think I'd tell you?"

"You did find something, didn't you?"

Lucy looked at her coffee.

"Aw, c'mon. Tell me. I hate it when people keep secrets."

"Grow up," advised Lucy. "Do your own homework."

"What, they imprint these phrases in your head when you give birth? It, like, comes with the anesthesia or something?" She leveled a long, cool stare at Lucy. "No. I don't think you've got a story or you wouldn't be sitting here overdosing on caffeine; you'd be writing it." She speared a cherry tomato. "We're obviously on the same track here—what do you say we pool our knowledge and see what we've got."

Lucy thought it over. Maybe Morgan had a point. She did have something of a relationship with the Boston cops, even if it wasn't as good as she thought it was. She had names and phone numbers, and maybe she could get somebody in the department to listen to her.

"Okay," said Lucy. "I'll tell you what I've got, and if we get a story out of it, we both get credit. Deal?"

"Deal." Morgan held out her hand and they shook on it. "So what have you got?"

"Harold Read tried to poison his first wife. . . ."

Morgan yawned.

"It's the same modus operandi and, furthermore, he had a whopper of a motive. He and Inez have been cooking the books and using Pioneer Press as their own personal checking account. Luther figured it out, probably when he was negotiating the National Media sale, and that's why Harold killed him."

"The cops have cleared Harold," said Morgan, interrupting her. "They've got a water bottle with Junior's prints."

"A water bottle? That's how the poison was delivered?"

"Pretty cold. Luther's choking and the murderer offers him a drink."

Lucy didn't buy it. There were water bottles all over the convention. It would be easy to switch one for another. "What about other prints?" she asked.

"Oh, it's got plenty of other prints, too, but the cops don't care. They've got Junior's, plus Junior alone with his father and Junior's motive. He wanted the sale to go through so he could start a magazine, and Dad was blocking it."

"So you agree with the police? You think it was Junior?"

"I'm not ready to say."

Lucy was indignant. "I thought we were working on this together!"

Morgan shrugged. "I changed my mind." She got up to go.

"That's not fair," protested Lucy.

"Let's just say I thought you had more than you did. I thought you were going in a different direction. You can't help me and I'm not going to hand my story to you."

"If you're thinking—"

"Sorry." She picked up her unfinished water bottle and slipped it into her purse, leaving her tray on the table. "Like my dad always says, I've got to see a man about a horse." She grinned. "I'm gonna break this story wide open; just see if I don't."

Lucy watched her leave and debated whether she should follow her. A little spark of resentment flared. Well, if she was going to be like that, more power to her. Let her go off alone to meet Deep Throat. Or maybe it was all a bluff and she was heading home to Framingham to do her laundry and touch up her dye job. Lucy crumpled up her napkin and tossed it on a tray, disgusted. A deal was a deal. The least Morgan could have done was run her story by Lucy and give her a chance to shoot a few holes in whatever stupid theory she had. Lucy didn't think for one minute that Morgan was any closer to breaking the story than she was. And at least she, unlike Morgan, knew when she was beat. She didn't have a story yet. All she had were some pretty good hunches. She might as well go back to the hotel and pack.

She picked up Morgan's tray and took it over to the trash bin, then decided to visit the ladies' room. It was there that she ran into Carole.

"What a coincidence," she exclaimed. "You know who else I saw? Morgan Dodd!"

"It's not all that surprising," said Carole, holding her hands under the hot-air blower. "I did a story once on the appeal of fast-food restaurants for women dining alone. Surveys show women feel a lot more comfortable in McDonald's or Burger King than they do in a more upscale place if they're by themselves." She smiled apologetically. "I've been in features too long. So what's our favorite girl reporter up to?"

Lucy was washing her hands. "She says she's solved the murder—but I have my doubts."

"Ah, the confidence of youth."

"Exactly," said Lucy. "Are you going back to the hotel?"

"No," said Carole with a sigh, "there's no rest for a working girl like me. I've got a meeting."

"At this hour?"

Carole gave a poor-me sort of shrug.

"That's not right," declared Lucy, thanking her lucky stars that she had a boss like Ted, who understood she had responsibilities outside of work. Ted would never expect her to work so late, especially on a Friday night. "You should give 'em hell."

"Oh, I intend to," said Carole, leaving Lucy standing in front of the hand dryer.

Chapter Twenty-one

Boylston Street was quiet, with only the occasional pedestrian and little traffic. Rush hour was over, and it was too early for people to begin coming into town for nightclubs or theaters. Lucy strolled along, determined to enjoy the sensation of having the city to herself on her last night in Boston.

She didn't envy Carole, she decided, even if she did have a fancy career and gorgeous clothes. Her life seemed so frantic, somehow. She was here, there, and everywhere, always on her way to some meeting or other. And all her hard work hadn't gotten her all that far. She was the features editor of the Hartford *Gazette*, to be sure, but the people on the news desk tended to think of features as fluff. It wasn't "real" news, like fires and automobile crashes and politics and world affairs. Of course, women hadn't been able to get jobs on the news desk until recently. Carole was a victim of her time. If she were starting out now, like Morgan, her chances would be much better.

Lucy couldn't help but smile when she thought of Morgan. That girl certainly knew how to get her goat, almost as if she were one of her children. That was when it hit Lucy: Morgan looked a lot like Elizabeth, with her spiky black hair and determined little chin. Of course, Morgan had a lot more drive than the lazy Elizabeth. She reminded Lucy of a feisty little terrier who wouldn't let go once she'd gotten her teeth into something. The something in this case was Luther Read's murder, and Morgan had set her mind on breaking the story. Lucy was convinced she'd succeed or die trying.

More power to her, thought Lucy. She had some leads of her own that she intended to follow up when she got back home. After talking to Louise she was more convinced than ever that Harold was bleeding Pioneer Press dry in order to keep up his lavish lifestyle. She wondered if Ted was having any luck with those annual reports. It might be worth the expense to have an accountant take a look at them. If it panned out, this could be a big story that the regional papers, and maybe even national press, would pick up.

The plan buoyed her spirits. It would be good to be home, to sleep in her own bed, cuddled up against Bill. She even missed his snoring, she realized as she passed a liquor store and remembered she needed vodka for his traditional Father's Day Bloody Mary. She dithered a bit, debating whether she should wait to buy it in Tinker's Cove, but decided she didn't want to risk it. She might forget; she might not have an opportunity once she was back in the thick of family life. She went in.

The vodka was in the rear of the store, tucked behind freestanding displays of wine. Lucy found Bill's favorite brand and brought it to the counter to pay for it, only to encounter Sam Syrjala, smelling like a distillery.

"Whaddya mean, you won't sell it to me?" he thundered, banging his fist on the counter.

"It's against the law to sell to inebriated persons," said the clerk, a thirtyish fellow who looked as if he played rugby on his day off.

"You think I'm drunk? I'm not drunk. Ask the lady."
Syrjala turned and focused his bloodshot eyes on Lucy.
"Hey, I know you," he declared, smiling woozily. "Do I
look drunk to you?"

Lucy watched as he swayed back and forth. "Actually—"
she began.

"Sorry," said the clerk, cutting her off and looking
steadily at Syrjala. "You're not getting anything here, so
you might as well leave."

"You're kicking me out?"

"Get out now, before I call the cops."

"Okay." Syrjala held up one hand and belched. "Okay.
I'm going."

Lucy and the clerk watched his unsteady progress
past the shelves of liquor and out the door.

"I'm sorry about that," said the clerk, ringing up her
vodka.

"No problem." Lucy handed him a twenty, took her
change, and tucked the wrapped bottle under her arm.

Which was where it was when Syrjala spotted her leaving the store. He'd been waiting outside, leaning against
a convenient trash barrel.

"Hey, lady," he said. "How 'bout we have a little party?"

"No, thanks," said Lucy, setting off briskly down the
street.

"I know you," he said, tagging after her. "News convention."

Lucy kept her eyes fixed straight ahead and marched
down the street. Syrjala, however, was faster than she
thought possible, considering his inebriated condition.

"I got a room, y'know," he said, grabbing her by the
hand.

Lucy whirled around and snatched it away. "What do
you think you're doing? Leave me alone," she said in a
snarl.

"You're no fun," he said, dropping his chin to his
chest and stumbling awkwardly.

"Careful there," said Lucy, watching in dismay as he lurched off in the wrong direction, stumbling against a fire hydrant. The man was headed for trouble, and she didn't want tomorrow's headlines on her conscience. "It's this way," she finally said, watching as he narrowly missed knocking over a garbage bin. "The hotel is this way."

Syrjala stopped and swayed backward, then turned around. "I'll follow you," he said.

"Right. All three of me and the dancing pink elephants, too," muttered Lucy, setting off once again.

She tried to keep her distance at the same time she kept a watchful eye on Syrjala, making sure he remained headed in the right direction. She wasn't happy about the situation but couldn't bring herself to abandon him, either. The man was in no condition to be wandering about the city alone, where chances were he'd get mugged if he didn't get hit by a car first. But as soon as they got to the hotel, Lucy vowed, he was on his own. There was no way she wanted to be associated with him.

The revolving door, however, proved more than Syrjala could manage, and he began pushing it in the wrong direction. A small crowd of amused onlookers had gathered by the time Lucy managed to extricate him. Embarrassed, she tried to explain that they were not together but found she was speaking to herself. The little knot of people had dispersed and she was alone with Syrjala. She led him to the elevator.

It was when they were riding together in the elevator that Lucy realized she had been presented with a real opportunity, a last chance before she had to leave Boston. Syrjala was dead drunk; she was sure he would pass out the moment he hit the bed. She would be able to search his room unhindered, maybe even find proof of Harold's financial manipulations. Tomorrow Syrjala would never even remember she was there.

Lucy drew the line at searching his pockets to find

his key card. Instead she instructed him to go through them one by one until he found it. Then there was the problem of getting it to work. When the little green light finally lit up, Lucy followed him inside his room, remaining cautiously in the doorway until he fell face-forward on the bed. He was out like a light; she was sure of it because he remained absolutely motionless.

Lucy shut the door behind her and set the bottle and her purse on the floor, ready for easy retrieval should a quick escape become necessary. Not that it would, she decided, advancing into the room. Syrjala was sprawled on the bed, dead to the world. In fact, Lucy wasn't posi-tive that he wasn't actually dead, and was relieved when he rolled onto his back and began snoring noisily.

She opened the closet and peered inside. Empty hang-ers, a pile of clothes on the floor. Grimacing, she bent to the distasteful task of checking the pockets. There was no vial of cyanide, no list of instructions from Harold. What did she expect to find anyway? she asked herself, as she moved on to the chest of drawers.

She'd know when she found it, she told herself. Budget projections, annual reports, cash-flow analy-ses—the editor-in-chief of a daily paper surely must need this information, but she didn't find anything. Except for a Gideon's Bible and a phone book, the drawers were empty.

That left the briefcase, propped on the chair, and the bedside table. Lucy peered into the briefcase, now full of papers, and pulled them out. She flipped through them but they were nothing more than handouts from the convention. There were no contracts, phony or other-wise, no pension fund transfers, no offshore bank ac-counts.

That left the bedside table.

Lucy looked at it, calculating the distance from Syrjala's hands. It was risky. If he regained conscious-ness he'd be able to reach her. It was a risk Lucy was willing to take. From the steady snoring it didn't look as if he was going to wake up anytime soon. She stepped forward and slid the drawer open, revealing a pint bottle containing a clear liquid.

Lucy reached for it, only to feel Syrjala's hand grip her wrist in a tight hold.

"Whaddya think you're doing?" he demanded, leaping nimbly to his feet despite his excess weight. His eyes were hard and his voice was steady, much to Lucy's dismay. If he really had been drunk, and she was beginning to wonder if it had all been an act, he certainly didn't seem drunk now.

"Just pouring a drink," said Lucy, attempting to smile brightly. "I thought this was a party."

Syrjala was having none of it. His grip tightened on her arm. "You were searching my room! What for? Cash?"

Lucy nodded. "I need bus fare home," she lied. "I spent too much."

Syrjala narrowed his eyes. "No," he said, "you're that hotshot reporter. You were looking for a story."

He let go of her hand and pushed against her chest, forcing her into the chair. Lucy was practically flat on her back, but when she struggled to sit up he punched her shoulder and pushed her back down. He was stronger than she thought; her shoulder ached from the blow.

"What story?" asked Lucy, hoping to convince him she was no threat. "I don't know what you're talking about."

Syrjala chuckled. "What story? *The story!* Luther's death, of course."

"There's no story," said Lucy. "The police have the right guy."

"You don't believe that, or you wouldn't be here, trying to pin it on me." His eyes flickered to the bottle.

Lucy noticed and tensed. What was in that bottle?

"That's crazy," she said. "The cops have got their case all wrapped up. Besides, you don't have a motive."

"That's a good one. I don't have a motive." He stared at her. "I hated Luther's guts." He reached for the bottle.

Lucy tried not to watch as he unscrewed the cap, but kept her eyes fixed on his. She didn't dare try to lift herself up and escape, but if he tried to force the liquid down her throat she'd spit it back at him. Maybe she could twist away and roll out from under him. Maybe not.

"He was rich, spoiled, arrogant. A real bastard."

"What did he do to you?" asked Lucy, watching as he tossed the cap onto the floor.

"He took my girl." Syrjala lifted the bottle to his lips and drank. He bared his teeth in a grimace, then smiled. "He didn't even have the good grace to keep her." He lifted the bottle again. "I would'na minded, y'see, if he'd made her happy. But he didn't. He used her up and when he was done with her he dumped her. He did that with everything. Uses it up, tosses it out."

Lucy slid her bottom backward and sat up.

"So that was your chance, no? Couldn't you catch her on the rebound?"

"She didn't rebound," he said. "Besides, who'd be interested in a drunk like me?" He tilted his head back and drained the bottle, then crumpled onto the floor like a heavy coat falling off a hanger.

Lucy was on her feet and almost out the door when she heard the bottle hit the floor with a thunk.

Chapter Twenty-two

Waking up Saturday morning, Lucy wished it had all been nothing more than a bad dream. Had she really gone to Syrjala's room with him? Whatever had she been thinking?

She shuddered, considering what could have happened. She could have been raped or killed. The thought of Syrjala's paunchy belly, pasty skin, and greasy strands of hair plastered over his bald spot propelled her out of bed and into the shower.

She turned the faucet as far as it would go, but somehow the water wasn't hot enough to wash away the stinging memory of her foolishness. She'd really been asking for it, a little voice in her head scolded. She'd used poor judgment; she'd put herself in a dangerous situation that could have had tragic results. And not just for herself, the voice continued. What about Bill and the kids? What would it be like for them if she'd been hurt—or worse, killed? She'd completely ignored her responsibilities, and for what? A story? She'd behaved disgracefully, and no matter how hard she scrubbed she still felt contaminated. Even worse was the realization that her risky behavior hadn't paid off. She'd left Syrjala's room no wiser than she'd entered it.

When she finally turned the water off, she heard the phone ringing and ran to answer it, clutching a towel around herself. It was Ted.

"Hey, Lucy, what time are you getting in tonight?"

"Around five, if I catch the noon bus."

"That late? Damn. I was hoping you could put in a few hours at the paper this afternoon. I'm way behind, thanks to the convention. I guess you'll have to come in tomorrow."

Lucy couldn't believe it. "On Father's Day?"

"Sorry, but it can't be helped." He paused. "Don't tell me you'll be waiting on Bill hand and foot for the entire day. Give him breakfast in bed and get yourself over here for a couple of hours."

"Bill isn't going to like this. He considers Father's Day only slightly less important than Christmas, and he won't understand why I have to work."

"I'm sure you can figure something out," said Ted in his boss tone of voice. "I'll expect you around noon."

There was a click and Lucy realized Ted had hung up. There wasn't going to be any discussion; he expected her to show up. On Sunday. On Father's Day. This was definitely a problem. She had promised Bill the best Father's Day ever, and she knew that this was one promise he expected her to keep.

Lucy mulled over her options while she dried her hair. Desert her husband on Father's Day and get herself divorced, or ignore her boss's demand and get fired. Faced with a choice like that, she was tempted to take the bus to New York City, or maybe all the way to Florida. Why not? she mused, as she studied her reflection in the mirror. Who wouldn't want a fresh start?

It was tempting. She had to admit she had enjoyed being on her own in the big city. It had been liberating to travel light, without her usual entourage of kids. No one to think about but herself. She could go where she wanted, eat what she wanted, even sleep when she wanted. It wouldn't be like that at home, where she'd be juggling the demands of five other people and the dog. Not to mention trying to fit her job in and get everyone fed. She had a feeling she had her work cut out for her, considering that things hadn't gone well in her absence. Toby and Bill were at odds, Elizabeth was running wild, the younger girls had been neglected, and she could just imagine what the house looked like: garbage bin overflowing, beds unmade, the family room strewn with newspapers and dirty dishes no one had bothered to tidy up. And then there was the matter of that upcoming dog hearing.

Lucy fastened her bra, pulled a polo shirt over her head, slipped into a pair of khaki slacks and stepped into her cute little red flats, clicking her heels together. This was better, she decided, firmly steering her thoughts back on track. There really was no place like home, even with the problems, and she missed Bill and the kids. She even missed the dog. She couldn't wait to get back. Really.

She had plenty of time before the bus, so she turned on the TV for company while she packed. She smoothed out the bedcovers and opened her suitcase on top of them, listening with one ear while she padded around the room, gathering up her belongings. She was taking home more than she brought, and she had to pack carefully if she was going to fit it all in. Plus, she wanted to make sure the vodka bottle was tucked in the center, where her clothing would serve as protective padding.

Most important, though, was her award. She couldn't forget that. She picked it up off the desk, where she had propped it against the wall, and admired the laminated wooden plaque which had her name printed in gold. She'd never won an award before, at least not since she left school. What should she do with it? Hang it in the kitchen? She chuckled at the thought. No, if she knew Ted, he'd insist that she hang it up in the *Pennysaver* office, where a small collection of similar framed certificates and plaques were arranged behind the reception desk.

First place. Investigative Reporting. She hugged the plaque and placed it on the bottom of her suitcase. On second thought, she removed it and wrapped a shirt around it for protection, then replaced it, arranging a pile of folded clothes neatly on top.

She wasn't really paying attention to the TV as she went to and from the closet to the bed. Even though she'd been in Boston for only a week, the news was already beginning to sound repetitive. Traffic was snarled on the central artery, hospital workers were on strike, a fire in a three-decker had left several families homeless, a woman's body had been found in the trunk of a car.

"Police have not identified the victim, pending notification of the family," said the newscaster. "She is reported to have been in her mid to late twenties. Police received an anonymous call leading them to the automobile parked at the Riverside MBTA station."

That's funny, thought Lucy; she'd heard somebody mention the Riverside MBTA station quite recently. It certainly sounded familiar, and she really had very little knowledge of the city's transit system. Somebody must have said something about it, but who? And when?

Lucy smoothed out the exercise shorts she'd tossed into a drawer and folded them, feeling vaguely guilty. She'd meant to take advantage of the gym by working out every day, but she'd gone only once. And then she'd plodded along on the Exercycle, hardly breaking a sweat, unlike Morgan, who had performed an intense exercise routine. And she hadn't even been staying at the hotel, Lucy remembered, but had sneaked into the gym. She'd been commuting to the conference from

Framingham, taking the T and leaving her car in a commuter lot. At Riverside.

Lucy dropped her hairbrush.

It was just a coincidence, she told herself, bending to retrieve it. A gleam of gold caught her eye, and as she worked to disentangle a pearl stud earring from the carpet pile she tried to convince herself that the dead woman couldn't possibly be Morgan Dodd. Young women got killed every day, she told herself, examining the earring. You could hardly open up a big-city newspaper without reading of some poor girl who'd gone home with the wrong fellow and ended up dead.

A previous occupant must have dropped it, she decided, placing the earring in clear sight in the middle of the dark-wood desk for the housekeeper to find, all the while continuing her private argument. Morgan was street-smart; she was a big-city girl. She knew how to take care of herself, surely, after covering so many rapes and murders. She'd be sure to park in a well-lit part of the lot, and she'd have her keys ready in her hand so she could gain quick access to the safety of her car. Why, she probably carried a little can of Mace or pepper spray, just in case. Not that she would need it, because she was physically fit. She'd probably taken a self-defense course and knew to go for an attacker's eyes, or was a master of some trendy unpronounceable martial art and could flip an assailant neatly over her shoulder and onto his back. Besides, it had been quite early when Morgan had left the McDonald's, and plenty of daylight had still remained.

"I'm going to break this story wide open . . ."

Damn, thought Lucy, Morgan might have the street smarts of a big-city girl but she wanted to get the story. She'd go anywhere with someone who promised her a lead. Good judgment would go out the window. Lucy knew it; she'd done the same thing herself. Fortunately, she'd lived to regret her rashness. She was beginning to suspect that Morgan hadn't.

Where had she gone? Who had she met? Lucy remembered they'd been talking about Junior. Had she gone to meet him? Were the police right: Was Junior really a murderer?

Before she realized what she was doing, Lucy was dialing the Reads' home in Tinker's Cove, praying that Elizabeth would answer.

"Hello." Lucy heard Angela's clipped tone.

"Hi," she stammered, "this is Lucy Stone. Could I please speak to my daughter—it's a bit of a family emergency."

"I'm sorry, but Elizabeth no longer works here."

"Oh." Lucy was stunned. When had this happened? Why hadn't Elizabeth told her? Drat the girl; she'd probably gotten herself fired.

"In that case, could I speak to your husband?"

"I'm afraid not."

"Is he there? Or is he in Boston? I really need to talk to him."

Lucy knew she sounded desperate and she sensed her pleas were falling on deaf ears.

"I'll tell him you called," said Angela, ending the conversation.

Ah, thought Lucy bitterly, the Read way. Invariably polite, presenting that smooth, impenetrable surface. Would she really give Junior the message? Lucy had no idea. She didn't even know if Junior was home. Maybe Ted would know. She dialed the *Pennysaver*, and Phyllis answered.

"Howdy, stranger. How's tricks?"

Lucy had no time for small talk. "Is Ted there?"

"He went out a bit ago."

"Is he with Junior Read? He was supposed to interview him."

"I don't really know."

"Is Junior in town? Have you seen him?"

"Can't say that I have, but I did hear that he's out of jail."

Lucy was disgusted. "I can't believe it. Everybody is supposed to know everybody's business in a small town. What's wrong with Tinker's Cove?"

"Well, since you asked, I think it's that shopping channel. Instead of keeping an eye on their neighbors, people are buying nonstick pans and genuine fake diamonds and—"

"I've gotta go," said Lucy.

She perched on the edge of the bed, clutching the phone, telling herself to be rational. For goodness' sake, she didn't even know that it was Morgan in the trunk. For all she knew the girl was sleeping in late, or eating pancakes for breakfast under her mother's doting gaze. As for Junior, she didn't know if Morgan had met him last night or not. And Junior wouldn't have killed her. Or would he?

She dialed home, hoping to talk to Elizabeth, but nobody answered the phone even though she let it ring and ring. She considered calling Morgan, even dialed Information, but there were twenty Dodds listed in Framingham, none of them named Morgan. Not even an M. Dodd.

She put the phone down and picked up the remote, flipping through the channels. She stopped when she saw Morgan's face filling the screen.

"A Framingham *Trib* reporter was found dead this morning. . . ."

Chapter Twenty-three

Lucy sank to the floor, her head in her hands. Each piece of information was like a blow. Cause and time of death had not been determined. She lived with her parents. A shot of a modest clapboard house. An interview with her editor. "A hard worker and enterprising reporter." His voice cracked but he got the words out. "She'll be missed."

Her fingers thick and clumsy, Lucy dialed Information and got the *Trib*'s phone number. She was connected to the newsroom, where the phone rang but nobody answered.

She had to talk to somebody. She had so many questions. But who? There was only one person she knew for a certainty couldn't be the murderer because he had an ironclad alibi. He'd been in Boston when Morgan was killed, and she could testify in court if she had to. She'd seen him with her own eyes.

She decided to pay him a visit. Maybe this news would shock him into talking, into telling what he knew. She got up slowly and tucked her key card in her pocket, then left her room and took the elevator down to Syrjala's floor. The door to his room was open, so she stuck her head inside.

"Anybody here?"

"Housekeeping," said the maid, popping out of the bathroom. She spoke with a heavy Spanish accent.

"He's gone?" Lucy hadn't expected this. She thought he'd sleep until they kicked him out of the room.

The maid shrugged.

"The man who was staying here? Has he left?"

The maid shook her head, but Lucy didn't need to talk to her. Syrjala's belongings were gone; there was no sign of him in the room.

Lucy walked slowly down the hall and waited for the elevator. When it finally came she went back up to her floor and into her room. She called the *Pennysaver*, and this time Ted answered.

"One of the reporters working on the Luther Read story is dead." Lucy blurted out the words, running them together. "They found her body in a commuter parking lot, in the trunk of her car."

"Who?"

"Morgan Dodd."

"The girl with the short black hair?"

"Yeah." Lucy's voice quavered. "Do you want me to work on it?"

"Absolutely not. I want you to get out of there as fast as you can. I don't want you dead, too."

"I'm not in any danger."

"Don't argue. Pack your suitcase. Get the bus. Come home. Period."

Lucy didn't answer, just slammed the phone down, furious that Ted was pulling her off the story. She wasn't a rookie; she knew what she was doing. This was the biggest story of her life, and Ted wanted her back in Tinker's Cove, working on obits and meeting announcements.

She tossed the last few things into her suitcase and

zipped it up. She slid it off the bed, onto the floor, and pulled the handle up so she could wheel it along. She picked up her purse and left the room.

She felt like a robot, pulling the suitcase behind her. A robot with low batteries. Who was she kidding? she asked herself as she stepped into the elevator. She'd never really been on the story; she hadn't produced any new information, written any stories. She didn't deserve the award that was zipped into her suitcase. It should have gone to Morgan, she decided, feeling hugely guilty.

The elevator bounced to a stop at the lobby level and she stepped out. There was a long line of people waiting to check out, and she dutifully followed it to the end, where she parked her suitcase beside her. She checked her watch and sighed. She was going to be here for a while.

It was the eternal conundrum. Time passed too slowly, and then it was over too quickly. Hurry up and die. She blinked back a tear.

"Have you recovered your appetite?" It was Fred Easton, one of the men she'd eaten with at Durgin Park.

"I couldn't eat for days," added his buddy, Bob Hunsaker. The two were just ahead of her in line, but she hadn't noticed them.

Lucy tried to smile, but ended up crying instead.

"Hey, what's the matter?"

Lucy dabbed at her eyes with Bob's big, snowy handkerchief.

"I'm sorry. I just heard about Morgan Dodd a few minutes ago. . . ."

"That girl reporter? What happened?"

"They found her body in the trunk of a car."

"Murdered?" Bob's face was white. "I was just talking to her the other day."

"Are you sure?" asked Fred.

"It was on the TV news."

"It's hard to believe," said Bob. "She was so interested in everything, always asking questions, always dashing around."

"The best reporters always are," said Fred.

The line inched forward.

"She told me she was going to break Luther's murder wide open," said Lucy, sniffling. "Was that what she was asking you about?"

"Not directly. She wanted to know all about the Pioneer papers in New Hampshire. She said she just wanted background, back story." Bob scratched his chin. "It was kinda funny. She was mostly interested in Luther and Monica. How they met, how long they'd been a couple, stuff like that."

"She couldn't have suspected Monica," said Fred. "She's the one person who's above suspicion."

"Because of her integrity?" Lucy had her doubts on that score.

"Not exactly," said Fred. "I admit she's got a pretty good reputation for a politician—but she's still a politician. No. I think the reason she's not a suspect is because she's so new on the scene. She and Luther had just hooked up a month or two ago."

"Really? Who was he with before Monica?"

"Who wasn't he with; that's the question you should be asking," offered Bob with a dirty chuckle.

"He dated a lot of different women?"

"Sure did. Usually employees. They'd be hanging on his arm and smiling one day; then next thing you'd hear the poor girl was looking for work."

"He fired them when he got tired of them?"

"Usually. He lost a lot of good staff that way. It was awkward, you know, breaking up. Embarrassing to keep running into old girlfriends. So he'd usually end up getting rid of them."

"That's why you should never date the staff," said Fred.

"That's awful," said Lucy, struck by the unfairness of the situation. "And you told all this to Morgan?"

"Sure did," said Bob. "It wasn't a secret or anything. Everybody knew what he was like." He scratched his chin. "You had to admire the guy, really. Considering his age and all."

"Viagra," opined Fred. "I'll bet he took Viagra."

What was with these guys? Lucy was beginning to get annoyed. She was trying to get to the bottom of a murder and all they could talk about was Luther Read's sexual exploits.

"So when did you have this little chat with Morgan?" she asked, taking another baby step closer to the counter.

"Lunch, day before yesterday, her treat," said Bob, sliding his suitcase an inch or two forward. "Did you say they found her body in the trunk of a car?"

Lucy nodded.

"Damned shame," said Bob.

It certainly was, thought Lucy, resisting the urge to knock Fred's and Bob's heads together. What a pair! So smug and complacent and so sure of their place in the world. They'd never had to battle the glass ceiling; they'd never had to prove themselves the way women did in the news industry. They were the ones who checked out the girls and made passes; they stared and ogled and commented and joked. All in good fun, of course. Safe in their thick-soled shoes and confident in their strength, they had no idea what it was like to be five-foot-two and one hundred and ten pounds, late at night, alone in a dark parking lot.

Lucy watched as Bob stepped up to the desk, pulling his stomach in and standing a bit taller as the pretty clerk with the blond curls smiled at him. He handed over his credit card and signed the bill, not even bothering to glance at the total. Well, why should he? It was tax deductible, wasn't it?

Fred at least looked at the bill, but Lucy suspected it

was simply a ploy to engage the blond's attention. He held the paper in such a way that the clerk had to lean forward to see the items he was questioning, giving him an opportunity to look down her blouse.

How long was this going to take? wondered Lucy, impatiently shifting from one foot to the other. Five minutes? Ten minutes? How long could he keep the checkout clerk dancing to his tune, a smile pasted on her face as he questioned the state room tax? Like he didn't know all about it.

Finally it was Lucy's turn. She crossed her fingers and handed over her card, hoping her bill wouldn't take her over her credit limit. Ted would reimburse her, of course, but she had to pay the bill first. It seemed to take a long time for the card to clear, and Lucy was beginning to fear her room-service supper had been a big mistake when the machine finally began printing out her receipt. Approved this time.

She stuffed the papers in her purse and grabbed her suitcase, eager to get on the move. Some of the faces of the people waiting in line were familiar—she waved a quick farewell to Carole and a few others—but she didn't linger to chat. She'd had enough of newspapers, of hotels, of Boston. She wanted to go home.

"Where to?" asked the cabby when she climbed in.

"Tinker's Cove, Maine," she said.

He turned and looked at her. "Come again?"

"What's the problem?"

"You said Maine. I don't go to Maine."

Talk about Freudian slips, thought Lucy, realizing her mistake.

"I meant South Station," she said.

Chapter Twenty-four

Traffic was heavy, and Lucy had plenty of time to think as the cabby maneuvered his way past double- and triple-parked cars and through gridlocked intersections, keeping up a lively dialogue with himself that was peppered with curses and punctuated with blasts on his horn.

"Don't even think about it," he growled at a SUV that was trying to make a right turn in front of him. Neatly cutting the behemoth off, he blasted the horn at a couple of young girls who were jaywalking, making them jump back to the safety of the curb.

"Whadda they think?" he demanded. "I'm steering more than a ton of steel here; they weigh maybe a hundred and ten pounds apiece. Who's gonna win? Me! They're gonna be squashed like bugs on the windshield. And what have we here? Want to turn left, do you? Not on my watch, buddy."

The cab lurched forward, blocking a Volvo station wagon, leaving the confused driver stranded in the mid-dle of the intersection with nowhere to go.

"Out-of-towner!" snarled the cabby.

Lucy didn't think his scorn was directed at the driver's effort to make a left turn; those daredevils seemed to earn his grudging approval. It was the hopeful blinking of the directional signal that he despised.

"Christ! An ambulance!"

Lucy turned around and saw the flashing lights approaching, slowly, as drivers tried to squeeze to the side to let the ambulance through. The ambulance driver encouraged them with blasts on the horn, occasionally adding the siren for emphasis.

Marooned in traffic and unsure whether South Station was just around the corner or miles across town, Lucy let her thoughts return to Fred and Bob. They weren't all that bad, just typical middle-aged businessmen who had managed, with society's connivance, to convince themselves that they deserved their success. They'd worked for it, they told themselves; it was their due. They blundered their way through life—guzzling gasoline and plastic and steak and alcohol—blissfully unaware of their privileged status.

Unaware was the word that best described them, thought Lucy. They spoke, but they didn't think. Without realizing it, they'd given her a likely theory that explained both Luther's and Morgan's murders.

Anger and hurt were powerful emotions, and so was the desire for revenge. And who would feel those emotions more strongly than a former lover? It hadn't been about business and money at all, or who was going to control Pioneer Press, she decided; it was about rejection and humiliation. Bruised feelings. A bleeding heart. Luther had died because he'd spurned someone who loved him. Someone who loved him too much to let him go.

Furthermore, thought Lucy, bracing herself as the cabby braked to avoid mowing down a bicycle courier, Morgan Dodd wouldn't have been wary of meeting a woman at night in a parking lot. She would have thought twice about meeting a man, but not a woman. Her defenses would have been down and she would have been easy prey for a murderer who feared she was getting too close.

Morgan must have figured it out, thought Lucy, chagrined to realize the spunky girl reporter had been way ahead of her. Close enough to spook the murderer, anyway. If only she'd opened up to Lucy last night in the McDonald's, maybe she could have warned her. Or gone with her. Maybe it would have turned out differently. Maybe.

"Thirteen seventy-five," said the cabby, and Lucy was startled to see they were parked right in front of South Station.

"Keep the change," she said, handing him a ten and a five.

"Thanks," he said, but he didn't stir himself to help her when she struggled with the suitcase. He merely waited, drumming his fingers impatiently on the steering wheel, until she yanked it free with a jerk. Then he pulled away so fast that the tires squealed.

Men! Men and women, somehow it was all screwed up. In a similar situation she would have rushed to offer assistance, without regard to age or sex. A child, a pregnant woman, an elderly man—if she could help, she would.

Men used to help others. She remembered her father shoveling snow for elderly neighbors and warming up the car for her mother on cold winter days. Her parents had always been a unit, a team. She couldn't imagine her father deciding he'd had enough of her mother. What had changed? When had men and women started having relationships instead of marriages? When had partners become disposable when somebody more attractive, or richer, or smarter, or more connected came along?

No wonder they'd put wheels on suitcases, thought Lucy, battling her way through the doors and into the station. They'd had to because nowadays everyone had to tote their own. Even little children, she noticed, were pulling brightly colored backpacks on wheels.

The enormous, echoing station was filled with people, and everyone seemed to know exactly where they were going. Lucy didn't. She found a spot against the wall, out of the flow of traffic, and looked for something familiar. This part of the station bore no resemblance to the bus terminal where she'd arrived. It must be here somewhere; the timetable specified South Station, but she didn't know where. And she had to find it fast because her bus was scheduled to leave in twenty-five minutes.

She needed to ask someone for directions, but who? Numerous kiosks dotted the station, but the salesclerks were all busy selling pretzels and books and newspapers and cookies to long lines of impatient customers who wouldn't take kindly to an interruption. Everyone was on the move and no one seemed approachable.

"Lady, you got change?"

Startled, Lucy turned to discover a homeless man sitting on the floor beside her, holding out a paper cup with a few coins in the bottom. She was ashamed to realize she hadn't seen him there; she'd become so used to seeing homeless people on the sidewalks, in doorways, and on benches that they'd begun to blend into the cityscape. They'd become invisible.

"Of course," she said, reaching for her purse and pulling out a dollar. "Can you tell me where to find the bus station?"

"Thank you, thank you kindly, ma'am," he said, snatching the bill with filthy stained fingers. "The bus station is over that way, on the other side of the tracks."

"Thank you," said Lucy, hurrying off in the direction he'd indicated. Indeed, when she got closer she could see the sign, high above a passage.

When she stepped through the doorway and onto a

train platform she saw more signs hanging from the roof, indicating the way to the station. She had to go the entire length of the platform, a long way, and didn't have much time to do it, so she quickened her pace, dodging and weaving around the people waiting for the train. Maybe it was late or something; it seemed as if the platform was awfully crowded.

Then a headlight suddenly appeared, and people who had been dotted around the platform began moving toward the edge, maneuvering for position. Lucy felt like a salmon, swimming against the current. Everyone was coming one way and she had to go the other, hampered by her suitcase.

"Excuse me, excuse me," she said, attempting to side-step a large lady with a shopping bag in each hand.

The woman wouldn't yield, but barreled toward her. Lucy leaned aside to avoid her and almost lost her balance, but caught herself. This was definitely not the place to slip, not with the train thundering into the station. Lucy tried to stay as far away from the edge of the platform as she could, but a woman with a stroller stepped into her path and she found herself stepping closer to the tracks. Then she was pushed—she felt two hands slam against her back—and found herself falling through the air. The train was roaring toward her and—ohmigod—she was going to be crushed to death.

A crazy kaleidoscope of faces spun before her eyes: Bill, Toby, Elizabeth, Sara, Zoe, her mother and father, the dog. Then she felt a strong hand grip her arm and pull her back just as the train whipped past her face, inches away. It was so close she could smell the steel and taste the grit.

"You ought to be more careful, lady; you almost got killed," said a big guy in a Red Sox hat.

Lucy couldn't say anything. All she could feel was her heart thumping in her chest, louder even than the squeal of brakes as the train slowed and then stopped.

"It wasn't her fault," declared the woman with the shopping bag. "That woman pushed her. I saw the whole thing."

A little crowd had gathered around them, and all eyes followed her pointing finger right to Carole Rose.

Lucy gasped, recognizing her. Carole Rose, who she thought was her friend. Carole Rose, who'd complained to her about the way Pioneer Press had treated her father. Carole Rose, who'd complained that Luther was all business. Carole Rose, who'd looked at the painting of Lucretia in the museum and said she should have killed the man who raped her.

Carole began to sidle backward, smiling apologetically, but her way was blocked by the crowd.

"There's some mistake," she said, attempting to retreat, but the guy in the Red Sox hat clamped a hand on her shoulder.

"Not so fast, lady. I think the cops are gonna want to talk to you."

A transit policeman was hurrying down the platform, talking into his radio as he came.

Lucy faced Carole as if seeing her for the first time. So many reasons to hate Luther: her father's injury in a press accident and his callous disregard afterward, her rejection when he turned his attention to another, her fear that she, like so many before her, would soon lose her job.

"Luther got what he deserved," said Carole, reaching ever so casually for the water bottle that was sticking out of her purse. She unscrewed the cap.

"Why Morgan?"

"She knew about me and Luther," said Carole, shrugging and lifting the bottle to her lips.

A bottle of clear fluid that was not water.

"Stop her!" yelled Lucy. "Don't let her drink it!"

It was too late. The bottle slipped from Carole's hands and she slumped against the man who had grabbed her arm. She sank to the stained and filthy concrete. Lucy knelt beside her, cradling her head as she gasped and struggled to breathe. When her blue-tinged lips twitched, she bent close to hear Carole's last words.

"Tell Daddy I love him," she said, just before she died.

Chapter Twenty-five

The single thing Lucy hated most about her job was calling survivors for quotes, and she could count on one hand the times she'd had to do it. She'd interviewed the mother of a college girl who'd been aboard one of the planes that crashed into the World Trade Center, the husband of a woman who had died while waiting for a liver transplant, and the father of a girl who had fallen asleep at the wheel after organizing an alcohol-free after-prom party. Each time she'd found the survivors grateful for her call and eager to talk, but she'd had great difficulty herself in controlling her emotions, spilling tears on the keyboard as she struggled to get every word exactly right.

This time she didn't have to make the call to Carole Rose's father. That was Brad McAbee's job. Lucy had called him at the *Globe* when she found herself stranded after the police finished taking her statement. They hadn't exactly hurried about it, either. As Detective Sullivan had told her, they wanted to get it right, and that took time. It was past seven when they finally released her, and the last bus to Maine had left at four.

The first bus in the morning wouldn't get her home until noon, and she didn't want to wait that long, not on Father's Day. When she called home to tell Bill she'd been delayed "as a witness" he'd urged her to rent a car, but she'd dismissed the idea as too expensive, considering her maxed-out credit card. After racking her brain she'd finally come up with the idea of offering Brad her exclusive story in exchange for a lift on one of the newspaper delivery trucks.

"So Junior's off the hook?" he'd asked, waiting expectantly for her answer with his hands poised on the keyboard.

"Absolutely," said Lucy, who was sitting on a spare chair in his tiny cubicle in the *Globe* newsroom. The idea made her smile. Trevor would have his daddy home for Father's Day.

"It was Carole Rose," continued Lucy. "She came prepared with the cyanide in a water bottle and was waiting for an opportunity. When she saw Luther coughing in the hallway outside the banquet she offered him the bottle, and he assumed it was water and drank it. He staggered into the men's room and she slipped unnoticed into the banquet hall and took her seat."

Brad whistled. "Talk about cold blood—"

"She had her reasons," interrupted Lucy. "They'd been lovers. Luther had a reputation for being quite a ladies' man, especially with women who worked for him. I guess these relationships were pretty intense at first, but when they cooled and it was awkward having them around, he fired them." Lucy paused, remembering their conversation in the Gardner Museum. "She was getting on in years, frustrated with her job—she hadn't been able to break out of features—and all of a sudden she's making pillow talk with the boss. She must have been shattered when it all ended. Plus, there was her father. . . ."

"What's he got to do with it?"

"He was disabled in a press room accident years ago. Pioneer pressured him to accept a settlement, which seemed generous at the time but hasn't turned out to be nearly enough to meet his needs. Everything's a lot more expensive now than it was twenty years ago.

"Carole tried to get Luther to increase it, but he refused, saying the company couldn't afford it. She even went to a lawyer about going to court, but he said the settlement was binding and they were stuck with it. If they'd sued at the time, they would have made out much better."

"And Morgan figured this all out?"

"Enough of it to make her suspicious," said Lucy. "The cops found story notes in her computer at the *Trib*, along with a list of questions she planned to ask Carole."

"I can't believe she met her alone in the parking lot. . . ."

"Carole was a woman, a colleague. Morgan didn't think she posed a threat. She knew about the relationship with Luther, but I'm not sure she'd pegged her for the murderer. There were no signs of struggle, you know. Just her prints on the water bottle. Like Luther, she didn't suspect a thing."

"But what about you? Why'd she want to kill you?"

"I think she overheard me talking in the hotel lobby when we were in line to check out; that's when I learned about Luther's relationships, and decided I might put two and two together. Besides, I think she panicked after she killed Morgan. She'd taken Morgan's notebook—the cops found it in her bag—but I'm sure she was worried that there might be other notebooks and computer files. She'd screwed up and she knew it." Lucy paused, thinking. "You know, I think she was worried about me right from the start. I won first place for investigative reporting, and I came from Tinker's Cove; she would have expected me to pursue the story. Now that I think about it, she seemed to pop up an awful lot in unexpected places, almost as if she was keeping tabs on me. She made a point of going drinking with me after a panel. I ran into her at the Gardner Museum, even McDonald's." She gasped. "The earring! I actually found one of her earrings in my room, but I didn't realize it at the time." Lucy remembered finding her notebook open on her desk. "She searched my room; she must have."

Brad whistled. "I still can't believe it. We were panelists together, you know, and she seemed so nice."

"She fooled me, too," said Lucy, shaking her head. "Boy, did she have me fooled. I liked her, I really did, until she tried to push me under the train." Her eyes fell on the telephone. "Are you going to call her father?"

Brad grimaced. "Got to."

"Would you let me talk to him? I've got a message to deliver."

Later, while she was waiting for the truck to be loaded, she called Ted to fill him in on the new developments. She was also hoping he'd take pity on her after her near-death experience and tell her she needn't come to work tomorrow.

"Gosh, Lucy, I wish I could but I need you more than ever. I've got a tiger by the tail. You were right about Harold cooking the books at Pioneer Press. After I talked to Ames over at the bank he did some investigating, and it looks like some of the shareholders are going to take Pioneer to court. He thinks they've got a real good case."

Lucy couldn't quite muster the enthusiasm to match Ted's. "That's a hell of a story," she admitted, "but getting involved in a lawsuit is going to be awfully rough on Junior and Catherine, don't you think? Especially after all they've been through."

"Well, I don't know. They seem eager to do battle

with Harold. And Inez, can't forget her. You can't blame them, really. They got hurt more than the others."

"I'm confused. Who's suing who?"

"Junior and Catherine and the bank and some of the other shareholders are all suing Harold, charging fraud and breach of trust and falsifying financial statements and failing to fulfill his responsibilities as chief financial officer and I don't know what all. They're also going after the accounting firm Inez worked for. It's gonna be big. They're talking millions."

"Wow," said Lucy, digesting this information. "This could be a whole new start for Junior and Catherine. And Pioneer Press, too."

"That's exactly what Junior said to me. A new start." He paused. "And we've got it ahead of everybody. It's a scoop, Lucy. And it all started with your investigating. I need your help on this. I'm counting on you. Don't let me down."

Lucy was stunned. Ted was actually giving her credit. Credit she deserved. If she hadn't seen Inez coming out of Armani and started poking around in the Boston Public Library, it might have been years before Harold's dishonesty was discovered. Maybe never.

"I'll be there," she promised.

The sun was up and the birds were singing when the truck driver dropped Lucy off at the end of the driveway on Red Top Road around six o'clock in the morning. She stood there for a minute, looking at the house. It looked neat and trim as ever, the grass was cut, the pickup truck and the Subaru were parked side by side in the driveway. Her heart sank a bit when she noticed that the spot where Toby's Jeep was usually parked was empty. She studied the house, looking for further clues about the family, but from outside the windows were blank and inscrutable. She couldn't tell what was going on inside.

The kitchen door was never locked, and she pushed it open with nary a squeak. Kudo recognized her immediately, rising from his mat in the kitchen and stretching before licking her hand and thumping his tail in polite doggy greeting.

She opened the door and let him out, making sure to attach his leash to the sturdy cable run she noticed Bill had installed, then made a pot of coffee. Surprisingly enough, the kitchen was neat and clean. There were no dirty dishes in the sink, and the trash barrel was empty and had a fresh plastic liner. She peeked into the TV room and found it neat as a pin, with pillows lined up neatly on the sofa, magazines stacked on the coffee table, and newspapers in the basket in the corner. There wasn't even a single sticky glass.

She returned to the kitchen and was pouring herself a cup of coffee when Elizabeth appeared, fully dressed in shorts and a T-shirt.

"What are you doing up so early?"

"My new job," she said, pouring herself a glass of juice.

"Angela told me you weren't working for them anymore. What happened?"

"Well, remember how I told you I was learning interesting words in many languages from the other au pairs at the yacht club?"

Lucy nodded.

"So was Trevor."

Lucy couldn't help smiling as she sat down at the table.

"So what are you doing now?"

"I'm back at the Queen Vic, and you know what? I actually like it. It turns out that making beds and cleaning toilets is a lot easier than chasing after a three-year-old all day. Plus, there are some interesting people working there."

"Interesting like with a tattoo?"

Elizabeth almost choked on her juice.

"What've you got, a spy plane or something? How do you know about Ernesto?"

"Sue told me. Is it serious?"

"I wish." Elizabeth sighed. "But I think we're just friends." She put down her glass. "Mrs. McNaughton gave me a raise, but I've got to be there at seven so I can help with breakfast."

"Even today?" wailed Lucy. "What about Father's Day?"

"I'm going to have to miss Dad's breakfast, but I've got a present for him. Sara's got it. And I got all those groceries you wanted." She stood up. "Gotta go, or I'll be late." She smiled—a rare, dazzling event. "It's nice to have you home, Mom."

That was one hurdle that had been easier than she expected, thought Lucy, as she started frying up the bacon and sausages. She had been wise, she decided, not to mention the bikini. There'd be plenty of time for that later.

"Mom's home!" It was Zoe, eager to welcome her with hugs.

Sara was more restrained, submitting awkwardly to Lucy's hug and asking, "What did you bring me?"

"First things first," admonished Lucy. "We've got to get your father's breakfast tray ready."

The girls produced a homemade place mat, woven from construction paper, and a paper napkin decorated in crayon with matching colors, which they arranged on the tray while Lucy scrambled the eggs.

"Do you guys know where Toby is?" she asked, keeping her voice casual.

"He's probably asleep," said Sara.

"His car's not in the driveway. Do you know what's going on?"

The two girls looked at each other, then shook their heads.

Lucy had a sudden desire to down the Bloody Mary she was mixing for Bill. Her worst fears had come true. Bill had kicked Toby out of the house. Her son was homeless and jobless, beginning a downward spiral that would lead to drugs, jail, and death.

"Mom?"

Lucy looked down at Zoe's worried face. She was overreacting. She didn't know what had happened, and Toby was a sensible kid. She'd sort it out later. Right now it was time to concentrate on Bill's special day. Even if she was furious with him.

When they opened the door, Bill was asleep, or pretending to be. He rarely slept past six, and Lucy suspected he was playing possum for Zoe's benefit.

"What's all this?" he asked, blinking and rubbing his eyes.

"It's Father's Day! We made you breakfast just the way you like it," announced Zoe.

Bill grinned at Lucy. "You're home! I didn't think you'd get in until later."

"I couldn't miss Father's Day," she said, refusing to yield to the anxiety and anger that were threatening to explode in a torrent of tears. "I hitched a ride on a news truck. I came in with the morning edition."

"That's the best present I could have," he said, lifting his Bloody Mary in a toast. "Here's to Mom—I wouldn't be a father without her."

The girls giggled and ran out the room, returning with a pile of presents for Bill. Lucy settled herself on the bed beside him. His warmth was comforting, despite her mixed emotions.

"This is from Elizabeth—she's at work," announced Sara, presenting him with a slim white envelope.

"This is nice—dinner at the Queen Vic. For two." He winked slyly. "Who shall I take?"

"It had better be me," said Lucy, handing him her package.

Bob shook it. "I wonder what this could be?"

"Open it and find out."

He did, expressing delight at the antique ruler she'd found on Charles Street.

"Do you really like it? I got it in an antique shop."

"Are you kidding? It's great. I love it."

"Now for our present," said Sara. "Zoe and I made it together."

"You made it yourselves? That's the best kind of present."

When Bill unwrapped the package he found a homemade scrapbook titled *Bill Stone: The Best Father in the World*.

He sat for a minute, fingering the book and, Lucy suspected, wrestling with his emotions. Finally he opened to page one. It was an old snapshot of him taken in the hospital, dressed in disposable scrubs and a ridiculous cap, holding a tiny, red-faced, newborn baby Toby. Underneath, Zoe had carefully printed the words *Bill Stone becomes a father for the first time*.

Looking at the photo, Lucy felt a rush of emotions: joy at Bill's proud expression, a flood of love for her firstborn child, and anger at the feckless and irresponsible young man he'd apparently become.

"Where is Toby, anyway?" asked Bill, voicing the question Lucy had dreaded.

He was answered by heavy steps coming up the stairs, accompanied by the click of Kudo's nails.

"Sorry I'm late," said Toby, who was dressed in waterproof fishing pants, as if he'd just stepped off the boat. "We had a bigger catch than usual and I couldn't get away."

"Bigger catch?"

"He's been working for Chuck Swift on his lobster boat," explained Bill.

By means of illustration, Toby hoisted a black plastic garbage bag. "I've got six nice ones, Pop. Happy Father's Day!"

"Thanks, Toby. Thanks, everybody. Now, if you'll excuse me, I'm going to eat my eggs before they get cold."

"C'mon girls," said Toby. "I've got some of Jake's doughnuts for breakfast. They're still warm."

Left alone with Bill, Lucy snuggled against him, resting her head on his shoulder. Drawn by the smell of the food, Kudo nosed his way into the room, sniffing at the discarded wrapping paper and finally curling up on the floor beside Bill's side of the bed, just in case Bill dropped a tasty morsel.

Bill chewed his bacon and swallowed.

Kudo sighed.

"The dog hearing's been postponed," said Bill.

"How come?"

"The dog officer, Cathy Anderson, is out on maternity leave."

"That's great news," said Lucy. "I'll have to send her something nice for the baby."

"You could stuff Kudo," suggested Bill, tossing the last bite of bacon to the dog, who caught it on the fly and gulped it down.

"It looks like you're doing that already," said Lucy. She reached up and stroked Bill's beard affectionately. "I'll admit I was worried, but it looks as if you were right and I was wrong. You managed fine without me—and you did it your way. Everything seems to have worked out. The kids are great, the dog's got a reprieve, the house isn't even messy. How'd you do it?"

"Just don't look under the bed," he said, shoving the tray aside and pulling her closer. "Welcome home."

Please turn the page for an exciting sneak peek of

Leslie Meier's next Lucy Stone mystery

STAR SPANGLED MURDER!

Prologue

He'd killed before and he would kill again. He couldn't help himself. It was more than an addiction; he was programmed to do it. It was in his DNA. He loved the rush of excitement when he spotted his victim and the sense of power he felt when he'd mastered his prey. They were so stupid. Going about their daily business unaware of the eyes watching them. His eyes. They thought they had it all under control, but they didn't. They would live or die as he willed. As he desired.

He sighed and rolled over on the sorry excuse for a bed that his captors gave him. There would be no killing today. He stared at the thick wire mesh that confined him. It was nothing more than a pen, really, but there was no way out. He'd tried, of course. It was his major occupation, considering the small amount of exercise his captors allowed him. He'd examined every corner, looking for a gap, a loose screw, a flaw in the concrete. So far, he hadn't found any.

So he'd just have to bide his time until they made a mistake. He could wait. He was used to it. He'd had to get used to it. But that didn't mean he'd given up. Oh, no. He was simply waiting for an opportunity. Hearing a door slam, he looked up. Maybe this was his big chance.

The woman was coming towards him carrying a bowl. His dinner. He got to his feet and watched as she opened the door and carefully slid the bowl towards him. "Hungry?" she asked, in a high squeaky voice. What did she think? Of course he was hungry. And bored. Eating was the high point of his day. Even the slop they gave him. He licked his chops, turning his attention to his meal.

And then he heard it. A shriek. "Mom! Come quick!"

She whirled around, slamming the heavy gate and ran for the house. He waited until she disappeared inside, then gave the gate an experimental push. It opened. This had happened before. She'd slammed it too hard and it had bounced back without latching. Stupid woman. Would she never learn? In a moment he was outside, sniffing the air, feeling the warmth of the sun on his back. It was a fine day, a fine day for killing.

He gave himself a good shake, then he was off, tail held high. His bowl of kibble remained untouched. Kudo was in the mood for chicken.

Chapter One

Lucy Stone wasn't usually a clock watcher. Time didn't pass slowly for her; it galloped ahead of her. As a part-time reporter—not to mention feature writer, listings editor and occasional photographer—for the *Pennysaver*, the weekly newspaper in Tinker's Cove, Maine, and the mother of four, her life sometimes seemed to her an endless chase after a spare minute. She was always late: late for meetings she was supposed to cover, late for doctor's appointments, late for picking up the kids. But not today.

Today her eyes were fixed on the old electric kitchen clock with the dangling cord that hung on the wall behind the receptionist's desk in the *Pennysaver* office. If only she could stop the minute hand from lurching forward, if only she could stop time, then she wouldn't have to go to the Board of Selectmen's meeting at five o'clock.

"Is there something the matter with my hair?" asked Phyllis, whose various job descriptions included receptionist, telephone operator and advertising manager.

She gingerly patted her tightly-permed tangerine do. "You keep staring at it."

"Your hair's fine," said Lucy. "I'm looking at the clock."

Phyllis peered over her rhinestone-trimmed cat's-eye glasses and narrowed her eyes. "Have you got the hots for Howard White? Can't wait to see him," she paused and smoothed her openwork white cardigan over her ample bosom, "wield his gavel?"

Howard White was the extremely dignified chairman of the Board of Selectmen, a retired executive who was well on in years.

Lucy laughed. "Howard's not my type," she said.

Phyllis raised an eyebrow, actually a thinly penciled orange line drawn where her eyebrows used to be. "Why not? He's not bad looking for an old guy, and he's rich."

"He also has a wife," said Lucy. "And I have a husband."

"Details." Phyllis waved a plump, manicured hand, nails polished in a bright coral hue.

"I don't want to go to the meeting. I wish Ted would cover the Board of Selectmen until this dog hearing is over."

Ted was the owner, publisher and editor-in-chief of the *Pennysaver*.

"Did I hear my name?" he inquired, sticking his head out of the morgue where the back issues going all the way back to the *Courier & Advertisers* printed in the 1800s were stored.

"Ted? Do me a favor and cover the selectmen's meeting? Please?"

"Trouble at home?"

"You could say that," said Lucy. "It's Kudo. He's been going after Prudence Pratt's chickens and I got a summons yesterday for a dog hearing. I just feel so awkward trying to cover the meeting with this thing hanging over me."

"Is the hearing tonight?"

"Next meeting."

"Sorry, Lucy, but I don't see a conflict of interest tonight. I'll cover the next hearing though."

"Do you have to?" asked Lucy, picturing her name in the headline. That darned dog was such an embarrassment. She felt like a criminal. "Couldn't we just skip that meeting? Pretend it never happened?"

"No," said Ted, flatly. "And if you don't get a move on, you're going to be late for today's meeting. It's five, you know."

Lucy checked the clock. It was five minutes to five.

"They never start on time," she said, slowly gathering up her things. "And town hall's just across the street. There's no hurry, really."

"You better get a move on."

Lucy hoisted the faded African basket she used as a purse on her shoulder and drifted towards the door.

"I'm not going to miss anything. Bud Collins is never on time and they always have to wait for him."

Ted yanked the door open, making the little bell jangle. "Go!"

"See you tomorrow," said Lucy, walking as slowly as a convict beginning the last mile.

The door slammed behind her.

Selectmen's meetings were held in the basement hearing room of the town hall. The walls were concrete block painted beige, the floor was covered in gray industrial tile, and the seating was plastic chairs in assorted colors of green, blue and orange. One end of the room was slightly elevated and that's where the board members sat behind a long bench, similar to the judge's bench in a courtroom.

What with the flags in the corner and a table and chairs for petitioners, the room was quite similar to the district court, thought Lucy. It wasn't a comforting idea and she tried to put it out of her mind as she took her usual seat, smiling at the scattering of regulars who never missed a meeting. Scratch Hallett, a gruff old fellow who had a plumbing and heating business and was active in veteran's affairs, was a particular favorite. She also recognized Jonathan Franke, the former environmental radical who was now the respected executive director of the Association for the Preservation of Tinker's Cove, and several members of that organization. They were exchanging friendly nods when Lucy's attention was drawn to a newcomer. Tall and gaunt, with her skimpy red hair pulled back into a straggly ponytail, it was none other than her neighbor Prudence Pratt, dressed in her customary summer outfit of baggy blue jeans and a free Blue Seal T-shirt from the feed store.

Lucy's heart sank. She hoped Pru hadn't gotten the date wrong, and thought the dog hearing was today. Or maybe she wanted to file an additional complaint. Kudo had gotten loose again the other day, and had come trotting home with a chicken feather stuck in his teeth. The memory made Lucy wince. She was at her wit's end; she'd tried everything she could think of to restrain the dog but he was some sort of escape artist. And whenever he got out, he went after her neighbor's chickens.

Lucy tried to catch Pru's eye, hoping to start some kind of dialog. Maybe if she apologized for the dog's behavior, or offered to pay for the damages, they could work something out and avoid the hearing. But Mrs. Pratt stared straight ahead, pointedly ignoring her.

A little flurry of activity announced the arrival of the board members, who filed into the room accompanied by their secretary, Bev Schmidt, who kept the minutes. They always came in the same order, with IGA owner Joe Marzetti going first. He was a bundle of energy, tightly focused on the task at hand.

He was followed by newly elected member Ellie Sykes,

a dollmaker and member of the Metinnicut Indian tribe whom Lucy had gotten to know when Indian rights activist Curt Nolan was murdered a few years before. Kudo had actually been Curt's dog and Lucy had taken him off Ellie's hands when he'd begun raising Cain with her flock of chickens. Ellie gave her a big smile as she sat down and arranged her papers.

Next came board veteran Pete Crowley, whose crumpled face and world-weary attitude seemed to imply he'd seen it all in the twenty years or so he'd sat on the board and nothing would surprise him.

Chairman Howard White always took the center seat, and was the only board member to wear a sport coat. He invariably shot his sleeves when he sat down, as if he were chairing a high-level meeting of movers and shakers instead of this oddly assorted group of public-minded citizens.

Bud Collins always brought up the rear. A retired physical education teacher and coach, he seemed to have used up all his energy urging Tinker's Cove High School students to run faster and jump higher. He often dozed off during meetings. Lucy would have made a point of it in one of her stories, except for the fact that she sometimes dozed off too, especially during presentations by the long-winded town accountant, who tended to drone on endlessly in a monotone.

"The meeting is called to order," said White, with a tap of his gavel. "As usual, we'll begin with our public comment session. This is the time we invite citizens to voice any concerns they might have, keeping in mind that once we begin the advertised agenda discussion will be limited to the issues under consideration."

Pru's hand shot up.

Lucy swallowed hard and sat up straighter.

"You have the floor," said White, with a courteous bow of his head. "Please state your name and address for the minutes."

"You know perfectly well who I am," she snapped, "and so does Bev Schmidt. Gracious, we were in school together."

Howard White was normally a stickler for detail, but after glancing at Bev and receiving a nod in reply, he decided to allow this breach of procedure. "Please continue," he said.

"Well, as you know, my property on Red Top Road goes back all the way to Blueberry Pond, which is owned by the town. It's conservation land, open to the public for swimming and fishing, duck hunting in the fall, and up 'til now there's been no problem."

"But now there is?" inquired White.

"I'll say there is. They're naked back there. Butt naked! It's a disgrace!" Pru was clearly outraged: her mouth seemed to disappear as she sucked in her lips and her pale blue eyes bugged out.

Lucy fought the urge to giggle in relief, concentrating instead on the board member's reactions. They also seemed to be struggling to keep straight faces.

"I think there has always been a certain amount of skinny-dipping at the pond," said Bud Collins. "The kids like to go there after practices, especially the baseball team. To cool off with a swim."

"I don't know who they are and I don't care. I don't like it and I want it stopped! Isn't there a law against this sort of thing?" demanded Mrs. Pratt.

White looked to the other board members, who shook their heads.

"I am not aware of any town bylaw that forbids nudity," said White.

"And a good thing, too," offered Joe Marzetti. "There's nothing the matter with a hard-working man stopping by the pond for a quick dip on his way home on a hot summer day. Or at lunchtime, for that matter. There's nobody there most of the time. What's the harm?"

"What's the harm?" Pru's eyes bugged out in outrage.

"It's immoral, that's what. It's time this town took a stand and stood up for public decency!"

"You're welcome to write up a proposal and put it on the town warrant for a vote at town meeting," said White.

"Town meeting! That's not until next April!"

"We could call a special town meeting, but you'd have to get signatures for that." White paused. "Bev, how many signatures would she need?"

"Two hundred and fifty registered voters," said Bev.

"Bear in mind that a special town meeting costs money," said Marzetti. "It's not generally popular with taxpayers."

"We'll see about that," said Pru. "I'll be back, you can count on it."

"We'll look forward to it," said White, casting a baleful glance at Ellie, who was struggling to suppress a giggling fit.

Lucy knew her duty as a reporter, so she followed Pru out of the room, catching up with her in the parking lot.

"Do you have a minute? I'd just like to get your reaction to the board's decision for the paper. . . ."

"My reaction isn't fit to print," snarled Pru. "That board's a bunch of godless, lily-livered, corrupt scoundrels. They'll rot in hell and so will you, Lucy Stone, you and that dog of yours." With that she climbed into her aged little Dodge compact and slammed the door.

"Can I quote you on that?" yelled Lucy, as she rolled out of the parking lot.

When Lucy returned to the meeting, Jonathan Franke was making a presentation with the help of a laser pointer and a flip chart. He had certainly adopted all the accessories of success, thought Lucy, who remembered the days when he was usually seen holding up a sign protesting government inaction or big business profiteering and sporting an enormous head of curly hair.

"As this chart shows," he said, indicating a bar graph, "Tinker's Cove is blessed with one of the few surviving communities of purple-spotted lichen in the entire state. Once abundant, this complex life form has fallen victim to a sustained loss of environment due to development and pollution. It is now considered endangered and is protected under the state's environmental protection act. I'm here tonight, with other members of the Association for the Preservation of Tinker's Cove, to request that the town take all appropriate steps to protect our priceless legacy of purple-spotted lichen."

Judging from their pleased expressions, Lucy understood the board members were congratulating themselves on their good judgement and wise management of a resource they hadn't actually known they had. Whatever they'd been doing, it had apparently been the right thing, at least for purple-spotted lichen.

"And how do you suggest we continue to care for this rare and wonderful little plant?" asked Ellie.

"That brings me to my next illustration," said Franke, flipping to the next page on his chart, a map of the town with prime lichen areas indicated by purple patches of color.

"As you can clearly see," he said, making the little red laser dot dance over the map, "one area of particular concern is out on Quisset Point. This is actually the town's largest community of purple-spotted lichen, thanks to the abundance of ferrous rock."

The board members nodded, indicating their high level of interest in an issue that was surely noncontroversial and certain to resonate positively with voters.

"That is why our organization, the Association for the Preservation of Tinker's Cove, is here tonight to request the cancellation of the upcoming July Fourth fireworks display."

All five board members were stunned, even Bud Collins, who had been nodding off. They had certainly not expected this.

"I'd like a clarification," said White. "Did you say you want us to cancel the fireworks?"

"You mean call them off?" demanded Marzetti.

"No fireworks at all?" exclaimed Crowley. "Isn't that un-American?"

"Believe me, we are not making this request lightly," said Franke, looking very serious. "We wouldn't consider it except for these facts." He lifted a finger. "A: The lichen is severely endangered throughout the state. B: The lichen is extremely fragile and easily damaged by foot traffic. And C: The lichen is highly flammable and one errant spark could wipe out the entire Quisset Point colony."

"I get you," said Crowley. "What say we move the fireworks off the point? Onto a barge or something?"

"Once again I believe there would be substantial risk from sparks."

Crowley scratched his head. "Okay, you say this is the best colony in the entire state, right? Well how come, if we've had the fireworks out there every year since who knows when? I mean, maybe this pinky-spotted moss likes fireworks! Have you thought of that, hey?"

"Actually, we have, and we've concluded that the continuing success of this particular colony of purple-spotted lichen is nothing less than miraculous. We've been lucky so far, but it's far too dangerous to continue endangering this highly-stressed species."

The board was silent, considering this.

"Can I say something?"

Lucy turned and saw Scratch Hallett was on his feet, his VFW cap in his hand.

"Please do," invited White, desperate for an alternative to calling off the fireworks.

"This just don't seem right to me," began Hallett. "A

lot of folks have fought and some have even made the supreme sacrifice to keep America the land of the free and the home of the brave. We celebrate that freedom on the Fourth of July, always have, ever since 1776, and I don't see what this purple-spotted stuff has got to do with it. We didn't know we had it, none of us did except these here environmentalists. I never noticed it myself, and I don't care about it. We defeated the Germans and the Japanese and just lately the Iraqis so we could enjoy freedom and you're telling me have to stop because of an itty-bitty little plant?"

"Mr. Franke, would you care to reply?" said White. "I think this gentleman has made an important point."

"Yes, yes he has," said Franke, beginning diplomatically. "And I and the other members of the Association value our American values and freedoms as much as anyone, and the sacrifices made by members of the Armed Forces. I want to assure you of that. But," he continued, his voice taking on a certain edge, "I'd also like to remind you that the purple-spotted lichen is on the list of endangered species in this state and is therefore subject to all the protections provided by the state's environmental protection statute, which includes substantial penalties to any person or agency judged to have caused harm to said species."

The board members looked miserable. If she hadn't known better, Lucy would have suspected they were all coming down with an intestinal virus.

"As much as I hate to cancel the fireworks, it seems to me we have a responsibility to preserve our environment," said Ellie.

"I think we have to look at the APTC track record," said Crowley. "They've been active in our town for a good while now, and Tinker's Cove is a better place for it. We've preserved open space, we've maintained our community character, I think we've got to give them the benefit of the doubt on this one."

"I don't know what community character you're talking about. It's things like the Fourth of July parade and
the fireworks that give our town character. I refuse to
vote against the fireworks," declared Marzetti, who had
grown hot around the collar.

"Well said," drawled Bud Collins.

"Is this a vote?" Howard White seemed uncharacter-
istically confused.

The others nodded.

"Two for and two against. I guess it's up to me."

The room was silent.

"My inclination is to hold the fireworks. It's been a
tradition in this town for as long as I've been here and I
hate to see it end." White sighed. "But I truly believe it
would be irresponsible and futile to ignore the state reg-
ulation. It would set a bad precedent and it would cost
us dearly in the end. It's with great sorrow that I vote to
discontinue the fireworks display."

He had hardly finished speaking when Scratch Hallett
was on his feet, marching out of the room. He paused at
the door. "This isn't the end of this," he declared, as he
set his VFW hat on hs head. "We may have lost the battle, but we haven't lost the war!"